# Dedication

For Karen E. Hodge
You made me see that nothing is impossible.
Until we meet again, I will take care, be good and remember to smile
because hey… God loves me.

&

For Fannie Offord (Motherdear)
You made it all possible.

## With Love

# Acknowledgements

To my creator and sustainer, everything that I am and ever will be is all a part of your ultimate plan. Thank you for loving me. Thank you for forgiving me. Thank you for your Son.

To my family who stands by me through it all. You have provided the solid foundation upon which I stand. Without each of you, I don't know where I would be. You are irreplaceable. Thank you for your unconditional love.

To Co-op E, the inspiration and push I needed to make this a reality came from each of you. I owe this completion to you. Thank you for your acceptance and encouragement.

To all my special moms, aunts, mentors, teachers and family in Christ, words cannot explain how much your support, prayer and guidance has helped shape me into the person I have come to be. Even when you thought I wasn't listening, I was. Thank you for your patience.

To the Delta authors and attorneys, you helped me keep my ducks in a row. Thank you for sharing your knowledge.

To the Duckteam, you all are the best. You were there when this was nothing more than a few pages on my computer. Each of you holds a special place in my heart. Thank you for your laughs. Umm hmm

To all the women of Delta Sigma Theta Sorority, Inc., the world is a better place with a Delta woman present. Thank you for your sisterhood, scholarship and service.

To all my supporters, I hope you enjoy this story as much as I enjoyed visualizing it. Thank you for your support!

To the family of Karen E. Hodge, thank you for sharing her with all of us.

# There Was A Spirit

# "The Article"

From miles away one could see the full moon. It was so white, round, and clear in the cloudless, dark blue-black sky. The northern sky illuminated the wheat and cornfields. In the plains, the area without trees for acres, the light from the moon made the night nearly as visible as the day. A slight peaceful breeze swirled about the late spring sky of 1901. Across the field, at the end of the Millhouse land, began the dirt road that led to the wider, better roads and the main one to the city. Sadie Mae Wesley was in that city. She had just finished scrubbing the floors of the new Municipal Hotel when she heard the crack of the back door.

"Sadie Mae," a male voice with a thick Irish accent said.

"Yes sir," Sadie answered. She rose from the floor wiping her wet hands on the dirty apron wrapped around her waist. She stood tall, at five-foot-ten inches. She was the tallest woman in her classes. In fact, Sadie had never met a woman as tall as, or taller than she. Her mother told her that height was the feature of a true leader. It was in this memory that Sadie found comfort when others would tease her about her lanky appearance.

"This ole' place closed now." The man wiped his thick red hair from his eyes and walked towards Sadie. "Ye bets get along home now girl."

"Sir..." Sadie started to ask him a question as he approached.

"Oh, now. Stop it. They only let me clean up this here ole' bloody place just like you. No ole' bloody sir," he said as he reached for the spot where Sadie was standing.

"You're new here." Sadie picked up her mop bucket. She noticed his eyes pan her dark brown skin, her hair, and her statuesque body. She felt uncomfortable.

"Ye better go on home now, it's late." He smiled and reached for the metal bucket Sadie gripped in her hands. "I'll take this."

"No, no sir. Don't need your help. I've got it." She hesitated realizing the roughness of her voice. "I mean, I better go like you said, it's late." She nodded politely, rushed past the man and out the room. Sadie removed her apron and placed it and the bucket in the sink area. Slowly she looked back and watched as the man inspected the room's furniture.

Moments later, Sadie returned to the bucket and dumped the dirty water into the sink. She thought how odd it was to see a White man cleaning. She had heard of the city's promise to hire more immigrants and thought, possibly, this was why he was there. Maybe, Sadie thought, this man with the fiery, red hair knew someone on the city's council.

It was Chicago's Mayor Carter H. Harrison who believed that men could be productive citizens if given the opportunity. The working example of this premise was the Municipal Hotel. It was established earlier that year to provide temporary shelter for homeless men of good character. However, the working citizens of Chicago knew that the real reason for the shelter was to relieve the overcrowded police station. Maybe, Sadie pondered, this new worker was an example of the Mayor's promise.

Minutes had passed when she found herself standing on the steps of the hotel looking down the road. She glanced back and waved at the man. His grinning face disappeared as she began her long walk home. She clutched the straps of her bag and walked into the night air.

Deep thought was definitely a characteristic of Sadie Mae Wesley. Often, when away from her studies at the University of Chicago, and especially when caught in the mundane nature of her job, Sadie buried herself into the depths of her mind. This night, she thought of the deed tucked down in her bag. The promise of a new life. She knew her father cherished the land the deed represented for over twenty-five years. Their farm was nestled in the small town of Casperton, Illinois, and the only home Sadie had known.

She was excited by the arrival of a letter and her only tie to her father. Reading small pieces between breaks, she held it all day. His barely legible words expressed the importance of the deed and what it meant to their family. Before Sadie left to attend the University, he explained how, besides what few items he carried in his knapsack, the deed was the first thing he owned after becoming a free man in America.

Along five acres of flat golden prairie land, the farm stood. Sadie's dream was to return to Casperton and build a school for Negro children on the corner acre. Her father, a man who sustained the first twenty-five years of his enslaved life on a dream of freedom and knowledge, understood his daughter's quest. Sadie's father mailed her the deed for reasons that she knew all to well. It was a reminder of the promise she made to the Negro citizens of Casperton. She was also aware of the White man's history of stealing land from their rightful owners. The most important reason was for safekeeping.

Within a mile, the hotel was a faint image behind her. As her long legs quickly strode along the dirt road, she occasionally felt the harshness of pebbles sticking through her worn shoes. A glimmer sparkled from the tip of his cane and against the moonlight. His steps echoed hers since her journey began. He had watched as she waved goodbye to the Irishman in the hotel.

So deeply contained in thoughts of the future and the father she adored, a smile eased across her face. She never heard the footsteps of the man behind her.

The blows were fierce and continuous. Sadie's world turned black. Her body slammed to the damp dirt. Her fingers clutched unsuccessfully to the bag he snatched from her grip. She never heard the laugh as he tossed it over in the dirt. Nor did she feel the weight of his body on top of her. Minutes seemed like hours. Her pain blended into the deepest part of the night.

And then the numbness. The air, the sounds, and the unfamiliar smell all ceased.

Her body engraved a trail from dirt - to - sand - to water. Reaching for life, her hand touched his. The diamond letter "B" sparkled from his monogrammed ring. Grasping at her death, he shoved her from the rock's edge. The water engulfed her body while he moved out of sight. Her struggle was hidden beneath the rocks and covered by the distant sand. In time she reached the shore.

Minutes blended into hours, and hours fell into the morning. Daylight hit the sand's edge when the small, yet strong hands of women pulled her high upon the shore. Fingers brushed her hair and the lake's life from her swollen face. They placed a light shawl over her darkened and bruised body. Its fabric absorbed the water's remains.

"Is she dead? Oh mercy, I think she's dead," a young woman said.

The other woman patted Sadie's face. She did not speak. She prayed for some sign of life then moved her head downward in anticipation of hearing a heartbeat. In a long second, her quest was rewarded with the faint beat of Sadie's heart.

"Do somethin' Anna! Haven't your schoolin' taught you somethin'?" The young woman pleaded.

"Hush! Go for help!" Anna Hattie Merriweather shouted to the young woman.

After pausing, in a panic, the woman rose from the sand and ran towards the University. Her bare feet made sharp indents as she conquered each piece of shore.

Anna noticed that the bruises around Sadie's face had been agitated by the water. She strained in recognition of the face. Through the tattered clothes lay the body of a classmate. It pained Anna to speak Sadie's name.

"Sadie," she whispered. Anna's arms embraced Sadie's lifeless body. Slowly rocking, Anna spoke soft, yet surprisingly steady.

"Sadie. Be strong Sadie," she whispered.

Sadie struggled to cough. She felt numb but fought to regain her voice. Anna, sensing Sadie's will to speak, quieted her friend.

"Don't," she said. "Don't try to speak. Help is on the way."

Sadie managed only a faint mutter. Anna began a deep, painful weep.

"Must…" Sadie fought hard. Slowly regaining only a blurred sight, Sadie strained to make out the silhouette of a familiar face. Consciousness continued to slip from her grasp. Yet, she fought.

Overhead the sea birds cried and the lake's waves rolled onto the shore. The beauty of the morning was lost to the two women. Minutes faded. Anna continued rocking Sadie, stopping only to check for breath. Anna shuddered as she thought of what may have happened to Sadie. The tears falling steadily from Sadie's bruised eyes broke her thoughts.

"Hold on, be strong." Anna felt a new sense of urgency.

Mustering her strength to grasp one lone moment with Anna, Sadie managed one word.

"Listen…"

"Sadie don't! You must hold your strength," Anna pleaded.

14

Anna knew the familiar safe haven of the University was a couple miles away. Even with the quickness of Augusta Washington, it would be a while before help would arrive.

Sadie could not hold life. She would not wait for assistance. She knew that these minutes were the last. With all her heart and soul, and all that God had given her, she spoke.

"Listen Anna!"

Anna was startled. She lowered her head to her dying friend's mouth. Sadie squeezed Anna's hand. She used every ounce she had within to draw Anna closer. Her words formed a promise to her awaiting friend.

More than ten minutes passed when Anna finally noticed Wilma T. Rogers, Alpha Lester, and a man running in the distance. Augusta was far ahead of the others. She stopped suddenly. She knew they were too late. The man knelt next to Sadie's cold, limp body. Anna stood with her friends praying for a miracle. They cried as they held hands encircling Sadie's body.

*In the beginning, there was a spirit*

# FIRST SEMESTER

# Sunday, August 12, 1973

Fire singed the edges of the newspapers as it quickly softened the eternal crystals of the coal. Flames shot slightly up from the back bedroom window of the red, brick, northeastern corner, Third Street house. A group of eight people gathered near and around the grill in anticipation of the smoked, cooked meat that would soon follow. It was August 1973 in Washington D.C. The sun was hot. The air was dry and filled with the smell of barbecues and crab feasts.

"*Till you come back to me that's what I'm gonna do...*" flowed from Aretha's mouth and then from the speakers of the small transistor radio at the edge of the back porch. There was a quiet chatter from the group and the normal noises of an occasional vehicle passing through the neighborhood. When the back bedroom window opened, the cracking of the old sliding wood made the group below stop and turn.

"Hey y'all, don't even think about eatin' up all the food before I get there. That's if it even tastes like anything," Najwa K. Jackson yelled from her bedroom.

20

"What you mean baby? Don't you know this food I'm grillin' is out of sight?" Dakota Phillips responded in his naturally deep voice as he wiped the sweat from his brown complexion.

To Najwa, Dakota resembled a wide receiver preparing a team meal for the Washington Redskins more than he resembled the kid next door. He towered over the barbecue grill with his six-foot-one, two- hundred pound, muscle frame. She watched him pile unusually large pieces of meat onto the grill.

For years, Najwa and Dakota shared the privilege of being neighbors. They attended the same elementary and high schools in the D.C. area and now attended the same college in Casperton, Illinois. Dakota, although the same age as she, was like a big brother to Najwa. In fact, Najwa never remembered having any neighbor other than the Phillips family.

As children, Najwa and Dakota walked to school every day. Dakota, as Najwa liked to think, was the big brother that all the neighborhood bullies were cautioned about when teasing her. This was probably why she never fed into the buzz of Dakota being the finest Black man at Casperton University. To her, this tall, handsome, slightly bearded man with short, wavy hair and perfect teeth was just Dakota.

To Najwa's parents, Dakota was their eyes away from home. Najwa slowly, but surely realized this after a long night of partying at a homecoming game in her junior year of high school. She vividly remembered how she and a group of her inebriated friends stumbled around the corner into the glare of her father. She smiled as she thought of how Dakota rushed in front of her and smoothly explained why they were two hours past curfew. So smooth, the incident was never again mentioned in the Jackson home.

"Yeah, whatever you say!" Najwa hollered back out the window. "There just better be a piece of somethin' when I get down there!"

"Well don't wait too long or you'll miss out." Dakota did not miss a beat basting the meat with his special sauce.

The childhood friends gathered around the backyard agreed with Dakota and continued slapping the playing cards on the rickety card table. Najwa laughed and closed her window. She turned and stepped over the boxes sitting around her bedroom. Finding a clear pathway, she walked over to her dresser and gathered the last of her clothes.

In the corner of her mirror, Najwa noticed two old photographs. Summer had come and gone so fast and now she was packing for school. Looking at the picture and then in the mirror at herself, she was stunned at how her college years changed her appearance. She remembered how she left home a slightly overweight and shy teen. Three years, thousands of college meals, a few looks from the campus athletes, and a couple of laps around the track later, she was now a shapely 5'10" woman with a perfectly round Afro.

However, Najwa was not a vain person. Her childhood memories were filled with teasing children calling her Baby Huey. Unlike many of her anonymous admirers, she did not see herself as one of the finer women on campus. Yet, her rich brown complexion, hazel brown eyes, and high cheekbones were the exotic, striking features that added to her quiet mysteriousness.

For three years she made the drive from D.C. to Casperton, Illinois for holidays and vacations with her eyes practically closed. During Najwa's freshman year, she spent most of her time in the library concentrating on school. With the exception of Dakota and those who shared classes with her, she was almost nonexistent to the social scene of the University.

The campus of Casperton University seemed to open to Najwa after her sophomore year. It was during this year that she explored the world of sisterhood and pledged the Black sorority, Omega Pi Alpha. Even then, many of the women hardly knew anything about their soon-to-be sister. Some even argued that she, in fact, was a transfer student. But quietly, the world of sororities and secret societies intrigued Najwa. The first sight of sorority sisters showing a seemingly unconditional love for one another made her work even harder for the high grade point average required to pledge.

Possibly handed down from her parents, she was always interested in being a member of an organization that dealt with the social and economic development of her people. Quiet, yet intimidating, Najwa was raised to be strong and speak her mind about what she felt was right. Her father, William Jackson, had been a faithful member of the Southern Christian Leadership Conference in the Atlanta area, and was known to do his share of protesting. Her mother came from the same background and in fact met William while they were both members of the Dexter Avenue Church. Being an only child, Najwa knew she was their sole pride and joy. She was

23

destined to carry on their spirit of social justice in some way or another.

Najwa smelled the rich aroma of barbecue seeping through her window. Although her mind was telling her to continue to pack, her stomach was begging to be fed. She raced down the stairs and out the back door.

"Let's get down to some serious eatin'!"

# Friday, August 17, 1973

As the sun took its first glance across the east coast horizon, Najwa was already up and packing the last boxes in the trunk and back seat of her Camaro. The black 1968 that had taken Najwa thousands of miles each year was a gift from her parents in her sophomore year. She named it Panther.

Looking forward to getting back on the campus, Najwa decided to leave two days early. Her mother, although happy to get Najwa's bedroom back for her sewing projects, was noticeably saddened by her only daughter's decision to leave earlier. Najwa's preoccupation with her sorority was Mrs. Jackson's biggest complaint. She constantly questioned her daughter's motive to leave the nest so early, but knew Najwa's stubborn nature would win.

One fact remained. She had been, and always would be nervous about her daughter making the eleven hour drive to the Illinois campus alone. The more she tried to convince Najwa to take the train, the more Najwa insisted the drive was necessary.

"You know we have the money. It's really not a problem," her mother pleaded. "Najwa honey, I know you like to drive so I'll just ride with you. I'll take a train back home. That way you won't have to be alone and I won't worry." A second plea came.

"Ma, I like to drive so I can think. If you ride with me then you'll talk all the way there. Then I wouldn't get the chance to be with myself and it would defeat the whole purpose," Najwa responded for the past three years.

Again, Najwa won the argument and was on her way alone. Again, her mother sat home by the phone for eleven hours waiting until it rang with Najwa on the other end saying she had made it safely. Najwa's father, on the other hand, gave up the fight after the first year. He made it his duty to not be at home when Najwa pulled out of the driveway due west. Mr. Jackson never made a big show. He always said his good-byes the night before, followed by his maintenance check of the car for any glitches, and of course enough money for just in case. Najwa knew her parents were proud of her and meant only the best. At least, Najwa offered, this would be the last year they would have to revisit this annual routine. June graduation was closer than imagined.

As the six o'clock morning hour set in, Najwa rolled out of the driveway, through her neighborhood, and on to Pennsylvania Avenue headed towards 495 North, the Beltway. Nearly four hours and three radio stations faded into the past before Najwa decided to take a rest stop just inside the Ohio state line. Every year, she stopped at the same service plaza for gas and food. Mindful of being a Black woman traveling alone, Najwa bought gas and a road trip meal of a hamburger and fries in pit stop record time. She climbed back into her car and within minutes she approached the Ohio state toll booth.

As she drove along the endless crops and farms, she smiled as she thought of the worldwide connection of Omega Pi Alpha women. Being an only child and not one of the popular girls in her high school, Omega Pi Alpha gave her the much needed popularity and sought after sisterhood. She thought of her chapter sorors and how the year ended. It certainly had not been an easy one. She wondered if the problems they experienced would carry over into the new academic year.

The chapter was going through a serious transition of members. Of course there were the usual arguments at the chapter meetings. Many of the eldest members graduated mentally, far ahead of their actual physical June date. This caused Najwa and her inexperienced line sisters to take on many responsibilities prematurely. Perhaps this worked for the best, Najwa assured them. She knew her extra work only prepared her more for the responsibility as President. But no matter what they experienced together, nothing would prevent them from going to the campus Greek party together that same night.

With a smile on her face, Najwa adjusted the car radio to a clearer station and thought back to the sorority rush in January 1973. She remembered that this would be her first time pledging a line and was anxious to dish out some of the punishment she had taken at her own rush. Najwa laughed to herself as she recalled mimicking actions of the most intimidating member of Gamma Chapter. These very actions almost made Najwa not pick up an application for membership.

"If I have to talk to that sista, then I just won't be a member of this sorority," Najwa remembered thinking. "That sista," would later become Najwa's special secret big sister during the pledge period. Oddly, had it not been for her, Najwa would have never made it through the pledge process.

Najwa shook her mind out of deep thought and glanced down at her watch. Looking at the overhead sign, she realized she had passed through Cleveland and was heading towards Toledo, Ohio.

"I'm right on schedule," she said.

She turned the volume up on her radio and sped down the relatively empty highway.

*A slight peaceful breeze swirled about the late spring sky of 1901. Across the field, at the end of the Millhouse land, began the dirt road that led to the wider, better roads and the main one to the city.*
*Sadie Mae Wesley was in that city.*

# Friday, August 17, 1973

Eight hundred miles away from Washington D.C., and a mere two hundred miles from Chicago, lay the college town of Casperton, Illinois. By summer's end, the small working class town came alive with the arrival of twenty thousand Casperton University students. The chimes of the campus' old wooden clock greeted incoming students from at least two miles away in each direction. At a glance, the city appeared covered with throngs of White residents. But, upon closer inspection in smaller clusters, different shades of people made up what a few enthusiasts thought was the beginning of a campus melting pot.

On the campus outskirts were scattered apartments filled with upperclassmen and graduate students. A dark skinned woman emerged from her apartment and looked down at her watch. Lynette Kendall stood on the balcony of her new apartment overlooking the football stadium and part of south campus. She turned and picked up the black satin banner that lay just inside the balcony door. She gently unrolled it revealing the large red Greek letters Omega Pi

Alpha. Below the letters was the quotation, "The soul of a new nation." in smaller letters. She smiled.

She eased further into the apartment and carefully tacked the banner above the couch. Lynette stood back and looked at it proudly remembering her past two years in the sorority's local chapter. Finally she thought, "I am the Dean of Pledges." She had the responsibility of grooming the next generation of Omega Pi Alpha women. Lynette knew these women had to continue the legacy of Gamma Chapter's unique blend of academic excellence, public service, and social grace. This was a direct reflection of her.

Memories of the past romanced Lynette's mind and her eyes glazed over. The acceptance letter, the chapter's serenade of the new initiates, initiation night, the fear, the pain, the laughter, the tears, and the closeness as she bonded in the circle of sisterly love all lingered. It seemed so long since she and her sands were in the forefront of all campus activities. From Black Greek president to academic All-Americans, Omega Pi Alpha women were always a positive presence at Casperton University. Lynette's fondest memories were of those times.

"O-Pi, O-Pi!" A familiar voice rang from the parking lot.

Lynette rushed to the front door yelling, "O-A, O-A!" She watched the tall and thin caramel colored woman run up the steps.

Their eyes met and in unison they exclaimed, "O-Pi-A!"

Carla Campbell had shoulder length, light brown hair with perfectly arched eyebrows that covered a faint childhood scar. She had a flair for the eccentric and was always conscious about her clothing and hair. Known for her silver jewelry, Carla's attitude was foretold in the menacing way she would twist the rings on her fingers.

The two women shrieked as they hugged. Carla, Lynette and Najwa were now the only three remaining from their line on the campus. Carla was always the most outspoken, Najwa the strong-willed one and Lynette the most sensible. Although the Omega Pi Alpha bond was shared with all their sorors, there was a unique bond in their relationship that set them apart.

Carla stepped back and looked Lynette up and down. "Girl look at you. You went and cut that fro down. Not only that, but you had the nerve to pick up a few pounds. Watch out!" She joked.

"Girl, I'm thinkin' about gettin' this hair pressed. Now, are you coming in or are you going to tell the whole complex my business?" Lynette replied.

Carla walked inside and immediately began admiring Lynette's new apartment.

"How'd you find out I was here?" Lynette asked.

"Now you know news on this campus travels quickly. Ron told me he saw you moving your stuff in the other day."

"So why didn't he stop and help me. That old sorry dog, he..."

"Don't talk about him too bad," Carla interrupted. "He is looking mighty good these days. But enough about our local Omega," Carla said.

"You know I got the Resident Assistant job at Garret Dorm. The person who was assigned this year didn't come back to school so I got the position." Carla's eyes began to glow as she walked further into the apartment. "You know what that means don't you?"

"Yeah girl, a larger room and more money so you won't be gettin' your dibs from me," Lynette replied.

"Well I guess those are some of the good points. What I'm talkin' about is the fact that I will be in the dorm with most of the girls who will be coming to the rush this semester." Carla walked over to leaning wooden paddles that bore their sorority letters.

"I can't wait to see the looks on their faces when they see their new Resident Assistant," Carla smirked as she picked up one of the paddles and slapped her hand with its glazed wood.

"I can't wait to see the looks on those White girl's faces when they see the new Black girl on the block!" Lynette knew that her outspoken line sister would definitely stir up a little dormitory excitement.

"So what's happenin' on campus?" Lynette asked as she sat on her small living room couch.

Carla sat in the chair in front of Lynette. "The annual welcoming party is next weekend. But you know what? I don't care who is having the party. I'm there! This is my last year and I plan on going out of this joint with a bang."

"I know what you mean. I was just thinking before you got here about how long it's been since we first pledged and how far we've all come. Any news from the Black Greek Council? We need to pick our party dates before the good ones are gone."

"As a matter of fact, I think there is going to be a meeting as soon as the reps are back from vacation," Carla replied.

"Why so soon? Is there a problem?" Lynette sounded disgusted.

Lynette knew the Black Greek Council had been very active in Casperton University politics the previous year. She also knew that if there was going to be an early council meeting, there had to be something that needed to be acted upon. Lynette's interest piqued as Carla relayed more information.

"Get this one. It seems as if the White Greeks are offering the members of the Black Greek Council a spot on the CU Fraternal Council with voting privileges."

For years at Casperton University, Black Greek organizations had separate councils from their White counterparts. Their missions and histories set them miles apart. Historically, Blacks had been denied admittance in the traditional fraternities and sororities. This made the legitimate admittance of the Black Greek Council into the CU Fraternal Council unbelievable. Not only was Najwa and her sorors suspect of any intention of the CU Fraternal Council but of the University as a whole.

"So what's the catch? I mean what do they want from us now? We're not backing away from that petition we signed last semester for more Black students and professors."

"Lynette, your guess is about as good as mine. I'm curious to see what will happen at our council meeting. We really need to stick together on this one. It took us long enough to organize that petition. The council is strong now and we've got to keep making steps forward. This is our chance to show the rest of the campus that we are really about the business of our people."

Carla was known to play. However, when it came to the business of the community, the revolutionary would come forward without hesitation.

"You know this is the University's way of getting us to shut up. Wait till Najwa hears about this one." Lynette shook her head and bit her bottom lip.

"Hey, where is my girl Najwa? I almost forgot about that cow. When does she get in town?"

"She should be in some time tonight. I called her yesterday. She said she was gettin' on the road this morning," Lynette replied.

---

That evening around six o'clock, Najwa exited the interstate just after the "Welcome to Casperton, Home of Casperton University Fighting Tigers" sign greeted her. Her apartment, only ten minutes away from the expressway, sat just four buildings down from Lynette Kendall's. Early in her junior year, Najwa was one of the few lucky students to acquire residency in the newly built apartment complex.

Like many of the upperclassmen, Najwa's detest of the dorm life caused her to jump at the opportunity to move into her own place. The privacy and serenity of simple things like taking a hot bubble bath were taken for granted until her freshman dorm experience. The idea of sharing four sinks and showers with ten other women who did not appreciate cleanliness as much as she was a source of constant aggravation and disgust. No one ever knew how Najwa was able to acquire an apartment so quickly or how she was able to work other things out so conveniently. Lynette especially never questioned her works. It was through Najwa that her name was placed on the top of the apartment waiting list.

After unloading bags and boxes from the car's trunk and into her dark apartment, Najwa began making her phone calls. The first was to her worried mother. Next, she called Lynette and Carla to announce her arrival on the yard. The only thing she had enough energy left to accomplish was to catch the tail end of the news. Within minutes, Najwa was asleep on the couch.

# Saturday, August 18, 1973

The next morning, Najwa awoke to a sharp pain in the right side of her neck. She had forgotten how uncomfortable the couch could be, unlike her grandmother's sofa back home. Shaking it off, she resumed unpacking and dusting the sleeping furniture. She then made her Saturday trip to the grocery store to replenish the refrigerator for a planned dinner with her line sisters. This evening was just for her girls. She would use this time to run her ideas for the chapter by them.

Najwa felt a sense of security from her line sisters and knew that there lay the heart of her support for the upcoming year. Lynette and Carla were the only two line sisters to whom Najwa connected on a deeper, personal level. Because of height order, they were the last three women who stood on the "Eight Wonders of the World" pledge line. Lynette stood in the number six position and Carla, an inch taller, found her home in the number seven spot. Najwa, just as during her childhood years, was the tallest. She stood at the end. She was the anchor of the line. The position that many wanted until they witnessed the responsibilities it entailed.

Najwa was responsible for being the anchor in troubled waters, the strongest link in the chain, and the strength for the entire line. When someone on their line threatened to quit, it was Najwa who convinced her to stick it out a little longer. On the night they endured their final rite of passage into the sorority and crossed the "burning sands," it was Najwa who carried the weaker members into Omega Pi Alpha land. Whenever Carla grew tired of standing during pledge sessions, it was on Najwa that she leaned. This was the introduction to sisterhood they shared. Najwa had their backs during the hardest six months of their lives. Now, they refused to leave her side.

By five that evening, Najwa marked off all the errands on her list as completed. She returned to her apartment and was doing some last minute cleaning when the door bell rang. She knew that it had to be Carla and Lynette because she had not talked to anyone on campus besides them. Najwa put away an empty box and rushed over in anticipation of seeing Lynette and Carla for the first time since May.

"Hey sands!" They greeted Najwa. Sands was the term that all Black Greek-lettered organizations on the campus of Casperton University used when referring to members of their pledge class.

Their first hour together was spent admiring the physical changes each made over the break. Lynette explained again why she had cut her hair and picked up the extra pounds. Carla went on about her new Resident Assistant job in Garret Dorm only to be interrupted by her own growling stomach.

"So what are we eating tonight? What you got in this

refrigerator?" Carla lifted herself from the couch and walked over to Najwa's small kitchen.

"You got any freeze pops? You know I like the red ones."

Najwa watched as Carla opened the icebox and dug towards the back until her hands felt a long freeze pop. Carla always made herself home in everyone's kitchen.

"I see nothin' has changed with you Carla. You're still just as greedy as you were last year. I bought some stuff to make hamburgers if that's okay with you," Najwa joked.

"Well what you waitin' on? Start making," Carla said, beckoning Najwa from the kitchen doorway.

"Ooo, she is so ignorant. Girl, I'll help you cook," Lynette joked as she walked past Carla and got her own sweet, icy treat.

"Just sit down and get out the way." Najwa took a package of ground beef out of the refrigerator and began heating a big black skillet.

Carla sat at the kitchen counter. Lynette joined her licking the freeze pop juice from her hand.

"Speaking of food, when is Dakota getting here?" Carla turned to Najwa and asked.

"Well, he gets to Chicago on Sunday. Mike is picking' him up from the airport. They should be here Sunday night," Najwa answered.

"Now, that brother Dakota knows he can cook. Remember that time when we were on line and he brought us all that food in your room Najwa? Girl that meal was righteous," Lynette said as she cut the head of lettuce Najwa placed on the counter.

Carla shifted the frozen sickle to one side of her cheek. "Um hmm, and he ain't been able to get rid of me at his dinner table ever since."

"Sands, I hate tell you but that's a problem we all have," Lynette joked.

"But what y'all didn't know was that he had cooked all that food for a chick he was dating down the hall from me. He saw us walking in the dorm looking pitiful as usual and felt sorry for us. It was right after we had gotten back from that last weekend on line. Do you know to this day, that brother says I was the reason why that chick refused to see him," Najwa added.

"You mean he felt sorry for you, Najwa. You know that brother does everything for you," Carla said with one brow raised.

Although not a couple, everyone knew of Najwa and Dakota's special relationship. Only her line sisters dared to ask why they were not dating. A few tried to persuade Najwa to pursue a relationship. Carla and Lynette, on the other hand, tried to persuade Dakota to make the first move. Both Najwa and Dakota refused all the offers of match making, arguing that they were just friends - like family.

"Oh no you don't. Not this year. You know the relationship me and Dakota have. We're friends and that's that." Najwa continued as she patted the hamburger meat. "We don't need any of you trying to play the dating game. But I will say this much. He is fine!"

"Oh wait, I thought you said you weren't interested in him Najwa." Lynette stood and returned a now half head of lettuce to the refrigerator.

"I said I wasn't interested. But I didn't say I was blind!" Najwa replied as the three laughed. Najwa felt the need to change the subject. She didn't want to say anything that would give her sands the green light to play matchmaker another year. "So has anybody talked to the neophytes?" Najwa asked referring to the newly initiated line of the chapter.

"Them heifers here," Carla answered. "I talked to 'em yesterday. You know they were trying to get back here to party."

"Well, I hope they are just as frantic to get out in the community. I'm sure they will be frantic to pledge somebody." Lynette sat back at the counter and opened a Budweiser. Lynette expressed how excited she was about her role as the Dean of Pledges. But, everyone knew she was not looking forward to being the police of the chapter. Memories of constant problems from the previous year lingered in everyone's mind.

"You think we'll have a lot of problems this year Lynette?" Carla asked reaching into the refrigerator.

"I'm trying to graduate this year. I don't have time for any mess. I made a promise to myself that being Dean of Pledges would not interfere with my future." Lynette, chemistry major, was finishing her final prep classes for medical school.

Najwa flipped the hamburgers and stood back as grease popped in all directions.

"Lynette, you're too organized to let it get out of control. With your classes will be a lot, but you got me and Carla to help you."

Najwa alluded to the Dean of pledges from the previous year. "Last year, that Donna just wasn't organized. She didn't care what was going on from day to day. She had her own program. As long as you and I are on the same page Lynette, this year is going to be a breeze. Right Carla?"

Najwa turned to Carla after she did not answer. "I thought you were on dorm duty tonight missy? Why are you drinking beer?"

Carla swallowed the mouth full and looked back in Najwa's direction. "Look, don't worry 'bout me. This year is my year. You just worry about those neophytes. And yes, this year is going to be a breeze for us."

"I hope so guys. Speaking of Donna, that wasn't cool the way she just walked away after elections. She still hasn't forgiven you for running against her for president," Lynette added.

Donna was always late for pledge meetings, never knew where the pledges were at any given moment and failed to keep order. The only thing Najwa dreaded more last year was chapter tradition. Tradition dictated that the Dean of Pledges always moved to the role of President.

"I bet she would love to see you mess up," Carla said.

"But that ain't gon' happen. We got to have our stuff solid. I mean we got to really stick like glue. We've been in this chapter the longest and we gotta keep it standing. We gotta train the neophytes. We're all leaving in June so we have to make sure they know the right way to run the chapter. It's bad enough I don't know where they all stand as far as I'm concerned. You know, I have been thinkin' all summer. Even though I got the majority vote for president, I know some of them didn't vote for me."

Najwa knew this year was dependent on her leadership. The last person expected to be president of Gamma chapter, Najwa could make or break the chapter. No one, not even Donna, would have the privilege of seeing her fail.

"I really don't think you have anything to worry about. Out of the three of us, those girls look up to you. They know all the hell you went through for their line." Lynette gave her best effort to reassure Najwa.

"I know, I know. I just want to get the chapter back on its feet. We need some new community programs. We don't have enough money to last us 'til November. Not to mention, the old problems of the Black Greek Council. There's just so much to do," Najwa replied

"You two are killing me. First Lynette and now you Najwa! Why are you so worried?" Carla interrupted. "We're Sands, remember? We are going to be there for each other. We are only as strong as our weakest link. And we have no weak link. If you fail, we all fail. Najwa you took a whole lot for us when we pledged. We couldn't have made it without you and you couldn't have made it without us. This is no different. We are going to do this and then go out of this joint with a bang. Now let's eat!"

"I hope you're right," Najwa replied as she lifted herself from the kitchen stool to take the hamburgers out of the sizzling greasy skillet.

Although this was not the first conversation the three shared regarding their fears for the chapter, this time was somehow different. Najwa felt this conversation go beyond the chapter and reached within their inner fears. She sat the rest of the evening with her sands knowing that although they had no idea what would be thrown their way, they were willing to face it. On this night, Najwa left the kitchen feeling as they had during their pledge process. This time, however, it was to achieve a higher level of sisterhood with an unknown cost. One she hoped in time they could endure.

# Friday, August 24, 1973

The center of the campus lit up for the first time since May. The Bradley J. Barkston recreation center provided the meeting place for students seeking a study relief. With its full service snack area, new bowling alley, and campus bookstore, the Barkston Center was the pulse of the campus. This night, the center's auditorium was flashing lights and bumping with the music from the sound system.

One by one, half of CU's Black population poured into the entrance. Everyone knew it was tradition to meet at the first party to catch up on summer's gossip. This event was always the AKA welcoming party. For years the sorority used the proceeds from this party to fund their book scholarships. Members of all nine Black Greek organizations gathered both in and outside the party sporting new paraphernalia, hugging their frat and sorors as if it had been years since their last embrace.

Their distinctive colors and symbols set their organizations apart, yet their purpose and more importantly, skin color, bound them together. The Alpha men in their black and gold hung closely with the AKAs. The brothers of Kappa passed out crimson and cream invitations to their after party, while the Zetas and Sigmas made a grand entrance. The Delta women gracefully worked the entire room, while the Omegas partied hard. The bright blue and gold of the women of Sigma and finally Omega Pi Alpha completed the entire Black Greek family portrait.

As the D.J. increased the temperature and made it a little funky with some James Brown, the Black Greek organizations were introduced to the crowd. Freshman looked on in amazement as each organization marched onto the dance floor. The members of Gamma Chapter were scattered throughout the party talking with old friends when the last members of the Eight Wonders line- Najwa, Carla and Lynette- all walked in together.

"O-Pi!" Najwa called out in her strong voice.

The other chapter members immediately turned to see who had just sent the familiar call of their beloved sisterhood. Diane Kimball, a neophyte and newly-elected treasurer of the chapter was the first to spot the three elders of their chapter.

"O-A!" Diane replied.

"O-Pi-A!" Other members of Gamma responded in unison.

They rushed from different corners to hug the only women left on the campus who had the honor of saying they "made" them.

"Now I know you all aren't just standing around here talking? Let's get down sorors!" Carla looked determined to follow through on the promise she made Lynette.

"This is a shame you need us old heads to get the party going. I hate to see what will happen when we graduate," Lynette jokingly said to the neophyte members of Gamma Chapter.

"Right now as president of this chapter, I am making an executive decision that all the members of Gamma Chapter need to be on the dance floor!" Najwa exclaimed.

Humidity steamed both the auditorium windows and the glasses of late comers. Finally, the crowd slowed down as the D.J. slid on a smooth Marvin Gaye ballad and newly formed couples for the night assumed the floor for the first slow dance of the school year.

Irby Winfield, a 1973 neophyte of Omega Pi Alpha, walked off the dance floor and over to her line sister, Kate Jones. As she approached, she moved the fine black hair on her forehead to wipe away the sweat.

"Kate this party is happenin! I don't ever remember this many new students. At least not Black ones! And these brothers look good too!" Irby declared. Being of Creole decent, Irby was pegged the pretty face on the campus.

"I told you that's not my name anymore. It's Keisha." Kate vainly spelled out her new name. "K-E-I-S-H-A!"

"KEEYSHAA!" She repeated. "And yea, I saw em.' The new men aren't that bad but the old ones from last year ain't that bad either."

"I know! Have you seen Ron and Kenny? Girl, they have come a long way from those two scrawny Omegas we used to know." Irby noticed Najwa and Dakota. "And speaking of Omegas, Dakota is fine! I wonder when Najwa is gon' stop playing and hook up with that brother?"

Irby waited for a reply. Moments later she realized her sands'
attention was elsewhere.

"I don't know girl. But if she knows like I know, she won't
waste her time. You have to go for what you want if you expect to
get it." Keisha stared ahead as she licked and bit her bottom lip.

"Oh boy, I don't like that tone. Who are you trying to snag now?
You know you always gettin' yourself in trouble with some man."

Irby knew her sands' reputation was not the best. Often she and
her line sisters found themselves taking up for Keisha. She somehow
always found herself in an unfavorable light on campus. The
majority of the time it was over a man and usually someone else's.
Keisha's need for constant attention took precedent over her mind.

At the same time, Candace Sommers, another member of the 73'
line, stopped dancing with her boyfriend and walked over to the two.
"Hey, Hey, Hey." She sang. "What are you two talkin' about?"
Candace said.

"Oh, nothing girl. What's happening? I haven't talked to you in
months sands." Keisha smirked. "How you and Mark doin'? Y'all
been together for about a year, huh? Time sure does pass by."

"Yeah, it's been about a year now but it doesn't seem like it's
been that long." Candace's face lit up as she talked about Mark.
"The summer we spent with each other here on campus really
brought us closer together."

"Well, you better watch him. I don't know what you all did but
you must be doing him some good. He is looking good girl," Keisha

replied.

Candace laughed. She turned and admired her boyfriend who stood across the room talking to his fraternity brothers. Irby looked on and listened intently. Thoughts rushed through her mind. She hesitated. Hopefully, she thought, Keisha won't get into any trouble she might regret.

On the other side of the party, Karen Walters, a Delta and the president of the Black Greek Council walked over to Najwa.

"Najwa! How you doing?" Karen asked as the two hugged.

Despite small conflicts, the Black fraternities and sororities on the campus got along well. Given the time and the lack of Black students at CU, unity was a necessity. Omega Pi Alpha and Delta often performed community projects together. In the fall the two sororities collected groceries for Casperton's impoverished Black community.

"Karen, I'm doing well. How about yourself? I hear we got some things to do this year on the council," Najwa replied.

"Yeah that's part of the reason I came over. Look, I'm sure you heard about the offer we received from the CU Fraternal Council. I'm calling a Black Greek Council meeting next week and I need everyone represented." Karen was fair and always about the business. This quality earned Najwa's respect.

"Just let me know the time and the place. Gamma chapter will be there," Najwa replied.

"I'll talk with you next week. For now we'll say Thursday night, eight o'clock at the Black House."

48

"I'll be there." Najwa saw some friends and politely excused herself.

The party went on with the sounds of laughter and music. It was midnight when the crowd finally poured onto the outskirts of the impoverished section of Casperton. The speakers shouted out the windows of the two story wood frame house known to all the Black students of Casperton University as "Kappa Land." One after another, people poured in and out of the front door. A red light glowed above a crowd of bobbing heads.

Gloria, a neophyte of Gamma chapter had just crossed Fern street with her sands, Diane. "Aww sookey sookey naw! Girl, it looks like its jumpin' in there!" Gloria declared, popping her fingers.

"We gon' party tonight!" Diane answered. Just as the two walked to the corner of Fourth and Fern, Candace Sommers emerged from the house.

"Hey Sands, where you going?" Gloria called out to Candace.

"Girl it is a sweat box in there!" Candace wiped the moisture from her face. "That house is packed wall to wall. You can have your fun but you're crazy if you think I'm going back in there."

"Who's here?" Diane asked.

"I saw some of our sands in there shaking their booties. My crazy man, Mark is still in there too. I told him I'd see him back at my room later. Where is the rest of the chapter?" Candace asked as they looked over her shoulders in anticipation of getting inside.

"You know where they are. Their all at Lynette's havin' a little sip, you know, before they come here. That's where we were before we got here," Diane replied.

"Well you don't have to worry about a drink, there is plenty Kappa punch in there. I'll see you two later. Oh, and don't party too hard." Candace laughed as she walked towards her dorm. She turned to her two sands and shouted from the corner, "And send my man home if he looks like he's having too much fun!"

As quickly as Candace had emerged, Gloria and Diane disappeared among the sea of bodies inside the house. Ten minutes passed when the remainder of Gamma chapter rounded the corner laughing hysterically, some of them barely able to stand.

Najwa turned to the group and tried to look serious. "Okay wait, wait, wait sorors! We've got to get ourselves together. We can't let the whole campus see us like this."

"Oh girl you better shut up with your drunk butt!" Carla waved her hand in Najwa's face and walked past her as the rest laughed even harder.

"I been waiting to get back to school all summer. Ain't you or nobody else gon' stop my fun tonight! These girls better watch their men cause Keisha Jones is here. The party can now begin!" Keisha exclaimed as she popped her fingers, switched up the stairs and through the door moving people out of her way.

"You mean Kate Jones is here!" Carla hollered back.

"Oh Lord, we got our hands full tonight sorors. Let me catch up with my sands before somethin' else catches up with her." Irby walked ahead pushing her way in behind Keisha.

"Oh so I guess no one is going to listen to me." Najwa said still standing at the steps.

"Girl, just go on in that party before we leave you out on these steps looking crazy by yourself." Lynette pushed Najwa up the first step and the rest followed.

The humidity of the Kappa house was unbearable. Sweat rolled down the brows of heads whether they were dancing or not. Nothing or no one could possibly avoid becoming the victim of steam. People were dancing in the packed room that served as a living and dining room during the weekday. Twice as many lined the walls socializing. The vibrating floor forced those stationary to move to the beat of the music. Both the kitchen doorway and the stairs to the second floor bedrooms were lit with red glowing lights. Many held cups filled to the rim with intoxicating red punch.

Looking over the heads in the crowd, Carla noticed two neophytes bobbing their heads to the music. Gloria and Diane staked their claim to a position on the wall between the kitchen and the dance floor. Carla grabbed the hand of Najwa who then grabbed the soror behind her. Together they pushed their way over to them.

Carla smiled and reached for the closest drink. "Hey! What's in the cup and hand it over while you talkin'."

"Aw girl, go get your own there's plenty more where this came from." Diane wrinkled her brow as Carla turned the cup up to her mouth. "Besides, you already drunk as a skunk!"

"I think you better remember your deference. You know the deal neophytes! Until you make a line, step back in line!" Najwa joked as she too sipped from Diane's cup.

"Yeah right. We know y'all are drunk now." Gloria turned to the rest and laughed.

It was known that as neophytes, they still not only had a lot to learn, but respect to earn. The word deference had been used many times before, from acquiring a bed for visiting sorors to a quiet mouth and listening ear in times of confusion, even drinks at parties. In Najwa's world, it meant complete respect.

The cup made its way down a line of five sorors. Lynette turned to the neophytes who were now waiting their turn to taste the remains. "Did you all see Kate and Irby come through here? They were right in front of us."

"Yeah Kate, oh I mean Keisha or whoever, floated past here right before you all did. She should be dancin'. Ms. Social Butterfly could be anywhere by now. Especially, since she got a little juice in her system," Gloria replied reaching for the cup.

"Forget her, I'm going to dance, this is my jam!" Lynette pushed her way through the crowd and joined the bodies gyrating on the dance floor.

They all agreed that this had to be one of the best after sets in recent memory. Everyone was having fun. No fraternity fights or girls arguing over men. Every now and then members of Omega Pi Alpha caught a glimpse of one another. Time blended like the music. Najwa looked down at her watch. They allowed the wee morning hour of three o'clock to creep upon them. Robin Turner, the chapter's public service chairperson, was the only soror standing next to Najwa. The rest had somehow gotten lost in the crowd.

Robin turned and said the words Najwa anticipated all night. "I am ready to go." She pulled the damp blouse off of her glistening chest.

"Yeah my high wore off about two dances ago when that freshman put his funky arm around my neck. Where is everyone?" Najwa stood on her toes and strained as she looked over the dancing heads. "Look there's Irby!" Najwa pointed ahead. She had not seen her soror since she rushed in behind Keisha.

"Irby! Irby! Over here!" Najwa called.

Irby's silky black hair was flat and laid down the side of her face. The cream ruffled blouse she spent two hours coordinating with the rest of her outfit clung to her sweat-drenched body. As she walked towards Najwa, men turned to catch the silhouette of her round breast. Pushing a drooling football player away, Irby managed to move closer to Najwa.

"Where you been? We're ready to go." Najwa informed Irby.

"I think I'm more ready than you are. I have to shower as soon as possible. It's hot in here! Oh, and to answer your question, I been trying to keep up with your soror Keisha," Irby replied in disgust.

"So where is she? As a matter of fact, where is every body?" Robin asked.

"The last time I saw Keisha, her butt was upstairs socializing as usual," Irby answered.

"You go look for her and tell anybody else you see upstairs that we're leaving. Shoot. I got to go home. I'm getting sick in here." Najwa headed to the kitchen where she knew she would find at least one soror wrapping her lips around a glass.

Robin walked in the direction of the dancers. Despite their attempts to grab the sleeve of her blouse, Irby managed to slide past half the basketball team and began climbing the cluttered stairway. Berri Matthews, the vice president of the chapter, was the first soror Irby encountered.

"We're ready to cut out. Any sorors up here?"

"Now?" Berri leaned over and whispered in Irby's ear. "I'm just starting to get somewhere." Berri's eyes cut in the direction of the tall, husky, dark skinned man standing before her.

"Look, it's going to take us a few minutes to find everybody. You got five minutes. Did you see Keisha walk past?"

"Yeah Kate went past about fifteen or twenty minutes ago. She went into one of those rooms in the back." Berri pointed and turned back to her waiting audience.

Irby turned, let out a long quiet sigh and looked down the hall. "Sands please don't let me have to come in there," she whispered to herself. With every step forward, Irby hoped the door would open before she had to knock on it. This night of all nights, Irby did not feel like being bothered with the trouble.

A bright light cut the soft red glow in the hallway. Irby covered her face as it pierced her eyes. A siren blared for a brief moment. The white light was accompanied by red and yellow. Uncovering her eyes, she knew immediately it was the police breaking up the party. Why they had not come long before now she did not know.

"The party is over kids! Let's Go! Your folks didn't send you here to party!"

Irby heard the familiar sound of the White policemen with their bullhorns. Then a piercing scream from outside the window. The music inside stopped and the crowd poured onto the street. She walked further down the hall past the door and looked out the window. Irby was surprised to see the large number of police gathered outside the house. The crowd running across the street was even more unusual. She watched three Casperton policemen cuffing a tall, slender, Black male body.

"What did he do?"

"I hate this racist town!"

"What am I being arrested for?"

"Pigs!"

One after another, shouts came from both the crowd and the student Irby recognized as the brother who sat behind her last year in Philosophy class. The officer pushed the young Black man's head down and forced him into the back seat of the squad car.

"What in the hell is going on out there?" Irby asked herself aloud in disbelief.

The Casperton police were known to break up parties thrown by Black students. The small, college town was the last place for any person of color to think of driving over the speed limit, let alone cause a disturbance. Moments passed and the crowd grew more despondent. Irby felt uneasy. Although three years had passed since the incident at Kent State University, any large gathering of students still made the campus police nervous. The safety of her sorors was

Irby's only thought. Immediately, she turned and ran down the hall.

"My sands!" She said aloud.

She stopped dead in her tracks. She turned to the doorknob of the room Keisha was last seen entering. Irby swung the door wide open.

"Keisha we got to..." was all Irby managed to utter before her bottom lip fell and eyes widened.

Keisha's head jerked. Her hands desperately tried to fasten the bra hanging from her shoulders. Her breast dangled in the air free as the wind. Her blue jean hot pants were unzipped and hugging her hips.

Next to her stood a male body zipping his jeans. He turned and looked over his shoulder. Irby recognized this muscle bound guy. This time it was not just some other girl's man. It was her sands. Keisha's victim was Candace. Keisha just betrayed the entire Gamma Chapter. Quickly, saying nothing, Mark grabbed the T-shirt his girlfriend and their soror had given him and slipped it over his head.

"Let's go Keisha!" Irby shouted.

"Sands, wait I can ex..."

"Keisha let's go, the pigs are outside!" Irby commanded.

She turned away while Keisha managed to pull her shirt over her head. All Irby could think was why, of all people, she had to be the one to make the discovery. How could Keisha do this to her own sands? Irby knew she undoubtedly was now in the middle of a mess.

Mark buckled his belt and brushed past Irby. Within seconds he disappeared down the stairway.

Keisha stood in the doorway trying to explain. "Irby, I'm really sorry you..."

"Keisha let's go! Didn't you hear what I said? The pigs are outside!" Irby blurted in utter disgust as she scrambled down the hall.

They raced down the stairway, out the front door and into the crowd. Black students rushed in all directions avoiding contact with a dozen policemen scattered in the area. As they hurried along the sidewalk, Irby could see her sorors waiting for them at the corner of Fourth and Fern.

"Hey Irby!" Berri called. "What took you so long?"

Irby walked past her as if she was marching to war. "Let's just go before one of us gets arrested," Irby pleaded. She opened the car door and lifted the seat for Keisha who had not said a word.

Keisha climbed in the car unsure of her sands' next actions. Berri walked to the driver's side, got in and sped away.

# Saturday, August 25, 1973

Najwa's clock read a little after four in the morning by the time she walked into the comfort of her apartment. She sighed, closed her front door, kicked off her shoes and walked toward her bedroom. Before she reached the threshold, she unbuttoned her damp shirt. Hastily, she peeled the remaining garments from her body. There was nothing standing between her and a hot bubble bath.

She made her way into the bathroom and flicked on the light. Thoughts of the police raced through her mind. Surely, there would be talk all over campus about what happened. She smirked at the thought that neither the National Guard nor the local news crew appeared to add fuel to the fire. Steam eased over the bathroom mirror as the falling water whispered her name. Najwa climbed into the porcelain tub and slid beneath a blanket of bubbles.

Minutes later, she rinsed the lather from her body and grabbed the towel hanging just above the toilet. As she began drying, she faintly heard the doorbell. "Who in the world is that?" Najwa asked herself clutching the towel.

"I don't believe this. It has to be a soror." Najwa walked quickly into her room, grabbed her red silk Kimono robe and wrapped her naked body. She tied the belt snugly around her waist and made her way to the door.

"Who is it?"

"It's me, Dakota," the husky voice responded.

"Dakota? What in the world?" Najwa whispered to herself. She opened the door to see the tall, wide figure standing in her doorway.

"What are you doing here?" Najwa asked still clutching the knob.

"I can't find Ron or Kenny. They're off somewhere messin' around with some women. I lost my keys at the Kappa house."

As Dakota explained his dilemma, a sparkle from Najwa's damp chest caught his eye. He noticed Najwa was only wearing a robe. His eyes left her puzzled face and focused on her full chest. Najwa grabbed the lapels of her robe and slowly pulled them together silencing Dakota's stare.

"Oh, so I guess you want to come inside?" Najwa said attempting to ease an awkward moment.

"Girl would you just let me in, it's late." Dakota effortlessly pushed Najwa to the side and walked inside the apartment.

"Besides," he continued. "I seen you in your drawers before. You know I used to change your diapers when you were little."

"You need to stop lying." Najwa closed and locked the door.

It didn't take much for her to give in to her childhood friend and big brother. For all the years Dakota defended her against schoolyard bullies, she would not leave him hanging. Their protective bond was instinct.

"Tell me, what in the world would your trifling butt do if I wasn't on this campus?" Najwa turned and asked Dakota who was now sitting on the couch.

"I'd just go over to one of my many women's houses. They won't give me a hard time like you do," Dakota said referring to his many admirers on the campus.

"You can always get up and go to their rooms right now," Najwa said sarcastically. She continued into her bedroom to gather a pillow and blanket. Returning, she threw them over Dakota's head.

Dakota untangled the wool blanket from around his head as Najwa laughed at the comical scene. Again, her robe slipped apart revealing cleavage. Dakota's eyes left her chest and roamed to the fullness of her hips. The silk design at the robe's hem robe stopped mid thigh and allowed him to imagine more than her mini-skirts could ever reveal.

"No I think I'll stay right here tonight. The scenery is much better. Girl, what you been doin'? You tryin' to look grown," Dakota joked.

"Boy please!" Najwa waved her hand at Dakota dismissing his comments completely. She shyly withdrew into the bedroom to put on her pajamas. Najwa felt embarrassed by the attention her body generated. Having been an overweight teen, she was not accustomed to hearing compliments on her appearance from any man.

"So what in the world happened at the after set?" Najwa hollered from her bedroom.

Dakota positioned the pillow at the end of the couch and took off his shoes. "The pigs got another brother, that's what happened. You know, Dave, my little brother from last year. He was the freshman I was assigned to by the Black Student Union."

Najwa slipped the shiny pajama bottoms on and pulled the top over her head. She walked back into the living room. "What did he do? Or should I say what did they say he did? We all know how those jive police around here are."

"I saw his roommate over by Mel's Chicken Shack before I came here. He said something about some pot."

"So he got arrested for a joint? If they went down to the Beta's frat house they would have found enough pot on those White boys to get the whole campus high," Najwa declared as she sat in her wicker chair.

Dakota lay comfortably wrapped in the wool blanket. "I don't know what they got him for, but that don't sound like the brother I know. He's still wet behind the ears. He wouldn't know trouble if it walked up and slapped him. That's why I know the Dean is going to have hell on his hands once this all goes down. Some of the cats in his dorm are going to collect money to get him out. I gave about five myself. That's when I realized my keys were gone." Dakota paused.

"And what was the haps with your sorors?"

"My sorors? What are you talking about?" Najwa looked confused.

"When the party broke up I saw Kate and Irby coming out of the

Kappa House like something was wrong. I tried to get their attention to see if everything was cool but they just kept walking. Maybe they didn't hear me or something. I don't know. This night was just wild."

Najwa thought to herself. It wasn't just her imagination. Her sorors were acting a little funny after all. Her suspicion, based on who was involved, was that their behavior was not due to the police.

"Yeah you're right, tonight was just crazy. Ka... I mean Keisha. Whoever. She was acting real crazy tonight. Oh, you know Kate changed her name to Keisha?"

"What?" Now Dakota was really confused.

"Don't ask. Just take your big head to sleep cause I need to go to bed." She stood and walked toward her bedroom. "And no I'm not cooking you breakfast," Najwa said.

"Goodnight, at least what's left of it." Dakota turned over and covered his head with the blanket.

Najwa cut off the living room lamp and disappeared into her bedroom. She sank into her bed hearing only faint sounds of birds chirping. Moments later she was asleep.

---

At that same moment a phone rang in the third floor hallway of Garrett Dormitory. Irby was already showered and had slipped on her nightgown. It came as no surprise that the hallway phone rang at the wee morning hour. She knew it was for her. She figured Keisha would call to plead her case. However, Irby was not sure that she even wanted to hear any explanation. She was sorry that she had gone to look for her.

The phone rang a third time and Irby still found herself hesitating to go in the hall to pick up the receiver. She knew that if she did not answer, Keisha would continue to call until they had talked even if it meant waking the whole floor. After the fifth ring, Irby emerged from her room and rushed to the end of the hall.

"Yes Keisha," Irby stated, confident of the call's origin.

"How did you know it would be me?" Keisha said in surprise. "Never mind that. Irby, I just wanted to talk to you about tonight. I know you're mad at me. But just give me a chance to explain before you start getting' ugly."

"Keisha, I don't know how you are going to explain what I saw. But go ahead. I'm listening."

"I know it was wrong, but hey it just happened. I'm sorry you had to see what you did. I didn't mean for it to go that far. One thing just led to another and well, before I knew it there we were."

"Keisha please! What kind of jive story is that? How can one thing just lead to another with another sister's man?"

"Look, I admitted I was wrong. I'm telling you I'm sorry. Now get off my back. What else do you want from me? I can't take back what happened."

"Keisha just what exactly are you sorry for? Messin' with Candace's old man or getting caught?"

"You know what I mean. You know I would never try to hurt Candace."

"So how did it happen Keisha?" Irby raised her voice and risked waking the entire floor.

"I told you it just happened. What can I say? Maybe we had too much punch. You know what alcohol does to my system."

"You know what? I expected you to say something that stupid. You really have a problem Keisha. So is that what you're going to tell Candace?"

"I'm not going to tell her anything. And you ain't either Irby."

"You know, I just don't believe this is goin' down. You decide to start the year off by messin' around with Mark and now you want me to get in this mess. It's bad enough I witnessed it but now you want me to lie?"

"What lie Irby? You're not lying by not telling her what happened," Keisha responded arrogantly.

"Keisha, I knew you were low. But I never thought you could be this low."

"Whatever you say Irby. Listen, you can't tell. I'll take care of it. If anyone should tell Candace it should be me. And you know what? I'm just not ready to tell her yet."

"Keisha, I really don't know what I'm going to do. I just want to get off this phone and go to sleep before I wake up the whole floor. Goodbye." Irby hung up the phone without waiting for Keisha's response. She walked back to her room.

Irby's roommate squinted her eyes as the hallway light cut the darkness of their room. "You alright girl?"

"Yeah, I'm cool. Go back to sleep." Irby replied.

Irby lay looking at the small beam of light peeping through the curtain window. She wanted desperately to fall asleep and awake to find that the night had all been a dream. But reality prevented this from happening. How could she possibly face Candace knowing Mark had betrayed her trust? How could she face Keisha without slapping her face?

The look on Keisha's face flashed in her head each time she closed her eyes. The nerve of Mark to think he could get away with this. Irby realized that if she had not walked in, he would have gotten away free. But most importantly, what was she going to do now that she was a witness to the biggest mess to hit the Casperton University gossip circle. Sorors sleeping with other sorors' men?

"I should have just stayed in my room," Irby repeatedly said bumping her head into the pillow.

The groggy roommate turned to Irby. "What you say girl?"

"Nothin'. Just go on back to sleep. I ain't said nothin'." Irby turned her back to her roommate and struggled to sleep.

*She stood tall, at five ten. She was the tallest woman in her classes. In fact, Sadie had never met a woman as tall as or taller than herself. Her mother told her that height was the feature of a true leader.*

# Wednesday, September 19, 1973

Three weeks passed. The town of Casperton was booming as it usually did during the first month of school. Students crowded the bookstore buying used textbooks and supplies. The Barkston Center was noisy with the campus social scene. Late arrivals on the admission waiting lists were still moving into the dorms. The Black student newspaper had already begun the stages of a support rally for the anonymous sophomore now on probation with the university for drug possession. Carla had just learned the names of all the women on her floor. Lynette had already begun to stress over her pre-med classes. Dakota had two new admirers whose hearts were set on calling themselves his woman. Irby was still sitting on the secret she knew eventually had to be told. Keisha had collected three new phone numbers and two dates from old interests. Najwa had written plans for the executive board of Omega Pi Alpha into the month of January.

As promised, the Black Greek Council of Casperton University met at the Black House to discuss the offers made to them by the

Casperton University Fraternal Council. For over three hours the group scrutinized a written plan given to Karen Walters, the Black Greek Council President. One vote on the CU Fraternal Council, two dates on the social calendar of the Barkston Center, participation in the Rush week activities, and most importantly, five thousand dollars were the rewards. This same privilege was offered to each CU fraternal organization. With most of their money and special favors coming from the contributions of successful alumni, the lives of the White Greek members were made relatively easy. However, this privilege was not offered to each Black Greek organization.

Instead, the entire Black Greek Council would only count as one umbrella organization for the entire nine. This meant one quiet but careful vote speaking for nine, two dates to have joint programs and five hundred fifty five dollars for each organization. Whether the benefits of "selling out" to the CU Fraternal Council were worth becoming the token models for the university was the number one argument of the meeting. With the arrest and school probation of the sophomore student, and the suspension of the Kappas, there were several skeptics among the decision makers.

Finally, the nine organizations agreed that the most important features of their offer were the two dates and the money. With the two dates, it was decided that the Black Greek Council could hold a rally for the Black students and possibly another fundraiser. Not to mention, the five hundred dollars that would normally take each organization over a semester to raise on their own, was the biggest perk. By taking these privileges and turning them into advantages for the Black community, the council felt that the stigma of token could be lessened.

For the first time in Casperton University's history, the voice of the Black student would be heard in the CU Fraternal Council's meeting. Dakota was unanimously voted to serve as the representative. Confident of their decision, the nine organizations strategically planned how they would take advantage of every benefit they could draw from the new affiliation. Most importantly, they needed a way to explain this new affiliation amidst a campus ready to explode in racial tension.

On the third Wednesday evening of September, Omega Pi Alpha had its first chapter meeting of the year. For years before the construction of the new student union, the Black House was the only meeting spot of the Black students. The historic walls of the three story wood frame house had been the host of authors, scholars, poets, speakers and civil rights workers. It was in this house that all the campuses racial issues were discussed. It was also the office of the only full-time, Afro-American studies professor and the Black student newspaper, *Tiger Pride*. Its' warm walls were a refuge for the Black organizations and a home to Mrs. Dixon, the secretary who had played mother to every Black student since the early fifties. Since the inception of Gamma Chapter, their monthly meetings were held in the basement hall.

Around six that evening, Najwa entered the tall doors of the Black House an hour prior to her chapter meeting. Najwa had ideas for upcoming school year events and wanted to be clear on what the other organizations were planning.

"Hey Mrs. Dixon," Najwa said as the old wooden floor of the main office creaked under her feet.

"Hi baby," Mrs. Dixon answered.

The heavy-set, gray-haired woman began to gather up her things and organize them neatly on the desk she seemed to occupy since the building was erected. She looked over the top of her horned-rimmed glasses at Najwa and began to speak.

"You here early for your meeting I see."

"Yes ma'am. I thought I would come by to see the event calendar and get our mail so I can do some planning. I got a feeling this is going to be a good year Mrs. Dixon."

"You're a senior this year aren't you Najwa?" Mrs. Dixon received a nod from Najwa. "My, my, my how time just seems to slip by me. You know, just when I get to know you kids well enough to get on your case, it's time for you to go."

"Yes ma'am." Najwa answered knowing that once Mrs. Dixon started talking these would be the only words she could sneak in the conversation.

"And just look at you Najwa, you're the president of your sorority now. And you're doing so many good things on this campus. I tell you, I'm just so proud of all my babies."

"Thank you. Mrs. Dixon you must have a lot of babies. You been working here for over twenty years," Najwa kidded.

"Twenty-six years to be exact sweetie. Seems like yesterday," Mrs. Dixon replied.

Najwa was amazed. The thought of doing anything consistently for over twenty years was incredible.

"So you been working here since you been in Casperton Mrs. Dixon?" Najwa asked curiously. She was actually ashamed that in all her four years at the university that she had never taken the time to learn more about this woman who helped most of the Black student population out of a squeeze.

"Oh no. I came to this old town in 1938 with Mr. Dixon. That was over thirty-five years ago! Right after we got married, I started working at the Town Hall 'til I came over here to the University. Everybody wanted to work for the University back then."

"So, Mrs. Dixon ..." before Najwa could finish, Mrs. Dixon had already interrupted.

"Still got a lot of friends over there at the Court building. As a matter of fact, just talked to my friend Martha today. We're getting ready for my Thanksgiving dinner. Are you coming' this year baby?"

"Well, Mrs. Dixon I don't..." again Najwa was interrupted.

"You know, Martha mentioned to me that they needed some part-time help over at the hall. You could probably use the extra money. You want me to give her your name sweetie?"

"Yeah, I can always use extra money," Najwa replied as she thought about the days of desperately calling home for spare cash.

"Good! I'll give her your information tonight when I talk to her," Mrs. Dixon beamed.

"Thank Y..." again Mrs. Dixon interrupted but Najwa did not

mind. Mrs. Dixon was the sweetest Black woman on the campus and had nothing but the best intentions.

"Now, I put all of your sorority's mail in your mailbox and oh, I have had some young ladies coming in here asking about your sorority. Looks like you may have a mighty big rush this year. And speaking of calendar, I think you better hurry up and put your event dates down 'cause some of the good spots are already taken.

"Now, Mr. Smith the custodian will be here at 'round about nine o'clock to lock up when you young ladies are finished with your meeting. And don't forget to leave the information for all your new officers on my desk so I can put them in the directory. Listen, if you come by tomorrow at about three o'clock you can get a piece of my lemon cake. I'm baking it tonight." Mrs. Dixon pulled her pink knit sweater off the coat rack and slung her shiny patent leather pocketbook over her shoulder.

"Yes Mrs. Dixon, yes ma'am," Najwa continuously answered in between Mrs. Dixon's short pauses for breath.

Finally, Mrs. Dixon made her way to the door still talking.

"Well baby, I hate to leave you but I got to get home to Mr. Dixon. You know he's not feeling well lately. Anyway, I hope you have a good meeting and don't forget to pick up behind yourselves before you leave. And oh, Najwa, did I tell you how proud I was of you girls? See you tomorrow baby!"

Mrs. Dixon hurried down the old rickety steps of the Black House and around to the driveway where her 1957 Buick Roadmaster was parked.

"Bye Mrs. Dixon." Najwa shook her head and laughed to herself as she watched Mrs. Dixon pull the huge dinosaur of a car out of the driveway. She mused herself by thinking that this gray haired woman would be one of the few people she would actually miss after graduation.

Najwa's thoughts focused on her impending chapter meeting. She picked up her black shoulder bag and walked over to the student organization calendar. September through June stretched across the main office wall. Each holiday was crossed out in blue ink and a red marker indicated midterms and finals. She smiled as she realized all the good party dates weren't taken yet. Pulling her spiral notebook from her bag, she jotted down the available dates and walked towards the back stairs leading to the basement.

By the time she reached the bottom step, she felt the cool basement air gently brush past her face. The house served an important role throughout the history of time. This basement was formerly a stop on the Underground Railroad and had been carefully preserved to capture its many stories in time. The center room was now the birthplace of CU's black consciousness. Preserving the memory of history and fostering the Blacks of CU was now its primary responsibility.

Scatterings of chairs were about the basement's room. The long table at the front served as the resting spot for Najwa and her bag. She placed copies of her agenda on each end of the table when she noticed Berri descending.

"Hey girl!" Berri exclaimed entering the center room.

"What's happening VP?" Najwa responded, acknowledging her vice president's presence.

"Guess who I just saw at the Chicken Shack?"

" Who? Chicken?" Najwa kidded.

"Naw Girl. My Dean, Donna. You know we've been looking for her since we got back?" Berri continued as she took her seat at the table.

Najwa rose and began organizing the chairs.

"She livin' way out there by the bus station. Wonder why she moved so far? No wonder none of us seen her." Berri joined Najwa in arranging the chairs.

Najwa, shrugging her shoulders replied, "What's happenin' with her?"

Berri eagerly answered with more information than Najwa cared to know. "She won't be making the meeting. Somethin bout' a report due. That Donna is all right with me. You know she made honors last semester?"

Najwa slightly straightened the last chair and returned to the front table. Her thoughts flashed back to the last time she saw Donna. Erasing the memory, Najwa realized she really did not care about the happenings of one Donna Davis.

"So, what do you think about the agendas?" Najwa changed the subject.

"Ooo-wee! Two page agendas, a calendar and what's this, a budget too? Looks like somebody's got some big plans for her last year," Berri answered.

Najwa smiled. "Berri, you know I don't like mess. I have got to be organized."

"As vice president my sista', I second that emotion."

For the first time they laughed.

Berri sat in the front row facing Najwa. "Seeing Donna sure brought back some memories. Remember how she would get mad and leave us in the hands of visiting big sisters. You would have to come over in the middle of the night to rescue us. Remember that?"

"Yeah, I remember," Najwa smirked.

"Trifling heifer was never around," Najwa thought. Najwa tried not to think about last year's unfortunate events but Berri was determined to force her down memory lane.

"That Donna..."

To Najwa's pleasure, Berri was interrupted by the sounds of Carla and Lynette's laughter.

"Hey Sands," Lynette and Carla said in unison as they walked in.

"Hey Berri," Lynette continued as Carla sifted through the agendas.

"We had to be here early to support our Sands' first meeting as the pres," Carla joked. "What's going on with you soror vice pres?" Carla turned to Berri.

Berri slightly smiled at the recognition Carla gave her existence. "Nothing," she responded flatly.

"As a matter of fact Sands, y'all are right on time." Najwa assured. She knew if they had not showed, Berri would have continued about Donna. Najwa wondered if Berri was trying to invoke a response or if the sight of Donna genuinely touched her. Upon the arrival of Najwa's sands, Berri's conversation ceased.

Within twenty minutes, the entire Gamma Chapter of Omega Pi Alpha Sorority gathered. Najwa conducted the meeting as if it were a well-written and rehearsed script. Leading the room through the traditional Omega Pi Alpha sorority song and the correspondence, Najwa never skipped a beat. She announced the names of all the committee chairpersons. Dates for every chapter event including the rush, public service programs, parties, and fundraisers were already chosen. Najwa left no stone unturned.

In exactly two hours, the meeting came to a conclusion. Everyone looked at their watches in amazement. Najwa managed to breeze through topics they normally would have argued about for hours. She noticed Carla and Lynette glance at one another in astonishment.

"Sorors new business is last on our agenda. Does anyone have any?" Najwa asked.

Keisha raised her hand. "Yes, I do."

"Oh Lord," Carla muttered.

"Soror, I would like the record to officially reflect that my name is not Kate Jones anymore. I believe I made it known when our secretary did the roll call. But I want the minutes to reflect my name change."

Keisha turned to her audience who struggled to contain their laughter. "Sorors my name is now Keisha. K-E-I-S-H-A. And, I will not answer to anything else."

Najwa went along with Keisha's grandstand moment. "Keisha, we'll make certain that the chapter's roll reflects your name change."

"Kate, why did you change your name to that stupid mess?" Carla blurted.

"My name is not stupid soror. I will have you to know that the name Keisha reflects my individualism, creativity and our African ancestry. And for your information, I have gotten more compliments on my name than you could imagine. You watch, pretty soon everybody will be naming their babies Keisha. And it will be all because of yours truly. Just think Carla, you can say you knew the woman that started it all."

"Girl you are pitiful," Carla said before she burst into laughter.

Regaining control of the meeting, Najwa interrupted. "Sorors, we will all be mindful of our soror's wishes. Seeing no other business I think it's fair to say we can close this meeting." Najwa pounded the gavel that had been passed down to her by the former president and announced that the first meeting of the 1973 school year was officially closed.

"Now that's how you run a meeting, in and out sorors, in and out," Carla kidded.

Lynette walked over to Najwa who was packing her bag. "Wow! You really worked this meeting tonight."

"I told y'all I meant business this year."

"I know, but you're moving a little fast aren't you. I mean you just had it all put together. All we had to do was just listen and say yes ma'am," Lynette joked.

"What do you mean? I didn't come off too strong did I? I know I set a lot of goals for us but I just want everything to go really well."

"I don't think you came off that strong. But, if I weren't your sands, I might be a little offended by the fact that you already picked the date for the rush that I am chairing."

Najwa immediately apologized not realizing in her eagerness to be on top of every detail, she had stepped on her sand's toes. "Sands you know I didn't mean..."

Lynette interrupted. "Don't apologize, it's cool. I know you are a little anxious to get the ball rolling'. Don't worry I am not offended. That's just one less thing I have to worry about."

"Lynette really. I just don't want any mistakes."

Unexpectedly, over Najwa's shoulder Irby whispered. "Um' excuse me Najwa, but when you get a chance I need to talk to you alone."

"No problem, Irby you want to talk now?" Najwa looked surprised.

"No. If you are going home, I can come by after I stop to get something to eat," Irby responded.

"Why don't you just pick me up something to and bring it over to my place. We can talk then?" Najwa wondered what was so important that could not be talked about there.

"That's cool. The Chicken Shack okay with you?" Irby asked.

"Cool," Najwa replied.

Najwa and Lynette looked at each other puzzled as Irby walked away. "What was that all about?" Lynette asked.

"I don't know girl, probably just something silly about her line sisters. Anyway, I'll call you later on. I might walk over if it's not too late. I want to go over some stuff about the rush."

"Uh, uh no you ain't. I got to study," Lynette immediately said. "Would you please just let me handle the Rush? I told you I got it under control Naj."

"You're right, you're right. Just let me know what you come up with sands."

Najwa returned to her apartment confident that the groundwork for her year was laid. Over and over she played her mental tape of the chapter meeting wondering if she had forgotten any vital points. Already, she began planning the executive board meeting. Despite the reactions Najwa received from the officers, she did not feel that next week was too soon for the committee chairpersons to be prepared.

Only the arrival of Irby with two chicken dinners from Mel's Chicken Shack snapped Najwa out of her meditative state. She changed into shorts and her sorority tee shirt and together they sat on the floor with fried chicken, coleslaw, and slices of bread spread across the coffee table.

Najwa licked her fingers and tore a wing apart. "Mel knows he can fry up some chicken."

"I know and it seems like the longer I'm in this town, the better it tastes," Irby replied.

Ready to hear what Irby had to say, Najwa finally indulged her dinner guest. "So, what did you want to talk to me about?"

"Najwa you know, you really had that meeting under control. I'm so glad you are president."

"Thanks Irby. But that's not what you wanted to talk to me about was it?"

"Well, no. But I just wanted you to know that I really do look up to you. I mean you were my secret special when I was on line and you really helped me through the pledge process. I feel like we are bonded Najwa."

"I feel the same way too. Irby, you know you are my girl."

"I feel like I can tell you anything Najwa. I mean you have really given me some good advice in the past."

"Irby cut it short. What's the problem?" Najwa was flattered by Irby's compliments, but she knew there was more.

"Najwa, I have been holding a secret for a couple of weeks now and I don't know what to do. If this gets out it could hurt a lot of people. That's why you have got to promise me you won't tell anyone what I am about to tell you. I mean nobody," Irby pleaded.

"I can't promise you that until I know what the problem is," Najwa answered.

"Najwa, I promised myself I would never tell but I need to lift this off my shoulders. Truth is, I can't think of anyone else in the chapter that I trust or respect more than you." Irby sat in silence.

Najwa waited for her to continue still not making any promises.

Finally, Irby took a long deep breath. She looked Najwa in the eyes. "Okay here goes. Remember that mess the night of the Kappa after set and how y'all sent me to look for Keisha?"

"How could I forget that night? It is only the talk of the campus. The Kappas will never be able to have another party."

"I went upstairs to find Keisha and well…" Irby hesitated. "I found her in one of the bedrooms with a man," she finished.

"And you think that surprises me? I'm going to be honest with you since we are sharing right now. I never wanted that girl in this organization to begin with. But no, sorors felt that with time and a little molding, she would be Gamma chapter material. I told sorors they couldn't change that girl. So as a neophyte, I just shut my mouth." Najwa ripped a piece of bread and soaked up the thick barbecue sauce on her plate.

"There's more Najwa. She was with someone we know."

"Irby this campus' Black population is not that big. I'm sure it would be someone we know. Who was it? That ole' sleazy Isaac? Or was it that creep Darrel who lives in the old dorms."

"No it was worse than that, Najwa."

"Well who was it girl?"

"Mark," Irby muttered.

"Mark?" Najwa responded. "Mark, who?" She asked hoping it wasn't the Mark they all knew.

"Candace's boyfriend, Mark."

"What?"

There was silence for a moment.

"Well how do you know they were doing anything?" Najwa asked.

"Najwa, they were both half naked when I opened the door. And I don't think they were comparing birthmarks."

"What did Keisha say when you walked in?"

"Nothing. She couldn't say anything. She called me later trying to explain. She said it just happened and not to worry she would take care of it."

Najwa was furious. "It just happened? Is that all she had to say?"

"That's why I needed to talk to you. She acts as if nothing happened. Like it's business as usual. The way she sauntered around the chapter meeting talking about why she changed her name just sent me over the edge. The nerve of her! Did you see how she sat next to Candace the entire meeting? I wanted to throw up." Irby had never been more honest with Najwa since they first met. She had, in fact, lost her appetite.

"I see why you had to get that off your chest. Something has to be done." Najwa stood and walked over to her wicker chair and sat. "I'm not havin' this in my chapter."

"Najwa you can't tell! Candace would never forgive me if she found out I knew and didn't tell her. I don't care about Keisha. She showed her true colors. It's Candace I'm concerned about."

"Who else have you told?" Najwa asked.

"No one. I have been worrying about this for two weeks now. Every time I see Mark he just looks in another direction."

"He should!" Najwa blurted.

"What do you think I should do?"

"Don't tell anyone. The last thing we need is to become the

center of the campus gossip circle. Give me some time to think over this one."

"And then what?"

"I don't know Irby. I don't know. As hard as it may be, don't you worry about it."

"Whatever you do, I think I should be the one to tell Candace. She's my sands and I think it's the least she would expect of me," Irby pleaded.

"Don't worry, I won't tell her."

Najwa lost her appetite as well. Her problems as president had just begun. Within an hour, Najwa drove Irby to her dorm. The entire eight blocks Najwa reassured Irby everything would work out fine. But she also reminded her that she would not allow rumors to spread around campus about Gamma chapter. During the short ride back to her apartment, Najwa fought to maintain a calm mind.

"This was supposed to be the perfect year. My perfect year," Najwa muttered to herself.

She knew she was kidding herself in thinking everything would go smoothly. In her apartment parking lot, Najwa sat in her car thinking. Her first instinct told her to call an emergency meeting with Lynette and Carla. Her second instinct said to just calm down and think a little longer before she reacted. After all, she did not want this scandal to get any larger than it already was.

Najwa was appalled and disgusted by Keisha's blatant disrespect for Omega Pi Alpha. This was a sisterhood. There was no room for Keisha and her mess. Each Greek organization's members took an extraordinary amount of criticism from Black students alone for their affiliation. Normal problems of campus organizations would magnify if it involved a member of a sorority or fraternity. For the past two years, the organizations banned together to prove that they offered more to the campus than just gossip circles and strings of controversy. Omega Pi Alpha was at the forefront of this fight. Keisha's behavior made the entire chapter look like hypocrites. Najwa could not allow Keisha to destroy the success she planned this school year.

*Deep thought was definitely a characteristic of Sadie Mae Wesley. Often when away from her studies at the University of Chicago and especially when caught in the mundane nature of her job, Sadie buried herself into the depths of her mind.*

# Monday, October 8, 1973

Just as she promised, Mrs. Dixon opened doors for Najwa at the Casperton Court House. Immediately, Najwa jumped at the opportunity to get away from the daily grind of the campus and make extra money by taking a part time job.

The mere fact that Najwa even sought a job surprised her mother. Usually, she only worked during the summer when there was no pressure of studies. While her mother expressed her concern with holding a full class schedule while working, Najwa still impressed her parents with her initiative. Lately, it seemed as if they placed a tremendous amount of pressure on her seemingly complacent attitude about plans after graduation.

"What page did he say to start at?" Carla thumbed through her notes like a mad woman attempting to keep up with Professor Duncan. She turned to her sands.

"Najwa!"

Najwa, finally acknowledging Carla, turned slightly.

"The homework assignment. What page?" Carla asked.

"Huh?" Najwa looked confused.

"Earth to Najwa. Literature 551. The homework assignment for this week. I need to know the page number," Carla whispered.

"Oh, okay," Najwa flatly replied. She turned the pages in her spiral notebook then looked back at Carla blankly. "What homework?" Najwa asked puzzled.

"Girl, where is your mind? Give me that notebook." Carla snatched the notebook off Najwa's desk and began looking for the homework assignment. After turning the first few pages she looked at Najwa.

"Where are your notes from today? All I see on this page are little scribble marks and notes that mean nothing. What's wrong girl? You know you got to help me through this class. You were the one who talked me into this, Ms. English major." Carla felt as if she was talking to a brick wall. "Hello? Najwa?"

"What are you talking about Carla?" Najwa again snapped out of her daze.

"Excuse me ladies, is there something you would like to share with the rest of the class. We would simply love to hear your opinions on the piece we just finished reading. Which I am sure you were just discussing," Professor Duncan interrupted.

"Absolutely Professor Duncan. As a matter of fact, we are so enthused about this course, we were just discussing how anxious we are to complete the assignment. We just want to be sure of the pages. Would you mind repeating that?" Carla quickly returned.

Carla never skipped a beat. Her satirical nature always kept her on her toes. This time as always, she was able to talk her way out of another compromising situation. Professor Duncan gave his usual summation of the day's lesson and sent the students away with five chapters to read and a writing assignment. Najwa and Carla left class together to eat lunch as they had every Tuesday and Thursday since the semester began.

Carla fussed as they walked across long pathways of the campus grounds. "You know I only took this class because of you Najwa."

"Me? I didn't make you take this class. I thought you said you needed the credits to graduate? All I said, was I thought it would be nice to finally take a class with my sands."

"I told you I needed some more credits. I didn't say I wanted to take the hardest Lit Professor in the school," Carla continued complaining.

Najwa found no humor in her sands usual sarcasm. "Well don't blame me that you can't keep up. Maybe if you slow down in the party department you can keep up with class."

"Whoa, calm down Naj. I'm just kidding with you. No need to bite my head off."

"I'm sorry Carla. I just have a lot on my mind." Najwa fumbled in her bag. "I have a whole lot of stuff to do and I'm getting a little behind."

"Are they overworking you at your new job?" Carla asked.

"Are you kidding? The only peace of mind I have is while I am at that job. At least it is quiet in that basement. I am struggling in this class just like you. I had no idea they would switch professors a week after registration. If I had known this class was going to be taught by Duncan, I wouldn't have given it a second thought. He acts like his class is the only one we're taking. Like we don't have homework in other classes!"

"I know. I'm barely caught up on the assignment from last week," Carla added.

"Then, my mom called me going on and on and on about my plans after graduation. She says that I need to stop fooling around and figure out what I want to do with my life. Said she didn't understand why I was spending all my time on sorority stuff and that it's not going to last forever. The usual. So, I went to see my advisor about a week ago to talk about options. You know, try to get a head start on jobs." Najwa calmed herself as they rounded the corner of the Barkston student center.

"And?" Carla interrupted Najwa's silence.

"We talked about jobs I could easily fit into and a few graduate programs. But I should have been doing this last year when I was fooling around with Donna and that damn line. I didn't realize how much I let slip by me. Maybe my mother was right. Maybe this sorority is taking over my life.

"My counselor ended up giving me an application for a graduate sociology program here at CU. There may even be the possibility of a scholarship. I think I have to write an essay and get recommendations. I haven't even looked at the application yet."

"If I know you as well as I do Naj, you can spit that essay out in a matter of minutes. It shouldn't be a big problem. I can give you some pointers. We can have this thing done in no time girl," Carla reassured Najwa.

"Thanks sands, but that's not all. The rush is coming up in a couple of weeks. I know we have had three chapter meetings and Lynette has things under control, but I am still concerned. I get the feeling some of our Alumnae may show up. I feel like they are lurking in the shadow just waiting for me to make a fool of myself."

Najwa and Lynette proceeded over to the tables in the "Greek Corner" of the Barkston Center cafeteria. This was the section of the cafeteria where each organization had an unofficial designated table.

"Lynette is on her stuff. So don't concern yourself with that nonsense. I can't believe you're worried. Is this all about Donna again? She is out of the picture so don't even worry about her." Carla said.

There was one other concern that had probably burned inside Najwa more than any other. She could not reveal the secret she and Irby shared.

"It's not her that I am concerned about. It's the other chapter members, like Keisha. You know she is a magnet for mess. I don't have time to keep looking over my shoulders to make sure she isn't pulling some crazy mess. I got a chapter to run."

"Najwa as much as I don't like that girl, did you ever stop to think that maybe you are just overreacting?" Carla said.

"If you only knew." Najwa thought to herself. "I may be Carla. I'm still going to watch my back. I advise you to do the same," Najwa replied.

"Oh don't you worry. I'm gon' watch my back, Lynette's back, and your back too. I got everyone's back covered...Oh no..." Carla's attention was diverted. "Here she comes!" Carla scooted down in her seat.

"Who? Keisha?" Najwa leaned forward to see to whom Carla was referring.

"No, its that girl. You remember! That girl that talked our heads off for an hour about how she wanted to be a member of Omega Pi Alpha. Don't move Najwa. She is right behind you maybe she won't see us."

Najwa sat still as a rock. Nevertheless, the young lady managed to notice them sitting across the cafeteria. Immediately, she rushed over and rattled about herself. After a few minutes of listening to her bragging about her accomplishments, Najwa excused both she and Carla from the table. She was not in the mood for this nonsense.

———————————

Hours passed since Najwa and Carla parted. Najwa's mind was still captured by their conversation after class. Now she sat in the refuge of her apartment. In thirty minutes, the executive board meeting of the Gamma Chapter of Omega Pi Alpha would convene in her living room and Najwa struggled to maintain her focus. She had yet to even glance at the application her academic advisor had given her. Now, it lay on the coffee table unopened. She knew, at some point, she would need to begin thinking about her future.

Najwa picked up the application and threw herself on the couch.

She removed the contents of the brown legal envelope and stared at the cover page. No matter how she tried, she still could not focus on it's contents. Instead, she began to wonder if she had her notes ready for the meeting. She shook her head and repeatedly told herself to stay focused. Her mind drifted to how she would handle the situation with Keisha and Candace. That was a time bomb ready to blow at any moment. She forced herself to read the instruction page. She read the first paragraph and then the second. Najwa still could not retain any information.

"Najwa you have got to focus," she said aloud. Again, she started at the beginning. Finally, after fifteen minutes of straining to concentrate, she managed to read the entire application.

"This is more than I thought," she sighed.

The essay she anticipated completing with a quick trip to the library was slowly looking like a larger task. She leaned back on the couch, closed her eyes and took another deep breath. Najwa grabbed her pen and spiral notebook, opened the pages and began to jot down a few ideas. Unsatisfied, she drew the letter X over her words and started on a new page.

Twice this pattern continued before the doorbell rang. The first arrivals for her meeting were at the door and at least for this moment, Najwa could prolong thinking of her essay. Within fifteen minutes, the entire executive board sat in Najwa's living room.

"Since everyone is here, I think we can start the meeting." Najwa addressed the officers positioned around the living room. As usual, she assumed her position in her wicker chair and took command.

"Ladies the first and most important order of business is our Treasurer's report."

Diane, the chapter's treasurer, gave a report of every financial transaction since the first meeting.

Najwa acknowledged the Public Service Chairperson. "Your turn Robin."

Robin was probably the most socially aware of all the chapter members. It was this trait that allowed her to run unchallenged for her position. The focus of her report was their traditional Thanksgiving Turkey Basket Giveaway.

Casperton was not only the home of Casperton University but was also home to the state's most impoverished Black community. Every year, Gamma chapter hosted a Thanksgiving family night at the Casperton Community Center complete with entertainment, games, and music. The culmination of the evening was the awarding of food baskets to two Black families to celebrate the Thanksgiving holiday. This same program won Gamma Chapter recognition from the Casperton NAACP. Najwa saw much more potential in this program and hoped that they would again win the prestigious service award.

"Robin if you noticed from Diane's Treasurer's report, we have no money. Sorors, we need to come up with some ideas tonight on how we are going to fund this project. We only have a month before the holiday. Any money we may get from the Black Greek Council or the University won't come in until after the holiday. So let's think ladies," Najwa pleaded.

After a few moments of throwing out ideas that only met resistance, Candace spoke. "Hey wait a minute. The Kappas had a party date planned for this Saturday. Maybe we can get the date from them since they're still suspended."

"You know, you're right Candace. I still have that date marked off on my calendar. That would be perfect," Najwa responded.

"Yeah, we can have a party. It will be something quick and to the point. We can raise all the money we need in one night. We would just have to really get the news out on the campus and in the neighborhood. Sorors we need at least one hundred dollars if we want to make this event bigger than last year. I think it is possible," Robin added.

"But we don't have the date. How are we going to get the date from them?" Berri asked.

"Ladies, never underestimate the power of your sorors. Don't worry about it. Let's just say Richard, the chapter's president, owes me a favor." Lynette winked her eye.

"Umm…watch out now! You think you can get that date, Lynette?" Robin beamed.

"Honey that party date is ours. You just start making the posters," Lynette responded. "But remember sorors the rush is on Sunday. Y'all still got to get up and help with setting up for the Rush. So that means no after party ladies."

"This would be the first time we have ever had a party so close to the Rush. We have to make sure we are on top of things ladies. I feel a whole lot better about this project now that we have everything almost worked out," Najwa added.

Najwa knew that the responsibility of holding offices and planning chapter activities was relatively new to most of the chapter members. The last thing she wanted was to have an executive board that felt their president was unreasonable, unapproachable or unsupportive. If this happened, she would find herself single handedly running Gamma chapter.

The remainder of the evening, the women spent their energies belaboring the details of the rush and pledge process. Lynette reiterated the fact that she needed a stress free term. She wanted no problems out of her sorors whom she knew all too well. The neophytes, especially, were ecstatic with the first sign of pledges. Lynette, on the other hand, emphasized that she had no intentions of repeating her senior year due to fallen grades. This year, things were going to run differently. No one would jeopardize Gamma Chapter's charter on the campus of Casperton University.

# Saturday, October 13, 1973

Using her charm and a promise to dinner before the holiday, Lynette acquired the party date. By Friday, the members of Gamma chapter had hung posters and invited the entire Black campus population to their Pre-Thanksgiving party. Their spirits were high with the thought that most of their work until December would be done. The only exception would be their volunteer work and pledging the line.

Everyone knew to be at the Barkston Center for the last Omega Pi Alpha party before the Thanksgiving break. Because there was really nothing much else to do in Casperton, the Blacks in the surrounding community always attended the campus parties. Calls were made to the sorors in the surrounding Illinois chapters to attend. With all in their favor, Gamma chapter knew they could raise the money they needed and then some to tie them over until after Christmas.

The Saturday started with every member of the chapter completing an assignment. While half concentrated on party decorations, the others ran around town finding last minute items for the Rush. At eight o'clock that evening they all assembled at the Barkston Center to greet the eager partygoers.

By eleven, the main party room was almost full. At her last count, Robin determined that they collected close to one hundred and fifty dollars. This was well over what was needed to make the Thanksgiving baskets. The party was the success Gamma chapter needed. For the first time in almost three weeks, Najwa rested easy in the fate of her chapter. The first accomplishment as president was achieved.

With her mind clear of this hurdle, Najwa felt she could concentrate on her future for a moment. For now, all she needed to do was make it through the rush. Thanksgiving was only a few weeks away and the break would give her all the time she needed to regroup and get back on the ball. Writing her graduate school application essay would surely be easy.

As the last hour of the party neared, Najwa, Lynette, and Carla sat at the front table collecting the last of the proceeds. Basking in the success of the party, Najwa felt she could ease off the chapter. She and her sands took over the door duty allowing the neophytes to enjoy what was left of the evening. Their motives were also a little selfish. For the first time since the semester began, they would have a brief moment to bond.

Besides the Rush, the only subject Lynette spoke of was her pre-med classes. Lynette's father was a prominent gynecologist in the Chicago area and it was her vision to follow in his footsteps. Lynette spent her entire four years at Casperton University attending summer school and taking every extra class she could. In between counting dollar bills, Lynette explained how studying for her classes kept her in the library with the exception of sorority meetings. With midterms around the corner, seclusion was inevitable. Despite, Carla was still able to secure a commitment from her sands to dinner before the break.

Having sat on door duty most of the night, Najwa excused herself to the bathroom. She ran down the crowded hall to the nearest ladies room only to find that there was a line out the door. Waiting for each women in the line to release themselves was not an option for Najwa or her bladder. Unable to wait another minute, she raced down to the basement bathroom and swung the door open.

"Yes, empty!" She exclaimed as she performed what she had penned the "pee dance."

While in the stall Najwa heard another person rush into the stall next to her. "She must have to go worst than me." Najwa thought to herself. On her way to the sink to wash her hands, Najwa heard the woman gagging.

"Are you okay?" Najwa called to the stall.

She received no answer. Only more gagging. Obviously someone was sick.

"Hello in there. Are you okay? Do you need help?" Najwa again asked approaching the closed door. The toilet flushed and finally the woman spoke.

"I'm fine. It's okay, I don't need any…" she was stopped

abruptly by another series of gagging.

Najwa still concerned, stood at the door until the second episode of vomiting was over. Again she approached. "Do you need me to get you some water or something?"

"No, I'll be okay," the woman quivered.

This time Najwa recognized the voice.

"Keisha?" There was silence. "Keisha is that you?" Najwa asked again.

"Yeah it's me. Who is that?" Keisha struggled to speak before again gagging.

"It's me Najwa. Girl, open this door. Are you okay?"

Finally the door crept open and a flushed Keisha emerged. She walked over to the sink and began running cold water in her hands.

Najwa handed Keisha a handful of paper towels. "Here wet these and put them on your face."

Keisha leaned over the sink, wet the long white towels and dabbed her face and cheeks.

"Keisha I thought we all agreed. No getting drunk tonight because of the Rush tomorrow. What happened?"

"Najwa I'm not drunk. Just don't feel well," Keisha responded between placing the cold compressions on her face.

"You don't look good that's for sure. Did you eat something that was spoiled?"

"I didn't eat anything today. Don't feel like eating these days. Just makes me sicker to look at food."

"Well if you aren't drunk and you haven't eaten then what's

wrong? You aren't pregnant are you? Najwa joked.

There was silence. Keisha looked at Najwa. The blank stare on her face told it all.

"Are you Keisha?"

"Am I what?" Keisha snapped.

"Hey, I was just jiving. You aren't pregnant right?" Najwa struggled to smile as if she really believed this possibility to be a joke.

Keisha turned from Najwa. She continued wiping her face with the cold towels.

"Najwa I don't know. I mean no. Now would you please leave me alone? I'm sick," Keisha said.

"You don't know?" Najwa insisted Keisha continue. "What do you mean you don't know?"

"I don't feel like talking about this right now."

"Oh, you are going to talk Keisha. If you are pregnant I think you need to say something right now."

"Say something for what? Who do you think you are? I don't need to tell you anything. You never liked me anyway. So why should I tell you? Since when are you so interested in my business?" Keisha snapped.

Najwa immediately counter-attacked. "Since you started wearing the Omega Pi Alpha letters, spreadin' your business all over this campus with every man you meet."

"I'm not going to stand here and listen to this." Keisha turned and walked away.

Najwa grabbed Keisha's shoulder and halted her grand exit. Her anger was at the boiling point. "No you need to start talking right now!"

"What is with you? You supposed to be my soror, my sister. Instead, you in here harassing me when you should be helping. Remember Ms. Omega Pi Alpha herself? I'm sure you remember, 'In times of strife, trouble, and pain, the spirit of my sister is all I have to gain.' You made us recite it on line every night."

"Since you are so good at quoting the rituals, then why don't you tell me the line where it says your sister's man is all you have to gain?

Keisha's head jerked. She glared at Najwa. "What are you talking about?"

"Don't play me for a fool Keisha. I know what happened the night of the Kappa party. And now you are pregnant?"

"It ain't his baby!"

A callous spirit took over Najwa's being. "How would you even know?"

"To hell with you Najwa. I know that big mouth Irby told you. So, who else knows? I want you and all of my so-called sorors to stay out of my business!"

"Doesn't really matter how I found out Keisha. Cause the whole campus will know in a few months when you start showing. How could you do this to your own sands, Candace? Are you that unconcerned with everybody else?"

"I didn't want to hurt Candace. That is my sands and regardless of what you think, she is my girl. Me and Mark didn't even go all the way. I told him I couldn't. That's when Irby busted in."

"You are a liar Keisha. You were a liar in your freshman year. You were the biggest liar on your line and you have proven yourself to be consistent this year," Najwa smirked.

"For the past couple of weeks I've been trying to figure out how I was going to fix this situation. How I would possibly explain why we had sorors in the chapter who were no less than common whores? But now you've made that impossible." Najwa said.

"Oh I feel so bad for you Najwa." Keisha sarcastically replied. "You think I care about you and how this affects your image and your chapter? What about me and my feelings? This is my life we are talking about here. My life is ruined. You think I wanted to come this far to get pregnant? I worked my butt off to stay in this racist school and nothin' is gonna mess that up! I sure as hell ain't goin' back home. I can't take care of a kid."

"What am I suppose to say to Candace? Your mistake affects all of us. Keisha, I just don't get you. What is it you want from us?"

"Nothin, Najwa. Not a damn thing!" Keisha turned and walked toward the door. She didn't bother to face Najwa. "Don't worry about your soror, Najwa. I already took care of your problem. I got rid of the baby. Probably why I'm sick. Now if you are finished, the chapter whore is going back up to the party." She slammed the bathroom door leaving Najwa standing still and speechless.

*The promise of a new life. Her father cherished the land the deed represented for over twenty-five years. The farm was nestled in the small town of Casperton, Illinois and the only home Sadie had known.*

# Sunday, October 14, 1973

"Half breed that's all I ever heard. Half-breed duh, duh, duh…" Candace shrieked through Cher's chart-raising song. She was setting up the stereo system to play background music for the Rush when Cher's voice sprung from the campus radio station.

Candace made another attempt to match Cher's unique squeal. "I think that's what they called me since the day I was born…oh," she continued.

"Candy! Turn that mess off! Don't nobody want to hear that junk in here!" Lynette hollered as she walked to the basement stairs of the Black House.

Candace shot a quick look at Lynette as she passed. She continued humming as Cher's voice blended into the sound of the station's disc jockey. Only after the last note was sung did Candace lower the volume and turn the station.

"Hey how about those A's," the new raspy voiced disc jockey said. Candace adjusted the volume to WRTX. "It's been weeks but I am still beaming over my team, the World Champion Oakland A's.

Now for all you cats who sat on the championship train, this one's for you."

For a brief second dead air filled the airwaves of the Black house main room. Candace did not care much for baseball but was a fan of "The Max." On Sunday afternoon, he was always good for a few hours of soulful Sunday tunes. In less than a minute Candace was pooping her fingers and humming again to the sounds of the O'Jays singing "Love Train."

Lynette emerged from the basement struggling with two stacked chairs in one arm and glancing at her wristwatch on the other.

"Three o'clock," Lynette thought. In thirty minutes the doors would open and two, maybe three hours later she could get back to her books. Lynette surveyed the room noticing her sorors straightening the displays.

"Let's get this show on the road," Lynette ordered.

The Omega Pi Alpha banner stretched across the back of the upstairs room. A generous portion of cookies and chips were placed next to the red icing cake with black letters. The written words in the long sheet cake were simple, yet complete, "The Soul of a New Nation." On the opposite side of the room was the punch bowl. Another table contained the chapter's history book and paraphernalia. The wooden scrapbook was opened to the black and white photographs of 1930's Gamma chapter. A couple of red and black balloons were tied to the front and back chairs of each row.

"Sorors!" Najwa gained the attention of her sorors.

Each member stopped what she was doing and turned.

"Sorors," Najwa started again at the front of the room. "Sorors, listen up. Lynette has some last minute words for us before the Rush." She nodded towards her line sister. Lynette laid the last chair against the wall and motioned towards the neophytes to put their chairs into the proper place.

"Sorors, I think we should take this time to pray before we get started," Lynette instructed.

They all bowed their heads, stood in a circle, and held hands.

"Dear God, as we embark upon this journey. Please help us to remember that many are called but few are chosen. Lord, help us to remember our purpose here today. Help us to remember the purpose of those who came before us and the impact we will have on those who are to come after we have gone. Just as your son's life was given for our sins, so were the lives of others here on earth given so that we may have this opportunity to convene here today. We take a few moments to remember them silently." Lynette's words were soft and calming. Each woman was silent as they held the moment in remembrance.

"Amen." Finally Lynette ended and each soror responded with the same.

Only the cracking of the front door opening broke the moment's significance. Every member of Gamma Chapter turned in disgust that some prospective member would intrude. But the body that slipped through the cracked door was not a prospective member. The five-foot-one framed body had already made the journey.

"Donna, you made it!" Berri exclaimed as she headed toward the door.

Lynette and Carla's eyes caught Najwa's. Their instinctive bond tightened.

Berri reached and embraced Donna who was watching out the corner of her eye.

"Hey sands! Our Dean of Pledges is here," Berri said.

All the neophytes moved toward the door with the exception of Irby who smiled slightly and moved to check the food table. Robin fumbled through papers at the sign in table.

Donna closed her eyes and hugged Berri tightly. She then hugged each of the sorors who had gathered around. Finally after hugging the last neophyte, Carla approached.

"What's happening old head?" Carla said as their eyes met.

Donna adjusted the short wool suit jacket over her oddly shaped body. "I'm solid girl."

"Come on in, Lynette's just going over some last minute stuff. You know how it is girl." Carla motioned Donna further into the room.

Donna glanced at Najwa who returned an acknowledging nod. It was clear who the presiding officer was.

"Sorors," Lynette said breaking up the chatter.

Berri sat in the front row next to Donna. The two nodded affectionately towards one another.

Lynette glanced at her watch. "Sorors we have ten minutes before the doors open. Remember what was said in chapter meeting. Best behavior! The program begins promptly at four. Use the first thirty minutes to personally speak to our guests. About five minutes before the program starts, we will convene in the library for our formal entrance."

"Lynette, I was thinking. Can I have a little more time to talk about service projects?" Robin placed special emphasis on the word service. "After all, service is the basis of our bond," she ended.

"That Robin," Berri whispered to Donna. "The basis of our bond is sisterhood, not service. Give some sistas a little title and they let it go to their head."

Donna smiled, leaned in to Berri and whispered, "I hate that power hungry mess!"

"Me too," Berri echoed.

Lynette sighed then conceded. "Okay Robin, five more minutes. We will only sing two verses of the entrance song. Cool sorors?"

The doors of the Black House opened at exactly three thirty to twenty eager young ladies. With the exception of only a few, introductions were not necessary thanks to the close-knit Black community of CU's campus. Only the socially deprived and new students were strangers to the women of Omega Pi Alpha. Dressed in miniskirts, dresses and stylish pants suits, some of the prospective women planned their wardrobe and attendance before the first invitation was mailed.

The first thirty minutes, in between sipping punch, the women walked around and talked to the various members of Gamma chapter. With this being their first Rush on the other side of the spectacle, the neophytes were frantic. With sly and cunning smiles on their faces, the neophytes introduced themselves to each young lady and then immediately began the inquisition.

"What is your major?"

"I haven't seen you before, are you a transfer student?"

"So why are you here?"

Najwa stood at the front podium adjusting her notes. Whatever she could find to occupy her time while the mingling occurred, she did. Unlike some of her sorors, Najwa found this time during the rush to be necessary, yet annoying. She did not care for the pretentious airs put on by either the women interested or her sorors. Najwa felt that the pressure to say all the right things, or at least all the things her sorors wanted to hear, was far too great to get to the heart of anyone's true intentions. So, just as she had done the year before, Najwa inconspicuously observed from afar noticing body language, mannerisms and any other signs she felt were important.

Najwa found herself observing her sorors more than anyone else. Donna in particular was an object of interest. It bothered Najwa that she couldn't quite place her finger on where Donna's mind could be. Her instincts told her to just sit and wait and eventually it would come into the open. Najwa knew that she needed to be one step ahead at all times. Never could she at any point let her guard down. Failing as president of Gamma chapter was not an option. This year would become a strategic game Najwa was determined to win.

Najwa felt she already knew part of the opposition's plan. Berri was obviously Donna's eyes and ears in the chapter. All she had to do now was observe any other little workers Donna may have employed. As Najwa thought more, she actually became annoyed at the realization that Donna would even dare check up on her performance as president. After all, this was just a sorority. No one was getting paid. Najwa loved her sorority dearly but her family and education were her top priorities. But as always she welcomed the challenge to outwit her predator. Quietly, she took all her mental notes and filed them away.

"Sands, you think we can get started now?" Lynette interrupted her chain of thought.

"This is your show girl," Najwa answered.

"Keisha isn't here yet and I had her on the program. Have you heard from her?"

"No. As a matter of fact I have not." Najwa answered.

"I can easily have someone else do her part," Lynette said.

Najwa was not surprised at Keisha's absence in light of last night. But she could not share her last conversation with Keisha with anyone.

"Last night at the party was the last time I talked to her. Maybe you should ask one of her line sisters. They may have talked to her this morning."

"Yeah, you're right." Lynette turned to the group. "Hey guys! Has anyone talked to Keisha this morning?"

"I asked her to take the deposit from the party to the night deposit box. She said she would be coming after that. At least that is what she said last night. You know how she can be sometimes," Diane answered.

"Well since she isn't here you think you can take her part on the program?" Lynette asked.

With an affirmative nod, Lynette was ready.

Najwa knew Lynette would solve this without a problem. She knew the sooner the Rush was over, the sooner Lynette could get some studying in for her Monday morning quiz.

Lynette stepped to the front of the room and gained the attention of all present. Formal introductions of the chapter were made. After this, each guest stood and introduced herself. Just as the program had generally gone in the past years, after the introductions, history of the organization was explained. Najwa stood before the group and gave a detailed and passionate account of the founding of the organization.

"It was the beginning of this century. Four courageous women started the journey that we still walk today. These women - Anna Hattie Merriweather, a medical student; Wilma Rodgers, an English student; Augusta Washington, a law student; and finally, the spirit of Sadie Mae Wesley, an education student - left a legacy of sisterhood and service for all of us to follow.

"Notice that I said the spirit of Sadie Mae Wesley. This sister's dream to educate her people in this very town that we are in today was abruptly cut when she met a very violent death. In the last moments of our precious sister's death, a promise was made. A promise to carry on a dream. Together, the remaining three women, at the University of Chicago, joined together in a sisterhood to fulfill a promise made to their sister. They set their goals to further the progress of their people as a whole. They sought the realization of success despite their oppressor. There was nothing they could do to bring their dear friend back. But they knew that in their work, her spirit would live on.

"Shortly after the founding of Omega Pi Alpha, they took their message to other campuses with Black populations. Out of this, Omega Pi Alpha has grown. Today we gather, carrying on in the spirit of not just one, but all the sisters who came before us. We are here in the spirit of love, the spirit of courage, and the spirit of struggle. This dream some of you will realize through membership in Omega Pi Alpha. Some of you will fulfill this dream in other works of life."

Najwa closed the notes that she never used and looked around the room with a blank stare before she ended with one last sentence.

"Ladies, you are about to embark upon the journey of your life."

The room was silent. Najwa captured her audience and left them in a trance. The fluctuation of her voice at the right point, her body movements, eye contact, and hand gestures seemed to be choreographed to every word she uttered. Not until she had taken her seat next to the podium did anyone dare to move. Najwa knew that she had hypnotized the group as some watched her slowly and methodically sit in her seat.

Berri followed Najwa with the history of Gamma chapter, which did not prove to be half as captivating. Robin followed with a detailed description of the public service projects of the chapter. She made certain that everyone noticed the several plaques and awards the chapter received over the years for their community work. By the time the Rush ended, each guest had acquired enough information on Omega Pi Alpha's founding, purpose and programs to start their own chapters.

"You know she did that on purpose," Donna whispered in Berri's ear.

"Who did what?" Berri turned.

"That Najwa. I told you about how she is always trying to be a star. Always upstaging everyone. I wonder how long she practiced that speech."

Berri chuckled.

Donna made her exit just as dramatic as her entrance. "Chiiiiile, I got to get outta here, 'cause I just can't take it no mo!" She looked at Berri. "You call me and let me know what's going on." Donna picked up her purse, walked to the door and waved to her sorors before the door slammed shut.

A few moments passed. The conversation focused on the young women who attended the Rush. As Gloria rearranged a few chairs, she caught a glimpse out the window. A Casperton Police car drove up the driveway and stopped in Mrs. Dixon's parking spot. Diane stood and watched, trying to make out the images in the car. An officer got out and walked around to the back door.

"What in the world is going on?" Gloria exclaimed as she recognized the woman emerging from the police car.

"What? What is it?" several asked.

"Come look! It's Keisha getting out of a police car!"

Some ran to the window while others ran to the front door open. The officer and Keisha made their way up the stairs.

Irby was the first to run to Keisha's rescue ignoring the officer.

"Keisha are you alright? What is going on?"

Keisha tried to reassure them. "I'm okay Irby. It's okay everyone." Her eyes were swollen from tears.

Again the questions were thrown.

"Officer, what's going on? Keisha what happened?"

"Ladies everything is fine now. Your friend is just lucky to be alive." The officer turned to Keisha. "Ma'am are you going to be okay now?"

Keisha nodded.

"If we get any information we will call you. I have to get back now."

Shutting the door behind the officer, again the questions poured.

"Sorors please let her sit down. We aren't going to get anywhere if we all talk at once. Lets go back inside." Lynette directed everyone back into the large room.

Keisha sat down as Irby handed her a small paper cup of punch from the table. She took a sip and a deep breath.

She began to speak. "Guys, I'm so sorry. I am really sorry. I just don't know what we are going to do now."

"Sorry? Sorry for what? What happened?" Lynette asked.

Tears fell from Keisha's swollen eyes. "The money is gone. I was robbed this morning," Keisha said sobbing.

"Robbed? What? Where? When? How did it happen? Who

robbed you?" They all asked.

"The money from our party!" Diane blurted.

Najwa finally spoke amidst all the noise. "Sorors, please! We need to calm down and let Keisha talk. Now take it from the beginning."

Keisha never looked up from the soaked tissue as she began to explain.

"Last night Diane gave me the party money to deposit. I told her I would take the money to the night deposit box this morning because I had to go over to that side of town anyway. I was almost at the bank when a man ran up behind me. He knocked me down and grabbed my purse. You know, my brown suede one I got last year."

Carla spoke. "Who knocked you down Keisha? Did you see who it was?"

Keisha took another sip of punch.

"No everything just happened so fast. I…I never even saw the dude's face. He just grabbed my purse and took off. By the time I was able to get up he had gotten so far I couldn't even chase him."

"No one saw the dude who did it? Was there anyone around when it happened?" Candace asked as she stood over Keisha massaging her shoulders.

"No. It was so strange. There was nobody around. Nobody walking. No cars coming. Nothin'. Just me laid out on the sidewalk. I am just so sorry. We worked so hard to get that money."

"Keisha don't even worry yourself about that money. Girl as long as you are okay we can always replace the money," Diane reassured.

Candace rushed across the room to get her jacket. "Look y'all, my man Mark knows a lot of cats in the hood around here. I am going to have him find out who did this. This town ain't that big. Sooner or later somebody is going to talk. I am going to go straight to his room now."

Keisha tried to stop her. "Naw Candace. The police took the report. They said they had somebody out looking already. I don't want anybody getting hurt 'cause of me."

"Keisha, since when the police around here care about some little Black chick from Casperton University getting her purse snatched? We gon find out who did this. Mark knows a lot of people, he'll be alright." Candace clutched her purse under her arm and ran out of the Black House.

"Be careful Candy!" Najwa hollered as the door slammed shut.

Najwa thought of the irony of the whole incident. The fact that Candace was so concerned about Keisha's well being that she would enlist the help of her man. Mark, unbeknownst to her, would probably have more interest in Keisha's misfortune than she could have ever known. Besides appearing a little shaken, to Najwa, Keisha seemed fine. Keisha spent the next minutes going over the incident, attempting to salvage any clue to who may have robbed her. Despite their confrontation, Najwa was still concerned.

"Keisha must be drained," she thought to herself. "Sorors, give Keisha a rest. There's nothing more we can do about it now. At least not until Candace is able to get some help from Mark." Najwa urged

113

everyone to finish cleaning.

A few reached down to give Keisha a hug and reassure her that all would be fine. The group then dispersed mumbling about the misfortune and picking up the scattered chairs.

Najwa sat next to Keisha and began to whisper. "Look Keisha... I was thinking about what we talked about last night at the party. You know, in the bathroom."

"What the hell does that have to do with this right now Najwa? Look I'm not going through that with you again," Keisha snapped and rolled her eyes.

"Keisha, calm down. The only reason why I even brought it up was because of your health. This guy did knock you down. I'm just concerned that you are really alright, that's all. Maybe you ought to go over to the University Clinic to make sure."

Keisha made it obvious that she was not impressed with Najwa's concern. "I'll be okay. I'm a little shaken up but that's about it. If I feel any different then I will consider going."

"That's cool. I just wanted to be sure." Najwa rose and gathered her things to leave.

"Diane, Lynette, and Robin can I see you in the other room?" Najwa beckoned as she led the way into one of the side offices.

"Listen, I didn't want to go into this in the other room but we have to meet now. You think you three could come over to my place? We got to figure out where we are going to get the money for those Thanksgiving baskets."

"There is no way we are going to get that money back in time for

114

the Thanksgiving project," Robin blurted.

"She's right. That money was all we had. We spent the rest of it on stuff for the Rush." Diane kept a very strict tally on all the funds that entered and left the chapter's treasury.

"Look we can talk about that when we get to my place. I just want to know if I can count on all of you to come." Najwa looked to each of her sorors for an affirmative response.

"Naj, I really don't need to skip studying. I don't think you need me at this meeting. You have the Treasurer and the Public Service Chairperson. That's all you need," Lynette said.

"Lynette we won't be long. You'll still have plenty of time to study tonight," Najwa assured knowing Lynette was determined to not give in.

"Naj, I just can't this time. I'm sorry. You call me tonight and let me know whatever you want me to do. But I just can't give up any more time to study."

Najwa didn't have time to debate. "Okay, this time sands. I'll call you tonight. The rest of you can just ride with me to my place."

"What about Keisha?" Robin asked.

"What about her? She's done about all she can do for today," Najwa snapped and walked away in disgust.

# Wedensday, October 17, 1973

For Lynette, every Wednesday was judgment day. On Monday, she took quizzes. The following week, grades were posted outside the chemistry lab bulletin board. At 11:00a.m., she would make the long trip down the hallway to see if her sacrifices paid off. This day was no different. She waited patiently to examine the chart while a few other students frantically searched for their scores. Her heart immediately sank.

"A 76?" she whispered aloud and then to herself. One less point and Lynette would have received an F on her quiz. Although she passed, her average would ultimately suffer. She scolded herself as she slowly walked away.

"How in the world could I have gotten such a low grade?" She pondered to herself.

It was a relatively easy quiz. So she thought. Repeatedly, she thought of every activity that could have been sacrificed in order to study. She had to attend the rush, but the party could have definitely been skipped. Now she would surely be invisible this coming weekend. Only an A on the next quiz could make her happy. Lynette pulled out her school planner and wrote the word "library" through the entire weekend.

In disgust, she walked to the Barkston Center where she was to meet Candace at noon in the cafeteria. Lynette picked over her lunch as she feverishly combed the pages of her quiz notes.

Candace appeared. "Hey Lynette! You here early."

Lynette looked up only briefly to see her soror's large smile before her thoughts returned to her notes. "Oh, hey Candace," she said, still disturbed.

"What's happening girl? You look busy. Another big quiz?" Candace sat her things on the table and then herself across from Lynette.

"There's always a big quiz. That's the story of my life. But that's not what we are here about so let me put these notes away so we can get started."

"Everything cool Lynette? You seem a little uptight. I know those classes are giving you the flux but you can handle it."

Lynette appreciated the encouragement, but she knew that ultimately passing those classes would be up to her. She needed to get serious about her studies. Nothing could interfere.

"As a matter of fact Candace, since you brought up the subject, these pre-med classes are kicking my butt. As my Assistant Dean, I need you to be my eyes and ears. I am going to be spending a lot of my free time studying. Fooling around with silly pledges is not even in the picture. I'll be there during the crucial moments. I'll take care of all the paperwork and make sure the business is handled. But, I will need you for some of the little tasks."

"Lynette that is what I am here for. I know your classes are taking up a lot of your time. I expected you to tell me I had to do more. I am ready whenever you need me." Candace perked up in anticipation. "So, what is my first assignment?"

"I give you one month with the pledges and they will be boring you to tears. We'll see what happens to all that excitement and energy then. I know this is your first line, but it is more work than fun. Trust me," Lynette said knowing Candace's excitement would soon fade.

"So when are the girls filling out their applications?" Candace eagerly asked.

"This Friday night," Lynette answered in frustration. "I need to postpone it until next week. But Najwa wouldn't like me changing the schedule without notice. So, I'm gonna need you to reserve a meeting room over at the Barkston Center. You know, one of those on the lower level. Where no one ever goes."

"Cool. I'll go when we get finished here," Candace replied.

"Make sure you reserve it for three hours. I think that's enough time. I'm not trying to be there all night. We can split up the names of the girls who will be invited. You take the ones that live closest to you. I already made out the cards. All you have to do is put them in their mailboxes." Lynette handed Candace a handful of white index cards.

"I got one question Lynette. Why do we need the room for so

long? I remember our application night only lasted about an hour before y'all kicked us out."

"That's what we need to discuss. We are doing this a little different this year."

"Go on girl. I'm listening." Candace sat closer. "Oooooo ... This is getting good."

"This year, instead of waiting a day or so to review the applications, we are going to do it right there. As a matter of fact, those who pass the application phase are going to get a little assignment that night. That's why it is important that we start on time."

"I'm with you. But what's this assignment?" Candace asked.

"Lets just say, we're going to get a little help getting our Thanksgiving basket money back. Speaking of which, has Mark found out anything about who ripped us off?"

"No, he says all the cats he hangs with know nothing about it. And if anybody would know anything it would be his friends," Candace replied.

"How's Keisha doing? She was on a serious guilt trip Sunday."

"I don't know. That girl is like a roller coaster. One minute she is up and the next down. I was trying to get her to tell Mark what the guy looked like but she didn't want to talk to him. She just froze up. She wouldn't even come out her room to talk. When, I saw her this morning going to her class, she was back to normal."

"Well, after Friday, we won't have to worry about our little money problems. Oh...I almost forgot the most important thing

119

Candace. What we discuss must stay between us. Understood?"

"No problem! We gon' have so much fun this year. Najwa is president. We are about to have a line. And we will get our money for that project and win the service award again." Candace sat back, grabbed a potato chip from Lynette's tray and laughed. "Girl, we gon' be the baddest chapter on this yard!"

───────────────

That same hour, Najwa walked into the Black House to take Mrs. Dixon a little token of her appreciation. Najwa was very grateful to Mrs. Dixon for thinking of her for the court building job vacancy. Actually, her mother encouraged her to go out and buy "a little something."

Najwa had no idea what could possibly show how appreciative she was. Nor did she have the money to back it. Desperate, she went down to the town market and bought a plant. An art student, who was also interested in her sorority, was all it took at add a decorate flair to the ordinary flowerpot. The bright fluorescent colors would stand out on any dreary day in Casperton.

Najwa peeked around the corner holding the gift behind her back.

"Hello Mrs. Dixon."

"Najwa! Hello dear. What are you doing here?" Mrs. Dixon smiled.

"I felt like I had not thanked you enough for thinking of me for that job. I really needed the extra money."

"Oh dear you have thanked me enough already. It is the least I can do for one of my babies," Mrs. Dixon said.

"I still wanted to give you something to remind you of how grateful I am." Najwa slowly pulled the colorfully decorated flowerpot from around her back and placed it in the center of Mrs. Dixon's desk.

"Najwa! Why, it is so beautiful. Wherever did you find this? And it is hand painted too! This must have cost you a fortune," Mrs. Dixon beamed.

"It is really nothing. I had a friend here at the school make it especially for you. I hope you like it."

"Like it? I love it! I am going to keep it on my desk until I leave this old job. Coming in and seeing something as bright and beautiful is just what I need to keep me going 'til these walls fall over!" Mrs. Dixon smiled as she turned the pot looking at the unique design and bright colors.

Najwa made herself home in the empty chair next to Mrs. Dixon's desk. "You've seen a lot of people pass through these buildings haven't you?"

"Baby I been here for every university president that has come through that door in the past thirty years. When I was at the Court House I even worked for that old Mr. Barkston. You know chile. The one they named that big student center after."

"The Bradley Barkston Center?" Najwa asked.

Mrs. Dixon seized the moment to show off her historical wealth of university knowledge.

"Sure did. They named that building after that old man Barkston after he died and willed all that money to the university. He was one of the founders of the university. Said he had something to do with the land that the first class building was built on. He had money but that was one old White man that gave me the hee bee gee bees!"

Mrs. Dixon closed her eyes as her mind took a trip down memory lane. "He had to have been old as dirt. He would walk around the Court house with that old shiny tipped cane ordering people around like we was back in the land of Dixie or something."

"Didn't he have something to do with the old campus clock too?" Najwa asked.

Mrs. Dixon wrinkled her face as if she had just eaten a lemon.

"Ooo...yes, and I cringe every time I hear that clock chime. It might as well play Dixie."

"In light of all that we went through last year, I am not surprised at all that the founder of our school was an old redneck." Najwa added.

"Oh he was more than that. That man was crazy. I say that to this day. He was crazy! There was just something not right about him honey." Mrs. Dixon shook her head. "That's enough about him. Lord knows I don't want to conjure up any old Barkston spirit. Listen, I heard about Keisha. How is she?" Mrs. Dixon asked.

"Fine. Just a little shaken up that's all." Najwa quickly shifted to the important concern. "They took all the money we raised from our party."

"That is too bad! You all must be careful baby. The important thing is that she was not hurt. Count your blessings sweetie. Money means nothing. You can always replace the money."

"Oh I am certain we will make up for the loss." Najwa stood and gathered her purse. "Well Mrs. Dixon, I better go now. I didn't mean to keep you from your work. I just wanted to show my appreciation."

"Oh baby you are more than welcome to come see me anytime. Thank you for my pot and plant, I absolutely love it! Oh…and watch out for those Barkston ghosts at your job!" Mrs. Dixon smiled and winked at Najwa.

# Friday, October 19, 1973

Fourteen women sat quietly in meeting Room C in the Barkston Center lower level wondering what would happen next. Each received a small card with a time, date, and location. The only knowledge shared amongst them was that this would be a meeting of a select few interested in Omega Pi Alpha.

Najwa and Lynette stood before the young ladies and congratulated them on making it to the application phase of membership into Omega Pi Alpha. The rest of the Gamma chapter stood around the room blankly staring. With the assistance of Candace, Lynette gave each of the fourteen interested women a black pen and thirty minutes to complete a two-page application and a 250-word essay.

"If anyone has a question, now is the time to ask," Lynette announced.

Too anxious to begin, and obviously too fearful of the limited time, none asked a question.

"All right then. You can begin."

The announcement started the chaos. Immediately, members of Gamma chapter began to laugh and talk loudly amongst each other. The applicants tried to stay focused.

Berri walked over to one. "So what is your name?"

The young lady's head snapped up to see who was standing over her.

"Uh, me? Oh my name is Melissa," she nervously replied.

"Melissa? Melissa? What kind of name is that for a sista?" Berri laughed. A couple of her line sisters stood over the frightened girl laughing.

"I never seen you around campus before. Where do you stay?" Berri continued.

"I stay over in Roosevelt Dorm, but I just transferred into CU this September," Melissa replied trembling.

"You a transfer student? Where did you go to school?" Berri was interrupted by Lynette's voice.

"Ladies, you have twenty more minutes. At exactly eight o'clock, I will be collecting the applications. If you are not finished then maybe we will see you again next year."

"Oh, looks like you don't have that much completed on your application." Berri chuckled. "That would not be good if you don't finish."

Distraction was the name of this game.

The young lady who sat three seats to the right dropped her pen. Diane ran over and picked it up. "Sorors, look what I found." She held the pen in the air. "A nice black pen! I wonder who it belongs to."

"Fifteen more minutes ladies," Lynette announced. She walked into the corner and continued talking to Najwa and Carla.

Another applicant reached into her purse and frantically handed her distressed neighbor another pen.

"Aw, that was so nice. Next time you may not be so lucky," Irby warned.

Frantically, the applicants continued scribbling. It seemed like only a second had gone by when Lynette announced the ten-minute mark. A tear fell on a blank page as the thought of not finishing crossed the mind of one.

"Ladies, if I can't read your application due to tear smudges, I will not hesitate to take points away," Lynette announced.

Najwa turned and whispered to Lynette. "Oh my goodness, this is going to be a special group Lynette. They don't seem to be handling this too well. Maybe we should call the sorors off of them."

"Najwa? Is that you? Do I sense you getting a little soft?" Lynette kidded.

"Yes, it's me sands, and no I am not getting soft. I just want more than two applications to consider that's all. Obviously, this group is not dealing with the pressure too well."

"Okay, okay, you're right." Lynette turned and made her last announcement.

"Ladies you now have five minutes to complete your applications. If I were you, I would be working on the essay. Sorors give the ladies a little quiet time while they finish." Lynette turned back to Najwa as the chapter looked at her in disbelief.

Berri stormed over. "Excuse me, but did I just hear you right?" She asked trying to keep her voice down.

Najwa and Lynette replied with identical blank stares.

"What's the problem Berri?" Najwa finally spoke.

Berri looked at Lynette in disbelief. "Did I hear you say for us to be quiet while they finish?"

"Yeah that's right. And what's wrong with that?" Lynette replied.

"I don't recall having the same privilege on my application night," Berri snapped.

"Well, now I am in charge Berri. Things are going to go a little differently this year," Najwa interrupted.

"So you trying to say somebody did something wrong last year Najwa? I do remember you being there to." Berri replied.

"Berri I never said anyone did anything wrong. I just said this year that I am in charge and things are going to go down differently." Najwa rolled her eyes and turned to her sands. "Lynette I think time is almost up now. Let's start collecting the applications."

Unmoved by the confrontation, Najwa calmly turned to Berri. "Why don't you help us out?"

Lynette smirked as she walked to the front.

Najwa impressed herself by maintaining calm with Berri. She knew that Berri was angry and probably a little embarrassed. She believed that now someone else had a first hand account and understood her uneasiness with Berri.

"Time is up ladies. We are going to come around and collect your applications. After you have handed them in please go to the meeting room next door and wait silently. There should be no discussion at all," Lynette directed.

Gamma chapter's twelve members walked around and collected the applications from the women. Most looked frustrated.

"What's the matter Pat? You look a little disappointed," Lynette said to one of the young ladies as she reluctantly handed over the application.

"I could have gotten a whole lot more done had I not been so distracted. That was not cool at all. How was anybody supposed to get anything done?" Pat angrily replied.

Lynette stopped abruptly in her tracks and looked in disbelief. Overhearing, Najwa directed the ladies out of the room before Lynette could reply. Any words that could have come next surely would have lead to an unpleasant sight.

The doors were closed with only a wall separating the applicants from the women of Gamma chapter. Two separate meetings of the minds began.

Lynette sat with the applications in front of her sorting them.

"From the looks of how much some of these ladies finished, this is going to be a quick process of elimination."

*One of the applicants broke the silence in the adjacent room. "Man. How many of y'all were able to finish? I barely made it to the essay part."*

"They say the first application is usually always graded the hardest. Having said that, where is the one from that sister who had a problem with distractions? I think her name was Pat?" Najwa extended her hand to Lynette.

*"Sista, I wasn't able to get anything down. Like I told them, that wasn't cool at all. And I don't care if they didn't like it that I told them!" Pat replied.*

Lynette thumbed through the pile until she came across the application that barely had anything on it. She handed it to Najwa.

"Oh here it is." Najwa took the application, ripped it up and threw it in the garbage. The chapter looked on in surprise.

"There, now that we got that first application out of the way. Let's move on to the others." Najwa continued as if nothing had happened.

*"If this is the way these sistas want to act, then I don't need this craziness. As a matter of fact, I'm splittin'. Anybody coming' with me?" Pat stood and walked to the door waiting for a response that would never come. "Hey that's cool. I don't think I like this sorority stuff anyway. You sistas hang tight." Pat slammed the door as she left.*

"Right on Najwa! Throw that mess away. I didn't like her anyway!" Gloria exclaimed.

"I say we let her on line and then get the pleasure of seeing her drop." Carla piped in.

"Humph!" was the only sound Berri uttered since her confrontation.

*"She can leave by herself. I ain't goin' nowhere until a member*

*of Omega Pi Alpha tells me too. I have been trying to make this line for two years now."*

*"Me either. I am not leaving. I don't think they are going to pick her anyway," another applicant said.*

*More broke their silence. "Forget her! We need them to pick us!"*

Lynette pulled the direction of the application review into perspective.

"Sorors, lets get started. I will read each application to you. We are looking for good character and academic standards among each person. We need to pay special attention to the essay and the question that asks what they would like to see done in the community. After each application is read, if anyone has anything to add then that would be the time to do so."

*"I know my spelling on that essay is going to mess me up. I just couldn't concentrate."*

*"At least you put something down on the paper. I only got about ten sentences down before they took my essay out of my hand."*

*"I don't think Berri likes me too much."*

*"Girl, would you stop crying. Get yo'self together. It's over now. If you made it, you made it. Ain't nothing you can do 'bout it now."*

Under Lynette's direction, the chapter thoroughly reviewed each application and voted in forty-five minutes. With the exception of the one application that had been thrown in the trash, to everyone's surprise, all remaining thirteen applicants made it to the next phase.

"Sorors, looks as if these are the names of the women who will move on to the next phase. I'll go and get them so we can share the news. Oh yeah. And give them their next assignment." Lynette gathered the applications and rose from her seat.

*"How many of do you think they are going to take?"*

*"I wonder if the ones who made it are going to start pledging tonight."*

*"Shhhh. I heard the door open. Somebody is coming."*

All thirteen women were called back into the meeting room and given the good news. The next assignment, raise one hundred fifty dollars in one week. By ten o'clock, Gamma chapter had completed the application phase and were on their way home.

*Sadie Mae was excited by the arrival of a letter and her only tie to her father. Reading small pieces between breaks, she held it all day. His barely legible words had expressed the importance of the deed and what it meant to their family.*

# Saturday, October 20, 1973

Najwa couldn't be happier at the early ending of the evening. Reviewing the applications had gone rather smoothly. Unlike previous years, all the women did exceptionally well. They were the cream of the crop and for once Najwa felt confident about most of their choices. Because there were so many other things on her mind, Najwa did not challenge her chapter's decisions. This night, Lynette was the force behind the successful application night. Najwa was happier than the entire chapter to get away so soon. This was the first quiet Friday night and sleep-in Saturday morning in almost a month. After dropping Lynette off at her building, Najwa headed straight to her apartment where she fell asleep ten minutes into her literature assignment.

The next morning at six thirty, the sun rose over the football field and softly cut through the open space in Najwa's curtains. Both she and her apartment lay silent in a deep sleep, only to be disturbed by the ringing phone. Najwa, half awake and startled, reached over and slapped the top of her Big Ben clock. She turned over thinking she must have forgotten to turn her alarm off before going to bed. Within less than a second the ringing sound came again, louder. This time Najwa sat straight up.

"What the…?" It wasn't the alarm after all. But some inconsiderate person who obviously had no concern for her sleep time.

Najwa reached for the phone. "Whoever this is it better be good. Hello!" She irately answered.

"Hello dear, is that you Najwa?" a serene voice replied.

"Ma?"

"Yes, it's me honey."

Najwa panicked. "Ma what's wrong? Are you okay? Is there something wrong with Daddy?"

"I'm fine honey. Calm down. We're just fine. Missing our little baby that's all! So how is our little girl?"

"Ma, I'm doing fine. It's just so early. You scared me. I thought maybe there was something wrong." Najwa's heart began to find it's normal rhythm as she laid back and took a deep breath.

"Well, it seems like this was the only time I could find you. I tried calling you all this week but you weren't in. I tried calling you last night and I got no answer. So, I thought I would try you bright and early on a Saturday morning."

"Ma, I'm sorry but I have been really busy. You know classes and sorority stuff. I should have called you this week."

"It's alright Najwa, just as long as you're doing well. That's all I am concerned with. I just hope you aren't letting that sorority stuff interfere with your studies. Remember, school is first Najwa."

"Please, it's too early for that conversation. We argued about that the last time. Not right now."

"Najwa, I am not going to argue. I pay for your education and I know what is right. I am your mother, remember?"

"Yes mother. It's just early," Najwa replied.

She had the utmost respect for her mother. She also knew that no matter what she said her mother was going to persist. For the next twenty minutes, Najwa's mother gave her famous priorities lecture. Najwa's only words were, "Yes, Ma," between pauses.

"So, now when will you be driving home? You know you can fly if you like." The family Thanksgiving plans were the next item on Mrs. Jackson's agenda.

"That's what I need to talk to you about Ma." Najwa hesitated. There was a silent pause. Najwa bravely continued. "I was thinking. I don't think I will be coming home for Thanksgiving this year."

There was more silence.

"Hello? Ma? You still there?"

Mrs. Jackson finally spoke. "I'm still here. I just don't believe what I am hearing."

"I'm sorry. I know the holidays mean a lot to you. But I think I need to stay here."

"Najwa I told you, if you don't feel like driving the distance, I understand. I'll just make the flight arrangements as soon as possible. As a matter of fact, I will get your father on it first thing today."

"Ma, no! I don't want to fly. I'm not coming home until Christmas." Najwa half honestly pleaded her case. "I just have a lot of things to catch up on. Stuff like assignments and applications for jobs."

Mrs. Jackson ignored her daughter's excuses. "Are you staying there for some kind of sorority stuff? Because if this is about that sorority, I hope you realize who your blood family is. I've told you time and time again Najwa that BLOOD IS THICKER THAN WATER!"

Her words were too familiar. Najwa knew her mother truly did not understand her allegiance to her sorority. She even suspected that her mother was somewhat jealous of her newfound family. Because the call came as a surprise, Najwa didn't have the time to carefully choose the words to break her mother's heart. Now she desperately searched for something to soothe the sting.

"Most of the sorors are going home Ma. Aside from me, the only other person staying is Lynette, and oh yeah, Dakota is staying too," Najwa quickly added hoping Dakota's name would calm her mother. "We all are seniors and have a lot of work to do. Thanksgiving is the best time 'cause nobody is on campus and…" Najwa could not finish before her mother again interrupted.

"And I am sure their parents are just as disappointed as I am. But if it is really for school, then I have to go along. Tell you what. You think on it some more and I will call you tomorrow. That way I can still make your flight arrangements on Monday."

Arguing any further was pointless. Knowing her answer would

not change, Najwa hung up after surrendering to another call on the next day.

As much as her body yearned for rest, Najwa's mind was elsewhere. She tried unsuccessfully for the next thirty minutes to sleep but only tossed. Frustrated that she was awake at barely 7:30 on a Saturday morning, Najwa moved to the living room. At least there, she could watch television and maybe eventually fall back asleep.

Another hour passed and Najwa still lie awake on the couch. By now she had watched morning cartoons and ate two bowls of cereal. Sleep was pointless. The conversation with her mother left too much on her mind. It had been close to two weeks since she looked at the application for the sociology school. She still had no recommendations and it was all due before the holiday break. Not to mention, she still was behind in her literature class. Najwa believed half her troubles would be over if she could just make it through the remainder of the semester. Concentrating on school had never been a problem for Najwa until now. It was her newest worst enemy.

Najwa's level of frustration was rising. For the past few weeks, she passed it off as just the pressures of holding the presidency of her chapter. She would never admit to her mother that possibly the sorority was starting to take up more of her time. Regardless, Najwa comforted herself by thinking everything would get back to normal once the next event was finished. The only problem was that the events and the responsibilities kept coming. Somewhere in between, school became second.

Finally, Najwa found herself staring at the blank pages of a notebook attempting to write the essay for her application. Maybe, the uncertainty of life after graduation contributed to the blank picture she drew in her mind. The two extra years she would need to spend at school to complete the program was not a benefit either. Fitting into the role of a social worker would be easy. Whether she wanted that role was her ongoing internal debate. She thought continuously of her line sisters who graduated and how they were able to acquire jobs immediately. Then she thought of Lynette and the sacrifices she was making to realize her dream of going to medical school. In the midst of her partying, even Carla had direction. Now, Najwa, the backbone of their line, sat uncertain of her future beyond Casperton University and Gamma Chapter.

Half the challenge in the essay was expressing, with an ounce of sincerity, a desire that Najwa could not claim. It took her another hour before she could concentrate long enough to write one page. Despite straining to express herself, she was almost convinced that she was making the right decision. Feeling prematurely triumphant over her frustration, Najwa decided to take a break. After all, for the first time in months, the entire day was hers to enjoy.

Not only was her future uncertain but Najwa's social life was suffering as well. The only words she shared with friends outside the chapter were in passing. Dakota was the first to cross her mind. She had not seen him in over a week and noticed that he too had been busy. They were long overdue for a good talk.

Najwa wanted one day to be free of any chapter concerns even if it meant not seeing her sorors at all. She reached for her phone. She figured she better catch Dakota early before he had the opportunity to make any plans for the day. Even if he had plans, Najwa decided that she would be the reason for him canceling.

"He...llo," the deep groggy voice answered on the third ring.

"Wake up big head! It's me. I'm calling to make your day."

"Are you crazy? Do you know what time it is?"

"Yeah I know what time it is. I'm calling to let you know you're going to lunch with me today."

"What are you talking about? Wait ... who is this?" Dakota was still half asleep.

"What do you mean who is this? Man, I know you don't have that many women calling that you don't know who I am. But then again, it's been so long since you talked to me, I guess you forgot my voice."

"Naj ... Shut up. I am asleep."

A second soft voice came from Dakota's end of the phone. "Who is that baby?"

"Humph! Who was that? Don't sound like you're asleep to me," Najwa remarked.

"Huh? What?" Dakota stuttered.

"Huh? What?" Najwa mocked.

"D, baby who's on the phone?" The voice asked.

"Look I got to go. I'll talk to you later okay," Dakota rushed.

"Cool! I'll be over at about 11:30 to pick you up. So I think you might want to have the broad gone by then. Okay D baby!" Najwa mocked.

"What? … Hey wait…"

Before Dakota could finish Najwa hung up the phone laughing. She couldn't wait.

At exactly eleven she was on the worn wooden porch of the house Dakota shared with his fraternity brothers. She had thrown on her bell-bottomed jeans, knit sweater, and black leather jacket for her casual lunch with Dakota. Standing at the door, patting down her Afro, she wore a grin larger than life in anticipation of surprising whomever Dakota had in his bed. Before she could knock, Dakota opened the door and matched Najwa's smile.

"What's happenin' baby? You right on time."

"Uh uh, actually, I'm a little early. So, who's here? I mean you don't still have company do you?" Najwa asked hoping she had interrupted. She got a kick out of making Dakota's women think she was his "other" woman. This had been a joke she played on him since they were in college.

"No baby. It's just you and me. Oh, and the guys of course. Did you think my visitor would still be here? Had I known you wanted to meet her I would have told her to stay. Oh well, maybe next time." Dakota laughed.

"Ha ha ha." Najwa mocked Dakota. "Let's go. I am starving."

"Your treat right? You lost that time. I think I'll have steak." Dakota said.

Najwa played innocent. "What are you talking about?"

Dakota laughed hysterically as he closed the house door. "Don't give me that! You came over here early to mess up my thing. But you lost this time. I was one ahead of you. So it's your treat today."

Since entering Casperton University, the two scored their little competition with each other like a football game. If one were to cause the break-up of a relationship, it was considered a touch down. While a simple argument only earned the three-point field goal. Quarter one of the "Relationship Bowl" began in their first year. The fourth quarter was proving to be the most eventful of all.

"Oh, I got a treat for you." Najwa ran to her car, slammed the door, and rolled her window down. "Walk!"

The tires of her Camaro screeched as she pulled off leaving Dakota standing at the curb laughing. Moments later she pulled back around the block. Smiling, Dakota stood in the same spot she left him.

"Get your butt in this car." Najwa laughed.

"They always come back. Damn, I am good," Dakota kidded.

The playful side of Najwa's personality had lain dormant. Getting out and enjoying her day with Dakota was just like the old times she missed. With him, she felt comfortable enough to be herself. The chemistry between the two of them was unlike any other. For the rest of the day, Najwa found comfort in knowing that her worries could take a back seat. At the local campus diner they sat across from each other for what seemed like the first time in months.

"So where you been? No one on campus has seen or heard from Madame President, Najwa in ages." Dakota's thick, brown, muscular arms reached across the table to grab the straw basket full of bread slices.

"I been around. It's you I need to be asking about," Najwa replied.

"No, really Najwa. I have been doing my usual. After all, I can't keep all the ladies waiting." Dakota joked. "But you, you been out of reach. We used to talk almost every other day or at least see each other on the campus. It's been almost two weeks. Omega Pi Alpha got you tied up a lot."

"I know, I know. I have been really, really busy. Turns out this president gig ain't the breeze I thought it was going to be." Najwa sipped on a tall glass of sweetened lemonade. "Seems like there is always something going on."

"I kinda figured that's what it was. I used to at least see you at all the Greek Council meetings. Now we are just graced with the Queen's appointed representative."

Najwa laughed.

"Stop it Dakota. Now you know that is not how it is. You know I ain't that high on myself. I really haven't been able to come to the meetings. I feel bad too. I know Karen has been trying to get in contact with me for over a week about our joint project with the Deltas. I'm going to have to send Robin, our public service person, over to her dorm as soon as I get home."

"There you go again, sending one of your foot soldiers." Dakota stuffed a half-buttered slice of bread in his mouth.

"Well then you must feel real special cause you got the Queen herself, right here."

"I do, yeah I do. And not just because this meal is your treat."

"Ha, ha, ha very funny." Najwa mocked. "Enough about me. So, who was the girl Dakota?"

"Why you all in my business?"

"Cause you ain't got no business, now who was it?"

"Look, you will find out when it is time. For now, none of your business!"

"Give me a hint. Does she belong to a sorority? Come on D Baby!" Najwa mocked Dakota's mystery houseguest.

Dakota tried to stop Najwa's investigation. "No she doesn't. Now that is your one and only hint."

"That's a start. Does she live on the east or west side of campus?"

Najwa knew if she kept the questions coming, eventually she would be able to unravel the mystery. Dakota looked out of the window as if he heard nothing. Knowing each of his weaknesses, she reached over and seductively slid her fingers up and down Dakota's forearm.

"Dakota, the east or west side of campus?"

After only a moment and a sweet chill up his arm, Dakota responded.

"East! Now stop rubbing on me. Not unless you want to find yourself in my group of admirers just like her."

Najwa jerked her hand back and frowned. "UGH! Forget I even asked. Don't nobody want your big head self!"

"Well that's not what she said. Besides, you'll meet her at the

Thanksgiving dinner." Dakota assured Najwa. "You are coming to the dinner aren't you?"

Najwa had almost forgotten that Mrs. Dixon extended a standing invitation to every Black student who stayed on campus during the holidays. "Are you crazy? Of course I'll be there. I'm not passing up on Mrs. Dixon's lemon cake!" Najwa's eyebrows rose. "So that means your girl is not from around here. That narrows it down for me some more."

At that moment the waitress walked over with their plates and gave Dakota his escape. "Shut up and eat Najwa. You ain't gettin' nothin' else out of me. Hey, wait a minute, you're asking about my love life. What about you? All the brother's on the campus talkin' 'bout Najwa Jackson. Hey man have you seen Najwa lately? Sister is fine!" Dakota mimicked.

"Love life? Humph. What love life? Dakota I haven't been on a date all semester. I don't know who those brothers are cause they ain't came to me. Besides, I don't think I am ready yet."

"Naj I know you not still hurt over that jive revolutionary Huey Newton wanna-be? That was over a year ago. Its time to move on."

"His name is Paul and I think I have moved on. It's just that…" Najwa hesitated.

Dakota paused between bites. "What?"

"Well, we kinda…talked over the summer."

"You talked to Paul after what he did to you?"

"Dakota it was nothing. He was in town covering a convention for the newspaper he writes for and he called me at my parent's house. We talked a few times even hung out once. I didn't tell you 'cause I know how much you hate him."

"Yeah and I still say you should have let me kick his ass a year ago. Well...what happened?"

"Nothing." Najwa sank into the booth further and starred out the window. She continued. "Nothing at all Dakota, just the usual. He showed up, made promises and then I never heard from him the rest of the summer."

"Naj, I'm sorry that happened to you. You deserve so much more. But I told you to leave that no good jive nigga alone."

"Dakota let's not talk about it anymore. Let's just eat." Najwa's appetite was actually gone. Any bite she did manage to take was forced. Her mind was now on what she thought would be a lasting relationship with a man she only dreamed of finding on a magical day such as this one.

Everyone who knew Najwa closely also knew that she was conservative in relationships. Her sands claimed she was just old fashioned and needed the right man to put something on her mind. Najwa stood by her belief that her love had to be earned. She had only given one man on CU's campus the privilege of calling himself her boyfriend. To this man she had given her virginity and her heart.

Najwa remembered vividly the day she met Paul in her sophomore year. While walking across the campus yard, a copy of "Tiger Pride," the Black student newspaper, was thrust into her hand. Najwa pretended to listen as a young writer in black-framed glasses and a black leather jacket pleaded with her to read his article on the student Revolutionary. That moment turned into an hour. An hour turned into Najwa's first love. Paul and Najwa shared everything. This college senior and revolutionary opened a new door in Najwa's heart.

Only after pledging did Najwa see the first change in Paul. He was insistent that it was Najwa who had changed when she joined her sorority. He felt that her need to be accepted by this new "uppity" class of Blacks was totally contradictory to the revolution they talked about until the early morning hours. Because Paul was a graduating senior and moving back home, he used this as an excuse to end their relationship. The closeness, the trust, and the feelings she shared with Paul could never be gained with any other man.

The waitress returned and dropped a little white slip on the table waking Najwa from her trance. As she reached, Dakota intercepted and grabbed the bill.

"What are you doing? I lost so I'll pay." Najwa said.

"Don't worry 'bout it. I got it." Dakota winked at her. "Now you have had your first date this semester."

Not able to say anything, Najwa smiled and surrendered. There was at least one ray of light and today it was Dakota.

---

Just a mile away, the old campus clock chimed and marked the fifth hour Lynette sat buried in her anatomy books in the library. Determined, she went back and forth from her book, to class notes, and back to her book. So intent, she never noticed her sands sneak up behind her.

Carla jumped behind Lynette and tagged her on the shoulder. "Boo!".

Every nerve in Lynette's body jumped as she jerked around to see who dared to interrupt her study ritual. "Carla! Girl what is wrong with you? You scared the living day lights out of me!"

"What's happening sands? I stopped through to pick up a book for my Literature class and I saw you over here in your own world." Carla walked around the table and picked up a chair to join her sands.

"Yeah well, I gotta do what I gotta do. I can't get another D on any of my quizzes. So I am sentenced to this library." Lynette started rummaging through her notes again. "And no offense, but if you plan on staying for a long conversation, then you got to go."

"Calm down. I just stopped by to see how you were doing. I'm supposed to be on duty back at the dorm right now. Besides, I got to wash my hair so I can get to that Alpha party tonight. I guess I can't even begin to peel you out of those books."

"Don't even think about it Carla. There is absolutely no way you are going to get me to a party anytime soon. How do you do it sands? I mean really. How do you manage to make every party on this campus and still maintain your grades?"

"Lynette honey, it's all in the attitude. I refuse to let this place get to me. I got a life. Like I said back when the year started…I am going out of this joint with a bang!"

"Well these classes are my life," Lynette replied.

"Honestly, I don't know if I could do it with the classes you have. So in your honor, I'll party for you tonight. Hey, you seen any of our little pledges today?" Carla asked.

Lynette shook her head. "Are you kidding? I've been over here all morning. I don't have time to baby sit. They have their hands full anyway. Raising that money by the end of this week is not going to be a piece of cake."

"You think they are going to pull it off? Carla asked.

"I don't know. If they have any kind of brains they will borrow it from anyone and everyone they can. I am a little skeptical about letting them raise the money. But sands I just don't have the time to be bothered with raising it again myself," Lynette said.

"Speaking of money, has anyone heard anything about finding the cats who robbed Keisha?" Carla asked.

"Nope not at word. Mark has combed the hood and nobody knows anything."

"Sands, somebody has to know something!" Carla insisted. "This town ain't but a minute big. Somebody around here is livin' high up on the hog with our money."

"All I know is the money is gone, I got to get back in these books and you need to get back to the dorms before you lose your job. You know those White girls are waiting on the chance to get you out of that spot." Lynette picked up her notes and again buried herself before Carla could respond.

"You're right. But I think I am going to do a little investigating for myself. See you later." Carla got up from the table and walked away.

Lynette never looked up from her books. Again, she was far immersed into the anatomy of the human body.

After a ten-minute walk back across the campus, Carla was sneaking through the back door of the dorm with her master key. She called up to her room from the campus phone to alert Irby who served as her look out. Once given the sign that the coast was clear, she could make her mad dash for the stairway.

Luckily, she had her routine down to a science. It worked like a charm every time. Carla knew she could count on her soror to look out for her. It also helped that she could offer Irby information on all the surprise dorm room inspections in return. They figured the White girls were doing it, now it was the sister's turn to have the inside connection.

Just as Carla reached the top of the fifth floor stairs, she pulled the door leading to the stairway slightly open and peaked through the crack. As the heavy door creaked, Carla made a mental note to get maintenance to fix that problem. A squeaky door surely would not be the cause of her loosing her job.

The hallway was deserted just as Irby had reported moments earlier. Carefully, Carla emerged from the staircase and walked down the hallway as if she had been on a routine room check. As she made her way to the end of the hall, she opened her already unlocked dorm room door and closed it gently behind her.

"Whew! Thanks Soror," Carla said to Irby as she plopped herself on the bed.

"I'm just glad you made it when you did. That White girl from the second floor, you know…Betty, she came up here looking for you. I told her you went to the bathroom and then you were going to the basement to get a mop."

"That's cool. I owe you one." Carla quickly paid the debt with an announcement. "By the way the next surprise inspection for your floor is Tuesday night."

"For real! Thanks Carla. I got to hide that hot plate I have in my room," Irby responded.

"No problem." Folding her clothes, Carla felt this was the perfect time to start her investigation.

"Hey Irby, how is Keisha doing? Has she said anything about the man who robbed her?"

Irby rolled her eyes and shook her head. "No. But then again I haven't really talked to her."

"Bingo!" Carla thought to herself. There was something behind Irby's demeanor and Carla was determined to get to the bottom of it. Irby was the one soror who was able to tolerate Keisha's antics long enough to get closer to her.

Carla dug deeper as she twisted the silver mood rings on her index finger.

"What do you mean you haven't talked to her? You're just about the only one who talks to Keisha on a regular basis."

"Just what I said. I haven't talked to her at all. And she hasn't told me any more than she did the day it happened."

Carla believed the robbery story was just Keisha's attempt to get attention. She felt that Irby probably felt the same. The only problem was that the money was really gone. Something happened but Carla just couldn't put her finger on what it was.

"Look Carla, I am not really thinking about Keisha anymore. I can't concern myself with her drama because it is causing me way more stress than I want to deal with."

Carla pushed further. "What has she done to get you like this Irby?"

"Just the other day, I heard her talking about some after party she wanted to go to tonight." Irby admitted.

"And what's so strange about that. You know Keisha is a party girl."

"This party is on the worst side of town. Not too far from where she was robbed. Why would you want to go back to the scene of the crime alone?" Irby looked at Carla blankly waiting for an answer.

"That's a good question. I don't know. What do you think?"

Irby finally finished. "I think our money is gone and we got to get it back." Irby's suspect attitude was the go-ahead Carla needed to move to the second part of her investigation.

# Thursday, October 25, 1973

Carla knew that she could not go to Najwa with just gut feelings. She needed proof. She needed hard-core evidence before she would accuse her soror of pulling off the biggest hoax of the year. No party or school social event could top the feeling of exposing Keisha to be the cheat and sneak Carla recognized. Kojak wasn't Carla's favorite television show for just any reason.

The pledges would be turning in the money that week assuming they succeeded. All the evidence had to be given to Najwa before the week ended. Knowing this, it only took Carla a couple of days to formulate her plan. She had it timed down to the second. Keisha could not be counted on to attend their chapter meeting scheduled for that week. But she could, however, be counted on to attend the weekly Round Table at the Black House.

Carla had one other major advantage in her favor. The Round Table was every other Thursday of the month and most importantly, there were men there to keep Keisha busy. Carla was a Resident Assistant with access to nearly every dorm room within her quad.

All she needed was the master keys to Keisha's floor to do a little room inspection of her own.

That Thursday evening, the Round Table started at eight o'clock like clockwork. Carla needed to make sure her soror was there and busy for at least another half-hour. Pretending to check the chapter mailbox in the Black House hallway, Carla scanned the room for Keisha. Just as she thought, Keisha was there with bells on, socializing as usual.

"Hey everybody!" Carla said walking into the large room.

Responses echoed. "Hi Carla."

Carla walked over to speak to Keisha personally. "Hey soror."

"Hey Carla." Keisha mustered up conversation knowing that appearances were everything to her sorors. "I'm surprised to see you here. Not on duty tonight?"

"That's later tonight. I just stopped by to see some familiar faces. You know, pay my respects and keep going." Carla cringed at the fact that she was actually having a conversation with Keisha.

"You can't stay? Oh that's too bad. We were going bowling after the round table. I am sure it is going to be fun," Keisha said barely looking at Carla.

Carla could not take it any longer. She had to end the conversation and get on with her mission. "Oh well, guess I am going to miss out on all the fun. I got to get out of here I have a couple of stops to make before I go back to the dungeon. Listen, you have a good time and don't stay out too late!" Carla put on her best fake smile, threw her bag over her shoulder and made her exit out the back door.

"Perfect!" She thought.

She felt she had plenty of time to get in Keisha's room but she didn't want to take any chances. Quickly, taking long strides, Carla jogged over to Madison Residence Hall. Gaining entry into the front door was easy. There was always an RA on duty. Now, the hardest task involved getting into Keisha's room without anyone noticing. Packed in her bag was the solution to that problem she hoped.

As Carla walked into the dorm's front entrance, she contemplated how she could get the keys. All the dorm assistants guarded their master keys with their lives. Loosing a set of master keys could mean big trouble and potentially unemployment. Never were those keys out of sight. Somehow, she would have to use her wit to get in that room.

Carla beamed as she saw one of the few White Residents Assistants that she actually liked. "Hi Sue!"

"Carly!" Sue responded.

The White dorm assistants gave Carla this nickname that she hated. She didn't understand why White people had the need to find a nickname for every person they met. Her mother didn't name her after a man. Her name was Carla. Nevertheless she played the game.

"What's happening? I was walking past and saw you on duty and thought I would stop by to say hi."

Sue smiled. "Everything is okay here on my end. How are things at your dungeon?"

Carla continued on with small talk with Sue for the next five minutes. Her mind was nowhere near the conversation but rather on getting up to Keisha's room. Sue was cool but Carla knew her place. She knew that Sue would not give her the master key to the floor without questions. It was too risky to just ask. Carla began to grow impatient with small talk. That was not getting her any closer to that room.

"I'm going to have to go up to the floor and take my chances," Carla thought to herself. It was not what she hoped would happen.

During the course of her conversation, Carla maneuvered around the counter and was standing by Sue's desk. She talked about anything and everything until she could think of her next move. Just as Carla had given up hope, she noticed that Sue's keys were actually sitting right in front of her face. It wasn't fair. It was as if someone was dangling a steak in front of a hungry animal.

At that instant, the dorm main phone rang. Sue excused herself to answer it.

"I got to get those keys." Carla kept thinking to herself. "Carla think, think," she mumbled.

She thought for a brief moment. "What would I do if they were my keys?"

"That's it!" She finally said to herself.

Carla hadn't noticed she was still clutching her own keys in her hand as she ran from the Black House. Discreetly, Carla laid the silver key ring with what had to have been about twenty keys next to Sue's.

Sue hung up the phone and turned back to Carla. "I am sorry

Carly. Now what were we talking about?"

"Oh nothing important. Hey listen, is Jody on duty tonight? I think I want to run up and say hello before I leave," Carla responded calmly.

"Yeah I think she is. Let me look at the schedule. Yep, here she is right here." Sue didn't bother with the normal visitor routine check-in with Carla. "Go on up. I'll see ya when ya get ready to go."

Just as Carla picked up her bag, she reached for Sue's keys and left hers sitting on the desk. Sue never noticed the switch. Her attention drifted to the visitors coming in the front door that needed to be checked in.

Carla's heart was beating overtime. She was not accustomed to the life of a private investigator. She quickly walked to the side door and ran up the three flights of stairs to Keisha's floor. She was half way there. This was prime time in the dorms. Carla knew she could not count on the floor to be without action. But she was prepared.

As she exited the stairway, there were only a couple girls in the hallway milling around to her surprise. She disappeared into the shower room to put the next phase of her plan into action. No need to mess up now. In her bag was a large towel and bathrobe. The extra large towel easily wrapped around her head like a turban. This, along with the long terry cloth robe would be her cloak until she found the right key.

After a few minutes and a prayer, Carla eased out of the shower room wrapped from head to toe. She kept her head down hoping no one would see her face. If she could just manage to only be seen at a distance, she felt like she could accomplish her mission. Last year one of the RA's was caught making the statement, "they all look alike." Carla counted on this phrase to ring true this night.

Because Keisha was an upper classman, she had the luxury of staying in one of the smaller one-person rooms. So, a roommate would not be a problem. Carla jetted past doors praying no one would come out. Her stomach felt like it was sitting in her toes. Surely, everyone could hear her heart beating. That alone could get her caught. A couple of girls walked out their rooms and then to the bathroom. Each time Carla strategically turned her back as she fumbled for the right key.

Finally, the lock clicked and the doorknob turned with ease. Carla took a deep breath, slid into the room and closed the door.

"I'm in!" She cheered quietly.

"Okay Carla, I don't know what we are looking for, but we got to find it," she said to herself as she began lifting papers on Keisha's desk. She combed the table top removing and then placing every item back in it's original spot. She found nothing.

"I got to hurry up," she thought. Not because she felt like Keisha would be back soon and not even because of the keys. Instead, she was growing nauseated by the loud smell of the Musk oil perfume Keisha bathed in before she went anywhere.

Carla had done a few routine room inspections that semester. Because the dorm room designs didn't vary much, she knew all the hiding places. She seemed to find everything she wasn't looking for. Cigarettes, a flattened twenty dollar bill under the mattress, a small plastic bag of marijuana, and a condom were scattered around. The risk seemed to be more than it was worth. There was one last spot that Carla needed to check before she quit.

Carla pulled back the wood sliding door of the closet and began digging through the piles of clothes on the floor. Nothing. Carla rolled her eyes and sighed as she entertained the thought that she would have no proof of her suspicions.

"I better get out of here," she mumbled in disappointment.

As she slid the panel back to the closet, it stopped mid way. She assumed it must have been caught on the clothes that were everywhere. As she bent over in the closet to move what she thought were clothes, Carla noticed a suede strap. A brown, suede purse strap. She frantically dug under the pile to pull the strap free. Carla plopped on the floor in front of the closet with her mouth hanging open.

"Well, ain't this 'bout a blip!" She said aloud. It was the same brown, suede purse that Keisha claimed was snatched the day she was robbed

"I knew it! That rat!"

Carla's patience paid off. She held in her hand the pot of gold she was seeking. She frantically opened the purse as if she expected the money to still be there. It had definitely been cleaned of its contents. Just not by a robber, as Keisha wanted everyone to believe. There was a used tube of lipstick and a little loose change at the bottom of the purse. In the side zipper pocket, Carla found a card to a clinic. She recognized the name immediately. It was a clinic on the north side of Casperton where a few of the White sorority girls and one of the girls on Carla's floor had gone for an abortion.

"Well I'll be…" Carla couldn't finish. She put the card back in the pocket and left the purse and closet just as she had found it.

Getting through the hall and back down the stairs was easy. With her robe and towel back in the bag, Carla emerged from the staircase as if nothing had happened.

"Hey Sue, I better get back now." She startled Sue who was reading a magazine at the front desk.

"Oh okay Carly. Hey did you see Jody?" Sue asked.

"No, but I saw some other friends. So I stopped to talk to them. Oh by the way..." Carla paused.

"I picked up your keys by accident. You know those RA keys, they all look alike to me," Carla smirked.

"Hey, you sure did. I didn't even notice. I'll see you at the next Resident Assistants general meeting." Sue handed Carla her keys and took her own back.

Carla's mind raced. She prepared herself for two days to sneak into Keisha's room. But she never thought about how she would handle the outcome. Her heart told her to walk to Najwa's apartment immediately. Her mind told her that she was on dorm duty in ten minutes. Walking to Najwa's was out of the question.

"Ain't this a blip? Now ain't this 'bout a blip?" Carla repeatedly said to herself as she walked across the quad and back to her dorm.

Her first stop was the dorm main office where only Residents Assistants had access to phones. She had to get this out at once. This was more than gossip. It was a big problem that had to be eliminated, and fast.

She flung her bag across the dorm office desk and shut the door. Her hands shook as she dialed the number of her sands on the rotary dial. She knew Lynette would be her best bet. Surely she would be at home studying.

Lynette answered after the first ring. "Hello."

"Hey sands. It's me, Carla. What you doing? Studying?" Carla calmly greeted.

"Hey girl!" Lynette was beaming. "No, I am not studying. Can you believe it? I am taking a break tonight. I got A's on my quizzes for this week and I deserve a break. I am going to watch a little television, talk on the phone, and eat. You know, all the things normal people do. You want to come by?"

"Thanks, but I can't. Look, I can't talk long. I am due on front desk duty in less than five minutes. Listen, I know I never do this but, I am calling an emergency meeting with just you, Najwa, and me."

"An emergency meeting? What's going on girl? You okay?"

"I'm fine. I got to go. I need you to tell Najwa. Where will the girls be bringing the money tomorrow?"

"They are supposed to be here at my place tomorrow by seven. I don't plan on them being here for long. I can kick everybody out and we can just meet here. I'll just say I need to study."

"Cool. I got to go. If I am not on that front desk in the next few seconds I am sure somebody will try to report me. I'll see you then.

Oh, congratulations on your quizzes!" Carla hung up and rushed to the front desk. The RA from the third floor glared at her tardiness.

Lynette hung up on her end. Carla never called emergency meetings. As a matter of fact, Lynette couldn't think of anything that was ever an emergency to Carla. There would be no way she would miss this meeting.

# Friday, October 26, 1973

Najwa walked down the old stairs leading to the basement of the Court House building. After clocking in, she assumed her position behind the one lonely desk at the bottom of the stairs. Every afternoon, Najwa took her place in the old, dusty basement and went over newspaper articles, deeds, birth and death certificates, and marriage licenses, cataloging them for archives. It was tedious, but interesting. In less than an hour, she was usually able to finish all the work in her in-box.

To pass the time, she would look up Casperton's intriguing history. The fact that during the first twenty years of Casperton's existence, its majority population was Black, was its best kept secret. She discovered that the town did not see a surge in the White population until the local trade school was declared a university. Najwa found amazing articles on the lives of people who she always thought to be as boring as the town. She humored herself at the fact that her old, wrinkly math professor, Mrs. Mason had been married five times. But this day, more than anything, she anticipated the reason for Carla's emergency meeting. She anxiously thought of everything Carla could possibly have to say.

"Well I guess there is no better time than now to do some research on Sadie Mae," Najwa said as she thought of a distraction.

The driving force behind the founding of Omega Pi Alpha intrigued Najwa the most. Little was known about this woman, who in her short-lived life meant so much to the organization. Working in the archive department of the town Sadie was raised was the best place to be.

For the next two hours, Najwa buried herself in the file cabinets and sleeping dust doubting she would even find anything. By now, she figured, any information still in tact was so old that it would crumble from the hint of fresh air.

Although Najwa knew that Sadie Mae was raised in the town of Casperton, she was not sure of her birthplace. She figured her best source would be the census records. Najwa combed through the files one by one. Only files dating beyond the turn of the century could give her any answers about her dear founder Sadie Mae.

Najwa was having a sneezing fit as she disturbed the sleeping dust on the dry rotted papers. But she figured after coming this far, she might as well continue. She dug and dug through the files marked with the letter "W."

"WASHINGTON…"

"WATTS…"

"WEBB…"

"WESLEY…"

"Wesley!" She shrieked.

Finally, the dust in her nose and the dirt on her hands paid off. She had it. She found a secret map to a hidden treasure. She looked in amazement. She was speechless. Before her eyes was a record for a Negro family by the name of Wesley. It only included three names. Najwa read the sheet of old brown paper that was eaten away at the ends.

"Richard Wesley, wife Elizabeth Wesley, and one child, Sadie Mae!" Najwa exclaimed.

She could not contain her excitement. It was just a census record, but it meant the world to her. She committed her life to working for a sorority that was founded on the blood of this woman. Najwa now held the proof of her existence beyond the passed down stories and history lessons. It was because of this woman, Najwa had a sisterhood upon which she could depend. Holding this sheet was almost as good as reaching out and touching Sadie Mae herself.

Najwa clutched the tattered paper to her chest as her heart raced with excitement. She studied the sheet intensely, not wanting to put it back in its resting place. She wanted to commit every inch, every letter, and every piece to her memory until she could acquire her own copy. By the time she had put the notice back in its place, it was well past her time to get off from work. Najwa could not wait to tell her sorors what she had found. Although she knew they would not be as excited as she, she still could not wait. Even more, she anticipated getting back to work so that she could find more records of her founder's existence in Casperton.

The day, however, was most difficult for Lynette. She anticipated not only the topic of this emergency meeting but she wondered if the girls had accomplished their task of raising the money. She briefly saw one of the pledges, Melissa, in the cafeteria of the Barkston Center. Ever since the application night, and being teased by Berri about her name, Melissa was petrified at the sight of any member of Gamma chapter. Yet, she was determined to join the ranks.

As Lynette walked in her direction, Melissa dropped the piece of fruit she was carrying. Briefly, they exchanged unimportant small talk. But she gave Lynette no indication of whether they had accomplished their assignment. As Lynette watched her scamper away like a guilty child, she wondered if Melissa had the temperament to pledge her sorority. Although she was a prominent writer with the campus' Black newspaper, she was entirely too nervous for Lynette's liking. She noted to herself that this would be something that needed to be dealt with.

The pledges were given strict instructions of how they were to proceed with the night. Lynette warned them, any deviation would bring consequences they did not want to endure. Thirty minutes before the honored guests were to arrive at Lynette's apartment, the chapter officers gathered in anticipation.

"Najwa, what happens if these girls don't come through?" Robin paced the floor.

"Soror sit down before you wear a hole in my sand's carpet,"

Najwa kidded.

"We'll cross that bridge when we get to it." Lynette moved over on the couch so Robin could sit between she and Najwa. "Now sit down you are making me nervous with that pacing."

Taking her seat, Robin realized how she must have looked to her sorors. "I am sorry but as chair of this committee, this kinda rests on my shoulders. I don't want the one year we don't win awards for our service projects to be the year I am chair."

"I understand where you comin' from sister but we are all in this together. Pacing that floor isn't going to get the money. Don't worry. If they don't come up with the money we will get it some kind of way," Candace reassured Robin.

Berri finally broke her silence. "That should be the least of our worries right about now. There is a bigger issue that no one has even brought up. "

"And that would be…?" Najwa asked. She had not dealt with Berri's attitude in a week. She was ready for her pessimism.

Berri polled the room. "Has anyone else in this room thought about the fact that we are asking these girls to raise all this money for us and they aren't even on line yet?"

Diane sat patiently on Lynette's beanbag chair listening to Berri's antics before she broke her silence. "So? What is your point?" She snapped before Najwa could answer.

"My point, sands, is that it is not right. What would our alumnae say about this?" Berri answered.

"And what have we done this year so far that hasn't been on the borderline of right and wrong? Were you not the one at the application night hounding everyone?" Diane asked.

"Two wrongs don't make a right and this is a big wrong." Berri answered.

"Berri you sound stupid." Diane flatly replied.

The rest were silent. The sorors sat on the couch looking as if they had front row seats to a tennis match. Najwa, in particular, found the argument to be quite entertaining. She was actually relieved that, for once, someone else stepped up to Berri's nonsense.

Berri finally spoke. "Excuse me Diane?"

"You heard me. You sound stupid. I am treasurer and I know exactly how much money we have in the bank. We have $16.21 to be exact. I also know we budgeted $115 for this project. Now, would you like to go in your pocket and donate the remaining $98.79?" Diane waited for an answer.

Lynette tried to bring calm to the room. "Sorors listen, we are all a little tense over this entire situation. Everyone just calm down, take a deep breath, and relax. My girls are going to come through."

"I agree Lynette. But let me ask you one question Berri. How would our alumnae even know that we had them to raise the money?" Najwa sat back and crossed her legs.

"I am just saying that we need to be careful that is all." Berri backed down from the opposition fiercely riding her back.

"Point well taken, soror. But I want to add that if everyone is on the same page as me, then we will be fine. Remember? We talked about the confidentiality of this matter a long time ago." Najwa ended the discussion.

As the topic was conveniently ended, Najwa sat thinking of how she was beginning to despise Berri. She was inconsistent and didn't have enough backbone to at least give Najwa a good run for her money in battle. Berri was brave to initiate a challenge but she was ultimately weak in Najwa's mind. Battle was a waste of time. Najwa found that her lack of respect grew because she believed Berri's own words were not hers. Obviously, Najwa's old adversary, Donna, was the source and Berri was the spokesperson. Berri was nothing more than a puppet.

Within ten minutes, the buzzer of Lynette's apartment pierced the room. Conversations ceased and all eyes shot to the door. Lynette leaped to answer it. Najwa silently breathed a sigh of relief as she saw that there were only two women standing on the other side. Only she and Lynette knew that the girls were instructed to send two representatives if they had raised the money. If they had not, all thirteen women were to report to the apartment. Lynette stepped outside in the walkway and closed the door. For five minutes, Lynette left everyone in the room besides Najwa in suspense. Finally, only Lynette emerged and walked in the apartment.

Robin scooted to the edge of the couch. "Well?" She asked.

Lynette stood over the group. "Ladies." Her expression never changed. "Looks like we will be doing that project after all. Diane, I have your $150 and then some. I told you my girls would come through." Lynette said confidently.

"Yes!" Robin exclaimed.

Lynette reached into the pocket of her blue jeans, pulled out the folded bills and handed them to Diane. Robin let out a long sigh of relief. The project was a go and Najwa could sleep with one less worry on her mind. Diane grabbed the money and stuffed it into her bra. Berri rolled her eyes.

"Not that it is really important but, how did they do it?" Robin asked.

"I bet they were begging their friends on campus for money," Berri blurted.

Diane interrupted. "I don't care if they had bets down at the pool hall. We got our money."

Candace turned to Lynette in anticipation of a new assignment. "So what's next for the girls?"

"Well, I'll have a little trick or treat surprise for you guys on Wednesday for Halloween festivities. And of course, since next weekend is Homecoming, I will have another little surprise then too. Until then their assignment is to lay low. " Lynette took her seat back on the couch.

"This sounds good! If this is anything like what we had to do last year, I am sure it is going to be crazy!" Candace beamed.

"Oh this is going to be better than last year ladies. You can trust me on that one. This is going to be one to remember." Lynette smirked and reached out her hand towards Najwa.

"You got that right!" Najwa acknowledged her sands by slapping her hand and then thrusting her own hand out for Lynette to reciprocate.

Berri touted her lips, grunted, and excused herself from the gathering as soon as all particulars of the service project were discussed.

As planned, the meeting was over in almost an hour and everyone was gone. Najwa left with the rest of the group, picked up Carla, and was back at Lynette's in less than fifteen minutes.

"Alright sands, spit it out." Lynette pushed. "I went the entire day trying to figure out what was so important that you, of all people, would call an emergency meeting."

"Yeah, me too. This is something I would do. What gives?" Najwa prodded.

"Did we get the money? Did the girls come through?" Carla prolonged the suspense.

"Of course we got it. Now come on, what is this meeting about? Lynette urged.

"That's good. It makes what I am about to tell you guys a whole lot easier to swallow." Carla said as she walked over to the refrigerator and pulled out a bottle of soda pop. She popped the metal lid from the bottle on the counter and then continued.

"Let me ask you guys something first. When Keisha was robbed, what did she say she had the money in?"

Najwa stood in the middle of the living room. "She said she had her purse, the brown, and suede one. Why?"

"That's just what I thought. Well sands, I think you better sit down cause I have something I think you might find interesting."

Carla sat on the floor. She explained to them step by step how she grew suspect of Keisha. She went on to explain the scheme to get in the dorms. Najwa and Lynette listened intently until Carla finished her entire story with the finding of the purse and it's contents.

Finally, Lynette spoke. "So wait a minute Carla. Let me get this straight. You are telling me that Keisha wasn't robbed after all? You think she stole our money?"

"Mmm, hmm." Carla responded before she swallowed the sweet, orange soda.

"But why? What the hell is going on around here?" Lynette was baffled.

"Think Lynette. Remember I said I found that card in her purse for the clinic."

"I'm just not getting this one. I really am not. Maybe my brain is fried from all that studying or something." Lynette still was in shock. "Our own soror robbed us? No wonder they never caught anybody! I need a drink!"

Lynette got up from the couch and went over to her kitchen counter and pulled out a pint size bottle. She poured a little orange juice in a glass and filled the rest with Vodka.

"Pour me one," Carla hollered.

"So Naj, say something. You been standing over there quiet ever since I started talking. I know you got something to say," Carla said to her silent line sister.

Najwa could no longer hide her anger through the expression on her face. She was obviously furious but there was more going on inside her head. She stared into space until Carla spoke to her.

"Damn!" Najwa finally answered.

"Yeah that was what I said too!" Carla took the short glass from Lynette who brought the entire bottle and sat it on the end table along with a glass of ice and orange juice for Najwa.

"You can say that again for me girl." Lynette sat taking a drink.

"Damn!" Najwa repeated as she finally sat on the couch and hit the armrest. "This is my fault! I don't know how I missed this." Najwa leaned over holding her face in her hands.

"Your fault? You didn't steal anything. How in the world is this your fault? You talkin' crazy now," Carla insisted.

"No Carla. I'm not. There is something I didn't tell you guys. I planned on dealing with it in my own way but I see this is much bigger than I thought."

Najwa began to tell them about the night of their chapter party. She explained to them how she walked in on Keisha vomiting in the bathroom.

"The whole robbery story was a fake just like I suspected. She had to come up with something after our talk in the bathroom. Carla, the card you found in her purse. That is where she probably went to have her abortion. That's where we will find our money." Najwa added.

"Naj we all know that Keisha is loose. This is probably not the first time she has been pregnant. So what did you mean by dealing with this in your own way? Did you know she was pregnant before that night?" Lynette asked.

"No. There is more. I think the father was Mark," Najwa announced.

Carla spit out Vodka and orange juice like a spout.

Lynette wanted assurance as she jumped up to get paper towels for Carla. "What! Mark who?"

Najwa shook her head. "Who do you think?"

"Aw damn! Here let me pour your drink 'cause I am 'bout to have another one." Lynette was floored.

Never had there been this much drama or excitement in their chapter. Carla cleaned up the mess she made as Najwa went into the long story of what had occurred the night at the after set. She explained how she promised Irby she would keep it all a secret. What Najwa thought was a small problem had now turned into the scandal of the year.

"You know what the funny thing is? Guess what the Round Table discussion topic was the other day?" After getting no answer, she continued. "The Roe vs. Wade decision on abortion and how it affects the Casperton Community."

"I bet Keisha had a whole lot to say about that one!" Lynette smirked.

"Poor Candace. Obviously, she doesn't suspect anything. She's so naïve. Let her tell it, she and Mark are practically engaged," Carla said.

"We can't let this get out. We would be the laughing stock of the entire campus," Lynette added.

172

"The chapter and Candace are our first priorities," Najwa said.

Carla looked to her sands for the lead. "So what's our next move Naj?"

"Keisha has to go," Najwa muttered.

"Candace can't find out about this. She wouldn't be able to finish the year." Lynette added.

"Keisha has to go," Najwa said again staring into space.

"This has gone too far. We got to keep this to ourselves," Carla said.

"Are you kidding? I am not opening up that can of worms," Lynette declared.

"Keisha must go!" Najwa repeated like a mad woman.

Carla turned to Najwa. "That girl has given us a bad name ever since she stepped her butt in that Rush. She does have to go. But how?"

"Haven't figured that out yet. But I will get her off this campus and out of our hair," Najwa responded.

Lynette was beginning to show the affects of her drink. "And out of everyone else's bed."

"Yeah that too. Just give me a few days to come up with something. Her days are numbered." Najwa rolled her eyes and downed her entire drink in one gulp.

*Along five acres of flat golden prairie land, the farm stood. It was Sadie's dream to return to Casperton to build a school for Negro children on the corner acre. Her father, a man who had sustained the first twenty-five years of his enslaved life on a dream of freedom and knowledge, understood his daughter's quest.*

# Saturday, November 17, 1973

Casperton was an old country town in every sense of its being - from the look, to the smell, to its feel. Halloween was just another holiday that reminded the students of Casperton University that there was actually a community surrounding the outskirts of the campus buildings. The rich autumn colors brightened the town and gave it a warm glow. Pumpkins lined the town's one-mile strip they called downtown. The students often wondered if it were not for the holiday season, would the town slip into obscurity.

There was the annual Casperton Pumpkin Fair. It started with the Pumpkin growing contest where farmers just outside of the town grew the orange giants to almost three feet. Next was the Pumpkin cutting contest, which always gave the town the Halloween feel. That was followed by the Pumpkin Recipe Contest, which included the special Pumpkin Pie Bake. The festive season ended with the Pumpkin Pie-Eating Contest. This was the prevailing theme at least until December, when Christmas would assume the responsibility of giving the town a purpose to be noticed again.

174

The rust orange leaves, blended with splotches of yellow and green on the tress still clinging to their summer dress, all made Najwa actually like this small mid-west prairie town. Totally contradictory to her fast east-coast home, it was peaceful, calm, and carefree. It was what she occasionally needed. But she thrived on energy, challenge, and a downright good fight. Chaos was her jump-start.

For Casperton University's campus, this was the time of chaos. The traditional Halloween campus festivities kicked off. Homecoming weekend was only days away. Midterms crept up like a thief, and the Omega Pi Alpha annual Thanksgiving Basket Giveaway was in full swing. The chapter had thirteen women trying to become new members and for a moment, they were the comic relief.

On Halloween day, Lynette had the entire group to dress like the characters of the Wizard of Oz, complete with props and Toto. The task was to go to each soror's dorm, apartment, or job to trick or treat. The only difference was that they were passing out the treats. If anyone requested a trick, they gave a short rendition of the entire movie. The sorors loved it. They were entertained and fed. That was all they needed to keep them happy and off Lynette's back to have a "special meeting" with the pledges.

Homecoming weekend was far from uneventful. The Black Greek Council used a portion of its first monetary installment, or what some called their "sell out money" for joining the CU Fraternal Council. Together they threw what had to have been the largest

175

tailgate barbecue the Black population of Casperton witnessed. That weekend, the Black Greek Council was the toast of the campus. The star running back of the football team, who was a brother, scored the winning touchdown in the homecoming game and parties flourished everywhere. The campus was running high into the week of midterms.

The basket giveaway was scheduled for the weekend before Thanksgiving. Robin meticulously planned the entire day down to a science. After meeting with their president, it was agreed that the Basket Giveaway project would be expanded to include the Deltas who also volunteered at the Casperton Community Center. Together, the two chapters would host a family night of Thanksgiving where the baskets would be given to two deserving families in attendance. In less than a week, the sorors, along with the help of the pledges enlisted the assistance of other students to cook and serve meals.

Over thirty families, who had no less than two children each, poured into the community center. The children were entertained with games and prizes while the fathers watched a football game, and the mothers received manicures at the direction of Carla. Afterwards, members of both sororities stood eagerly waiting to serve full course meals. The culminating event was the basket giveaway. Robin bought a turkey, fresh vegetables, fruit, and canned items for each basket. There were so many in attendance, it was decided that the family with the most children would receive the first and largest basket. The second was raffled. Every child left with a small gift in hand and the hearts of every member of Gamma

Chapter were warmed by the experience. The night was such a success, Najwa wasn't rattled in the least bit that Donna and a few of the chapter's alumnae showed up with Berri to volunteer their services.

"Congratulations, Najwa," Donna leaned over and said as she bent to pick up a rolling paper cup.

Najwa, still warm from the smiling children's faces, looked around. "Huh? Oh Donna...congratulations for what?"

"The giveaway," Donna said. She patted Najwa on the shoulder. "It was a success. Congratulations."

Najwa looked towards Robin who was across the room, and winked.

"Donna your congratulations should go to Robin. She put this all together. She is the one who deserves all the praise." She was demanding of her chapter but she always gave credit where credit was due.

"Yeah Robin does deserve praise but I am sure she took some of her direction from her president. I just wanted to give you your credit," Donna remarked.

"Well thanks Donna. I really appreciate you coming out and helping us too. Helping out causes that are bigger than ourselves and ignoring all the petty things that sometimes get in the way is more important. That's what it's all about."

Najwa knew she could not let down her guard and this was her way of letting Donna know that she remembered their past. Najwa found it odd that Donna actually said something nice to her for once.

But, with the overwhelming success of the entire night, how could she do otherwise.

"Yeah, well Najwa that is right. Things like this are more important. No matter how you got the money to do it." Donna's words cut Najwa like an old rusty butcher knife as she walked away with a snide look on her face.

It was too good to be true. Najwa knew her instincts were right. The entire chapter vowed that they would not discuss the way in which they recovered their loss from Keisha's misfortune. It was no secret Berri was the leak in the bucket. Although Berri was the least of Najwa's concern, this was still another little fire that Najwa was determined to extinguish at once. She was not going to fail as president.

# Thursday, November 22, 1973

The energy behind the basket giveaway carried Gamma chapter into the reading week. Midterms settled upon the campus and abruptly calmed the holiday surge. The campus was virtually desolate. The student body buried themselves within the confines of the library and the dorm study lounges. Despite the success of the service project and the praise received by the center's director, Najwa only celebrated her victory one night, then focused on the next challenge by immersing herself in both class assignments and problems facing the chapter.

Twice, that week alone, her mother called to convince her to make the journey east. Twice she hung up the phone in disappointment. Najwa tried unsuccessfully to make the blow a little easier for her mother with the consolation of a long Christmas break. Going home, for Najwa, would mean facing questions of plans after graduation. Questions Najwa painfully asked herself. She convinced herself the answers would come by the semester break. Midterms were no breeze and she still had not figured out how to handle

Keisha.

The week went so quickly. Najwa didn't have the opportunity to see Carla before she left for home. The last time they spoke was to share notes for their Literature class. The two and a half hour midterm was so intense, they only managed a drained, "I'll see you later," before leaving the room. The only sorors of Gamma chapter who remained on the campus were Najwa, Lynette, and Irby. The rest jumped in the first car, bus, or train headed for home cooked meals.

Knowing the dorms would be virtually empty, Najwa invited Irby to stay with her over the holidays. Irby more than happily packed a bag and took up house with her soror. Outside chapter events, Najwa didn't have the chance to spend time with her special since the day she broke the news of the Keisha affair. Their days were spent kicking back and watching soap operas in their pajamas. They vowed not to mention Keisha's name the entire weekend.

Thanksgiving Day, Najwa and Irby slept in late as usual. Besides calling her mother to wish her a happy holiday, Najwa only moved to turn the television channel to the football game. Mrs. Dixon's Thanksgiving dinner started at five that evening and Najwa could taste the famous lemon cake all day. Thirty minutes before they were to be at Mrs. Dixon's house, Najwa bathed and changed into a mini skirt and black turtle neck sweater. Her leather black boots zipped up the side to her knee and made her legs look especially long and shapely. Irby, feeling festive, wore an orange knit dress that had to be as bright as the pumpkin that won the award in the Casperton

Town Fair.

After picking up Lynette, at exactly the designated time, Panther pulled in front Mrs. Dixon's large, wood-framed house on the outskirts of Casperton, holding three hungry passengers. From the sidewalk they could see the shadows of people walking about inside. Several cars lined the long driveway that led around the back of the house. Najwa expected that there would be several people at the gathering. After all, Mrs. Dixon lived in Casperton all her life and was revered as one of the pillars of the community. There was no telling to whom those shadows may have belonged. Najwa had only heard the many stories of school and town dignitaries breaking bread at the Dixon's table. Tonight, digging into a plump, juicy turkey was more important than rubbing elbows with the rich and famous of Casperton.

"Looks like a full house tonight," Lynette commented as they moved towards the front door.

"Just as long as there is food. I don't care who is here," Najwa replied.

"Girl, just wait 'til you see the spread Mrs. Dixon lays out. She clowned last year. If it's anything like that, you are going to have to roll me back out to this car," Lynette assured Najwa.

Najwa rang the doorbell anticipating the legend of Thanksgiving dinner.

The warm laughter and talking crept from under the doors and for a brief moment made Najwa think of what may be happening back in D.C. at her mother's table. Guilt tried to move its way into

Najwa's spirit. Only a moment passed when the door finally opened to reveal the anticipated meal that had been touted to be better than a critically acclaimed play in town for one night.

"Hello babies! Happy Thanksgiving and come on in!" Mrs. Dixon rang out with her thick southern accent that stayed with her after she left her home in Livingston, Tennessee on a blind quest for love with Harry L. Dixon.

Each took their turn giving Mrs. Dixon a hearty hug as they walked under the threshold of the home of a feast. She was their mother away from home and deserved no less.

Mrs. Dixon's smile shined brighter than the silver hair on her head. "I'm so happy to see you girls here! Let Mr. Dixon take your coats. Come on in and make yourselves at home."

Najwa could feel the warmth in Mrs. Dixon's home and was pleased she came.

"Najwa baby, isn't this your first time here for Thanksgiving dinner since you been at the university?" Mrs. Dixon inquired.

"Yes ma'am it is. I heard so much about it that I couldn't let my last year go by without witnessing it for myself," Najwa replied as she handed her jacket to Mr. Dixon who hung it on the extra rack.

"Oh you stop it. It's nothing but a regular ole' Thanksgiving dinner honey," Mrs. Dixon blushed.

"Now come on, Mrs. Dixon, you know you get down in that kitchen!" Irby joined.

"That's right. My mother is still trying to find out who this Mrs. Dixon is that has kept her baby here at school every holiday for the past three years," Lynette added.

"Well I hope I live up to it today. You know it is the least I can do for my babies at the university. Now come on in here and join everybody else. I got to go check on my cake." Mrs. Dixon hurried around the corner and disappeared into the kitchen.

The girls could see guests sitting around the living room talking while others were off in the dining room. There had to be over twenty people milling around. Najwa recognized many who were students, the one Black professor from the university and other faces of community leaders she remembered from the Tiger Pride Newspaper.

Her growling stomach pleaded as she noticed everyone walking out of the dining room with small plates filled with vegetables, cheese, and little chicken wings. As she walked into the dining room, Najwa was mesmerized by the size of the table filled with trays full of food. Never in her life had she seen so many different cheeses, little bite-sized sausages, luncheon meats, vegetables, and every item on earth that had ever been pickled. At the end of the table was a fountain that was streaming a red juice.

"Whoa!" Najwa said loud enough for only her sorors to hear. Her eyes were wider than they had been since her first Christmas.

"Did I lie?" Lynette said under her breath as she nudged Najwa and waved to some classmates.

"Whoa!" Najwa said again still in disbelief. "Now this is a spread."

"But Najwa this ain't even the half of it. This is just the

appetizer. You know, a little something to tease your taste buds 'til the real deal comes," Irby whispered.

"Yeah just wait 'til you see the main course," Lynette added, still looking around the room at this year's attendees.

"I don't know if I will make it to the main course," Najwa chuckled.

After making their rounds speaking and introducing themselves, the girls got plates and joined the crowd in enjoying part one of Mrs. Dixon's Thanksgiving saga. The wooden chairs borrowed from the Black House that lined the walls, served as the resting spot for Najwa and Lynette. Irby, on the other hand, needed to walk around as if her bright dress didn't announce her arrival when they first walked in the door.

Najwa was trying to devour the pickled beets in the most lady-like manner until she heard a laugh that she could never mistake.

Najwa leaned over and whispered to her sands. "Lynette, Dakota is here."

"Where is he? I don't see him," she replied.

"He just came in the door. I know that stupid laugh anywhere. This is the moment I been waiting for."

"Oh that's right. You get to see this mystery woman he's been hiding away."

"Knowing him, he was probably just kidding when he said he was going to bring her," Najwa hoped.

"Well since we are on the subject sands, tell me, and don't take me wrong, but do I sense a little jealousy?" Lynette smiled looking out the corner of her eye.

"Excuse me? Are you out of your mind? Jealous of what?" Najwa replied with frustration as she forced more vegetables into her mouth.

"So what is the big deal then?" Lynette replied.

"He has been keeping this chick a secret for a while. If that had been me, he would have been all up in my business."

"Cool it sister! You don't have to convince me of anything. I know what the real deal is," Lynette snickered.

At that instant, Irby rounded the corner of the dining room hurrying over to her sorors. "Ooo Najwa…Ooo Najwa…Girl, Dakota is here!" Irby tried to contain her excitement.

"I know Irby. I heard his stupid laugh when he walked in the door," Najwa said as she nonchalantly continued eating.

"But Najwa, wait 'til you see who is hanging all over his arm!" Irby declared.

"Who girl? Who?" Lynette pleaded.

Irby was so excited, her body uncontrollably rocked back and forth. "Uhh uhh. I'm not saying a word. I want you to see for yourself. Ooo…wait 'til you see." She repeated.

"Well then, what you come over here for? Go sit down somewhere. You looking' crazy," Najwa said.

Irby laughed as she pulled up a chair to witness the reaction first hand.

"Okay Naj, but not as crazy as you gon' be looking when you see this."

"You remember this when you need a ride to my apartment tonight." Najwa had to laugh because she knew her reaction would probably be just as Irby expected.

The mystery of Dakota's disappearance from existence was about to be revealed. This moment had to be perfect now that Irby had made so much out of it. Najwa wondered to herself what was taking him so long to come into the dining room. She wanted to get up and go to the other room and meet him head on. This was made impossible by her legs that had no feeling. If she were to rise, surely she would end up on the floor. Her butt was glued to the seat and her eyes to her plate. Najwa lost control of her senses and could not understand what was going on in her head that made her so nervous and anxious to see this sister who had taken her spot as Dakota's confidant.

"Oh…oh my…. oh my goodness." Lynette whispered leaning closer to Najwa.

Najwa continued to stare at the vegetables on her plate to prolong the moment. Finally, she slowly looked up and caught the first glimpse of the young woman. She looked intensely at every inch of the woman's body, feet first. She wanted to survey whoever this woman was that had made her home with Dakota.

"She is mighty thin for Dakota's liking." Najwa thought, observing the thin ankles that led up to the long slender legs. "Hmm …and she has on that ugly, cheap, pink knit skirt. Dakota hates that color. And her chest is rather flat," she continued. Finally, their eyes met and Najwa's expression never changed.

Irby nudged Lynette. "Here they come. Here they come."

Dakota walked over smelling shower fresh and dressed impeccably as usual. "Ladies. Good evening. Najwa how are you?"

Najwa acted surprised. "Dakota. Hey!" She looked over at the woman clinging to Dakota's arm. Najwa knew very well who this mystery woman was. She had the privilege of ripping up her membership application just a few weeks prior. As a matter of fact, she had not seen Pat since she was sent next door to await the chapter vote. Her disappearing act was the perfect excuse Najwa needed to get rid of her without an explanation. Other than lack of respect, Najwa really had no other reason to dislike Pat.

"Najwa, I would like for you to meet someone. I don't know if you have ever seen her around the campus but this is Patricia."

"Nice to meet you Patricia." Najwa extended her hand to shake Pat's as if they had never met. The interested ladies invited to the application night were told never to mention the experience to anyone. Obviously, Pat followed that instruction because Dakota never knew he was introducing old acquaintances.

"Humph…" Pat smirked. "I go by Pat. I think we have seen each other on the campus before sister. But nevertheless it's nice to meet you to." Pat still held Dakota's arm never returning the favor of shaking Najwa's hand.

Dakota finished his introductions. "These are her sorors, Lynette and Irby."

Blank stares and silence took over the moment.

"Umm well, excuse us ladies." He turned to his date. "Baby lets go get something to eat."

Najwa and her sorors rolled their eyes as Pat switched away.

"Don't say a word!" Najwa stopped both Irby and Lynette just as they were starting the commentary. "I don't want to hear it now. I just want to enjoy the rest of this holiday. We will talk about that cow in my car on the way home," Najwa announced as they all laughed.

Mrs. Dixon's house welcomed at least fifteen more people before she announced that dinner was served. Knowing the routine, everyone picked up their chairs and migrated to the basement where there were several tables set up in a circle. Unlike typical clammy basements, Mrs. Dixon's looked like a second large dining room. Each table was set, complete with tablecloth, silverware, and festive decorations. Najwa figured that Mrs. Dixon had to have started last week getting everything prepared. Surely it couldn't be done in less time.

Along the wall were four long, rectangular tables that had enough food to nourish the town of Casperton. Each table was arranged according to its contents. The first table had nothing but meats. Two perfectly baked, plump turkeys sat in the middle surrounded by what seemed to be the rest of the farm. Chitterlings, baked ham, duck, and even ribs were waiting. The second table was devoted to the vegetables and beans. Najwa didn't know that there were as many kinds of greens. There were collards, mustards, turnips, spinach and even something Mrs. Dixon called, the "wild ones growing in the garden." The last two tables were adorned with macaroni and cheese, dressing, rolls, cornbread, sweet potato pies, cobbler, and the jewel of the crown, the lemon cake.

"I think I just walked through the pearly gates." This time Najwa could not contain her excitement as the entire room broke into laughter.

Mr. Dixon led the room in a prayer and after the loud unified "AMEN," the feast began. Together the group of over thirty people sat as a family at each table enjoying the meal Mrs. Dixon prepared with the help of her sister who had come in town just for the occasion. Najwa wanted to thoroughly enjoy her meal and made a point to make it to every dish for at least a sample. She could have shown her appreciation even more by opening at least one button on her skirt. Being conscious of the large group, she reluctantly declined this pleasure. A pillow or even a spot on the plush couch upstairs would have done the job as well. But the party was kept alive as Mr. Dixon pulled out beer, Crown Royal, dominoes, and several decks of cards. The trash talking began.

Najwa along with several other ladies began helping Mrs. Dixon take up the dishes and food.

"Mrs. Dixon I am never, ever going to forget this Thanksgiving," Najwa declared climbing the steps carrying a naked turkey carcass.

"Good baby. I am glad you were pleased."

"How do you do it? I mean when do you find the time to fix all this food? I don't think I will cook that much food in my lifetime."

"Oh I started two weeks ago. I do a little cleaning and picking here and there. All the vegetables I grow right out in my garden. Some of the other stuff I just freeze until I am ready for it."

"Well whatever you do Mrs. Dixon, you have made a lot of people full and happy tonight," Najwa laughed.

"Baby I've been doing this for years now. It is second nature to me now. Plus I have my sister and some of the ladies from the church that come over to help me." Mrs. Dixon smiled and placed her hand on the shoulder of a short, stout lady bending over the sink.

Najwa glanced over at the clock. They had been at Mrs. Dixon's house for over four hours and yet it only seemed like moments since Najwa's nose caught the smell of a home cooked meal.

Najwa politely excused herself back to the basement. There the men were engaged in loud bouts of slapping dominoes on the tables. The women on the card tables were giving them a run for their money. Najwa's eye scanned in search of her sorors. She thought she managed to avoid Dakota and his date all night when she felt a tug at her arm.

His deep voice came from over her shoulder. "Hey stranger." Najwa slowly turned knowing exactly who was standing behind her.

"Hello, Dakota. And why am I a stranger? " she replied as if she didn't know.

"Well it seems like you've been avoiding me all night. I tried to sit with you guys to eat but when I turned around your table was completely full."

"Oh really. I didn't notice. I am sorry. Next time I will be sure to save you a place. Besides, I thought you two might want to be alone

190

at a more romantic table. " Najwa joked knowing that she intentionally sat where neither she nor her sorors would be in the presence of Dakota and his date. With the history the three shared with Pat, no one wanted to entertain that couple.

"Ha, ha you are just so funny Najwa," Dakota replied.

"So, where's your shadow," Najwa asked looking around Dakota's broad shoulders.

"She went to the bathroom and she is not my shadow. Her name is Pat."

Najwa laughed aloud. "You mean she could unlatch her paws from your arm for one second to pee!"

"Najwa that's enough. She is my date and I won't allow you to disrespect her just like I wouldn't allow her to disrespect you," Dakota snapped.

Najwa's looked Dakota up and down. "Oh, so Miss Thang had something to say about me?"

"No, Najwa just forget I even said that."

"No, what did she say Dakota? I want to know for future reference."

"Future reference? Najwa what is wrong? What is really going on here? Do you two know each other? I don't understand where all this tension is coming from."

Najwa began to realize how silly she might have sounded. "Oh, just forget it Dakota. I guess it's just a woman thing." After all, Dakota's date meant nothing to her she convinced herself. Najwa pointed over to a group. "Look, your date is out of the bathroom.

Why don't we go over there?"

At least among others she might not be forced to actually interact with Pat directly but just enough to make Dakota happy. Dakota and Najwa walked over to a group of familiar students engaged in a heated discussion about the emergence of marijuana on the campus.

A professor raised in Casperton and home for the holidays from Indiana University, pulled Dakota closer for his opinion. "Dakota, you are the representative of the Black Greek Council on this campus lets hear what you have to say bout this."

"This young lady here, I believe her name is Pat, is saying that the Black Greek-lettered organizations shouldn't play a part in ridding the campus and community of what I see as a surging drug problem. Basically, she is saying that we don't do anything for the community but promote elitism. And, until we can solve that problem, we have no place in the trenches. I am a Kappa man myself and brother, I just wanted to know what you think about that?" The professor waited for Dakota's response.

Najwa stood closer anticipating Dakota's reply. She didn't want to miss a single beat of this conversation. "Hell, I may even throw my opinion in this one," she thought as she looked at Dakota's surprised look.

"Uh well…brother, I would have to say that she is wrong. But obviously that is just my opinion and hey, she is entitled to hers," Dakota carefully replied.

"Oh no she didn't just say that when she just applied to my

sorority a month ago," Najwa thought to herself. Besides, she wasn't going to let Dakota off that easy.

"Hold on sister, what right do you have to even make a comment like that? I mean who are you to judge where I come from and whether I have the right to help my people?" Najwa asked calmly.

"Now that's what I'm talkin' about. Now we got a debate going here," the professor proclaimed.

Dakota's eyes rolled in the back of his head.

"I have every right to make a comment like that. I have lived in Casperton all my life. And I can tell you that the last thing we need is another pompous, elite Negro like you so-called Black Greeks to tell us how to live our lives," Pat blurted.

Najwa stood firm and anchored for battle. Not often did she bow down and tonight was not going to be one of those rare occasions.

"Well let me ask you this sister. You say you come from this community, right?" Najwa asked.

"That's right. I grew up less than a mile from the University," Pat replied.

"Okay. Well let me ask you this. When was the last time you went back home besides the holidays? Since I don't have any business in your community, tell me, what have you done? I am really interested in knowing." Najwa waited.

Pat folded her arms and turned up her nose at Najwa. "Excuse me?"

Najwa looked Pat in the eyes. "I'm just wondering because I have volunteered at the community center on a weekly basis for the past four years and I have never seen you there."

"Well just great! You go to the community center. But the Casperton Community Center is not the only way to help out this community." Pat blurted. She turned to the professor and continued. "See what I mean professor, you Greeks think that you can put a band-aid on a sore. You go out to the community center and volunteer for a couple of hours and you want awards for it."

By now Irby and Lynette made their way over to hear the conversation.

"You are absolutely right about the band aid solution. You have a valid point. And I guess the answer to my question was that you haven't done anything in the community. That's cool. Well let me ask you this sister, what is your major?" Najwa remembered from her membership application that in fact, Pat had no major at all.

"I don't have a declared major. I am a general studies student. What is your point?" Pat snapped.

"No major huh? Let's cut to the chase and take a real look at this whole situation. You don't have a major, so therefore you aren't preparing yourself with any expertise to take back to your community. You live on the campus, so how could you even know the living hardships of your community? You are dating a middle class brother from the suburbs of Washington D.C. who also happens to be a member of one of those elite organizations. So how would you even know the struggle of the Black man in this community, when you won't give him the time of day? You didn't even care to dine in your community on this good holiday. So may I just ask what makes you any different from any of us standing here in this room?" Najwa stared Pat down.

"That's right sister! You said it! Give me five on that one." The professor put out his hand and Najwa slapped it.

"Right on! Right on!" Irby hollered from behind.

Dakota tried to throw water on the sparks that would surely burn the house down. "Look, I think we should end this conversation. Hey baby let's get outta here. I am ready to go."

"Dakota, I do not have to take this garbage." Pat was fuming. Najwa called her out in front of the professor, her man and every other Black student in the basement.

Dakota quickly grabbed Pat by the elbow and nudged her towards the basement steps.

"Why are you pushing on me? I know you are not just going to let her talk to me like that?" Pat continued to fuss to the top of the stairway. "I don't need this…"

Najwa beckoned Lynette and Irby. "Sorors lets go. I think I have said enough here."

They said their good-byes to Mrs. Dixon and were on their way out the door smiling from ear to ear. Najwa felt a special thrill. Not only because she was leaving with a full stomach having eaten the best dinner in her entire life. Not even because she was leaving with a large slice of Mrs. Dixon's lemon cake. But the thrill of watching Pat quiver as she claimed yet another sweet victory with words was enough for Najwa.

# Monday, November 26, 1973

Thanksgiving break was over sooner than it began and the campus was back to normal. News in the gossip circle was Dakota's date and what was now known as "The Argument." Carla's arrival back on campus was met with several versions of the evening. Needing to get the full affect of exactly what happened, Carla found herself at Lynette's apartment with Najwa. She was a captive audience as the two went on about the evening.

Carla held her side she laughed so hard.

"Najwa you have got be jiving about Dakota and Pat!"

"They came in there looking like Willie Tyler and Lester," Najwa smirked. She never was a big fan of the famous ventriloquist whose claim to fame was a black wooden dummy with an Afro sitting on his arm.

Lynette fell over on the couch laughing.

"You are lying to me girl!" Carla hollered.

"Have you talked to him since the dinner Najwa?" Lynette asked.

"Naw. He is probably still mad at me for telling his woman off. He will get over it though. I think I am going to give him a call later this week if I don't see him on campus."

"I still can't believe she had the nerve to come in there bad mouthing when she had just tried to pledge," Lynette commented.

"All I have to say is it was a good thing I wasn't there cause you know I would have snatched her up so quick!" Carla added.

"Yes it was a good thing sands. But it's cool 'cause I took care of it," Najwa arrogantly declared. "Actually, I am glad the little scene happened cause it gave me an idea about a solution to our little Keisha problem."

"You know I was thinking about that the entire time I was home. What you come up with Naj?" Carla eagerly asked.

"Whatever we do, no one can find out that she was ever pregnant by Mark. That would be the biggest embarrassment of the year," Lynette said.

"Exactly. We all agree that she has to go right?" Najwa looked around to her sands and waited for each of them to acknowledge. After receiving quick nods, she continued. "Let's say our Keisha becomes a victim of the campus drug controversy by having a little pot in her dorm room."

"Najwa, it's 1973, EVERYONE has pot in their room," Lynette pointed out.

"Yeah but no one ever goes looking for it. And if you are black, on this campus you don't want to get caught with any." Carla added her resident assistance point of view.

Najwa revealed her master plan. "Listen, the whole argument at Mrs. Dixon's started over marijuana in the Black community. They even brought up the situation with the brother who was arrested back in September. It made me think. What if our Keisha gets caught with a little marijuana in her dorm room? She gets kicked out, but not for anything we aren't all guilty of. Everyone on this campus smokes a joint or gets high at some point when they step foot in Casperton."

"But not everyone sleeps with their soror's man and then steals the chapter's money to have an abortion. I am with you Najwa. The lesser of the two evils. But how?" Carla asked.

"Aren't there room inspections some time around Christmas break?" Najwa asked Carla.

"There's one the last day before Christmas break when everyone is just about gone," she answered.

Najwa looked to Carla. "I need you to get into Keisha's room the same way you did before. You know, drop off a little package right before the inspections."

"I don't know Naj. It wasn't that easy getting in there that night. I could lose my job and get kicked out on my own butt if I get caught," Carla replied.

"Carla has a point. What is she supposed to say if she gets caught? Oh well, see, I was in here trying to set my soror up cause she stole our chapter money?" Lynette mocked.

"She'll say the same thing she would have said had she gotten caught the first time. This time is no different. Come on guys. Don't chicken out on me now. We've come this far. We got to see this through." Najwa believed this was the solution to their problem and was determined to see her plan to the end. "If it makes you two feel any better, get me the key. I'll do it!"

Lynette was not completely sold on the plan. "Najwa I want to see all three of us graduate. You don't need to get caught either! Why can't we just try to forget all this ever happened and hope…"

"And hope what Lynette? Hope she doesn't steal anything else from us? Hope she doesn't get caught with anyone else's man? Hope she doesn't have to visit the abortion clinic again next semester? Or just hope no one ever finds out?" Najwa interrupted.

"I'm with Najwa, Lynette. She stole our money. Let's not forget how we had to get it back. Did you forget that? How many more messes are you going to have to make the pledges clean up behind her?" Carla added.

"Guys, how would I explain to my parents that I gave up my dream of medical school for this? Revenge is not my priority. I want to graduate!"

The three looked into space as if the answer to their problem would miraculously appear in mid air.

Najwa gave her final plea. "It's all or nothing Lynette. If we do this it is going to be all of us. Remember we are sands."

"I am scared," Lynette replied.

"So are we," Carla said. "Lynette, if I get caught, you have my word. I would never hurt your chances of going to medical school. I know how much that means to you and how hard you have worked."

"You have my word too," Najwa added.

Lynette hesitated. "Guys you know I am not just thinking of myself I don't want any of us to get caught doing anything."

She sat silent for few seconds.

"You two are out of your minds! I agree. She has to go. Let's do it." Lynette finally surrendered to her sands who had fire in their eyes.

"Christmas break. It's done," Carla ended.

# Wednesday, November 28, 1973

Najwa avoided Dakota for the next two days knowing he was angry with her about "The Argument." It was more infamous on the campus than the Watergate scandal. She knew eventually, they would have to meet. She knew the special meeting of the Greek Council, which called for the attendance of all chapter presidents, would be their first encounter. The university approved the largest funding for the Black Greek Council and would be dispersing the next deposit that month. With the money, the Black Greek Council decided to have its first "Snowflake Ball" with all proceeds benefiting the Casperton Community Center and a scholarship. The council president, Karen Walters, wanted to make certain she had the support of all the chapters. This would undoubtedly be the largest function organized by any group of Black students on CU's campus. Not to mention, the largest fundraiser ever for the Casperton Community Center.

With criticism still lingering in the air from joining the White fraternal council, this event was the perfect opportunity to make good on the promise of the entire Black community benefiting from their "sell-out" money. On the other hand, many of the other student organization's leaders were just simply pleased with the idea of a social event before the break that did not involve cookies and punch. This was not the regular Christmas social held in the Black House every year. This ball would be complete with catered food, a live band and DJ.

Najwa strategically arrived a little after the meeting began and quietly positioned herself in the back so that Dakota would not be able to see her. She knew her old friend could not stay mad all semester. But still she hoped that somehow she could miss him altogether tonight.

Karen tapped her gavel and brought the special "open meeting" to order. As expected, Karen, in her charismatic nature, announced the intentions of the council to have the ball and opened the floor for comments from all the organizations present. Surprisingly, the idea was met with overwhelming support from everyone. Hearing no objections, Karen announced that Dakota Phillips would serve as chairperson.

Dakota's broad shoulders emerged from the front row and moved to the center podium. He turned to address the applauding group of students and caught a glimpse of Najwa sitting in the back corner. He winked at her, smiled and began speaking to the group about the ball plans. Najwa's heart felt a little lighter. She would not have to worry about eating too much crow with Dakota. The signal that all was forgiven was received.

Najwa waited for ten minutes after the meeting while Dakota answered every question of each representative individually.

"Congratulations, Mr. Chairperson."

"Do you have a question for your chapter?" Dakota blankly starred at Najwa.

She was puzzled by Dakota's response. "Uh...no...I just wanted to say congratulations."

"Thanks Najwa, your approval means so much to me," Dakota blurted.

Najwa thought Dakota had forgiven her. Obviously she was wrong. "Huh? Dakota I know you are not still mad about that little episode are you?"

In that same instant, her heart found itself even deeper in her stomach than it was when she first walked through the door.

"Nothing ever changes does it? You still just can't admit when you are wrong and just apologize can you?"

Najwa stood with her eyes almost as wide as her open mouth. He really was angry this time, she thought to herself. He had never been so angry at anything she had ever done that she could remember. And, it hurt. There was nothing that Najwa could think to say that would possibly make the situation better. She didn't know whether to react to him being angry or to her own hurt feelings.

"I guess you can't then. Goodnight Najwa." Dakota turned, picked up his jacket, and walked towards the door.

Najwa's body was numb. Her entire being was in shock. The best half of her entire childhood was walking out the door and she had to stop him, even if it meant giving in.

"I'M SORRY!" Najwa blurted.

Dakota stopped and whisked around. "What did you say?"

Najwa had never, in the 15 or more years she'd known Dakota, said those two words in the same sentence.

"I said…I'm sorry," she muttered looking at the floor.

Dakota walked back. "Damn baby, I know I am a good actor but I must deserve an Oscar for that one." Dakota laughed. "You have never said anything like that to me or anyone for that matter!"

This time he really got Najwa back and it was a cause for celebration.

Najwa was not amused. "What!"

Dakota flopped down on a chair laughing hysterically at his victory. "I was just joking. I got you that time! Man, did I get you!"

"You got me. You won. Now if you don't mind I am going home." Najwa walked over to the chair where her purse still lay and began gathering her things to leave.

"Oh I know you are not trying to have an attitude after you made me the laughing stock of Thanksgiving? An apology is the least you owe me."

Najwa hoped that Dakota did not notice how much he affected her with his performance. "You are right Dakota. Tell me what it is you want me to do and I will do it. I don't want to hear about this anymore."

"You did apologize. And for you that is a big. But I can think of one more thing." Dakota waited. Finally, Najwa stopped fidgeting with her coat and looked at him. "Whatever it is, if I agree to it, will we be even?"

Dakota smiled. "Even, Steven."

"Fine. Now what did I just agree to?"

"Ms. Jackson, you just agreed to be my escort to the Snowflake Ball. You can pick me up at about 6:30 that evening."

"What? Escort? Oh no! I wouldn't take your rusty butt to the corner!"

"All right, well then, I guess the deal is off."

Najwa cringed at the thought but conceded. "Okay! Wait! Ugh! I'll do it. But don't expect me to hang all over your arm like that pathetic Pat. Why don't you take her? Oh, I forgot. She wouldn't be caught dead with us high falootin' Negroes would she?"

"See, now that is what got you into this mess in the first place. You just don't learn do you?"

"Answer me. Why aren't you taking her?" Najwa smiled for the first time since they exchanged words. "Don't tell me there is trouble in paradise?"

"We are not seeing each other anymore if you must know. And I don't want to talk about it, so lets just go." Dakota stood and walked towards the door.

"Touch Down! Fourth quarter and the score is now 24 –7. I am still ahead!" Najwa hollered. Her sense of humor returned as she alluded to the "Relationship Bowl."

"Well you know what? I could have scored more by now but…oh, I forgot...you've only had ONE boyfriend since we have been here." Dakota ran out the door ducking as Najwa threw a pen at him. The reality was that she was just happy to have her friend back.

*Minutes had passed when she found herself standing hotel steps looking down the road. Sadie Mae glanced back and waved at the man. His grinning face disappeared as she began her long walk home.*

## Friday, December 7, 1973

Finals were over and the students were free for the holidays. For the past week, every soror of Gamma chapter scouted the town with the few dollars they had left, in search of the perfect dress. At the last minute, both Najwa and Irby were able to find dresses at a small boutique on the outskirts of Casperton. Najwa did not think the ball would garner as much attention as it did. Every Black student delayed the journey home for Christmas for one day just to attend the ball. Najwa had to admit that even she grew excited as she ran into her apartment to hurry and get dressed. With such an attendance, in a small town like Casperton, if the Pumpkin contest could make feature story, surely a benefit of this magnitude would be headline news in the local paper.

Najwa could not believe that she was Dakota's escort for the Snowflake Ball. But, when the thought of his reaction played back in her memory, it was the least she could do. Now, she found the whole incident to be quite amusing.

Knowing Dakota was serious when he told her what time to pick him up, Najwa sat in front of his house at 6:30 sharp, blowing Panther's horn. There was absolutely no way that she would go so far as to get out the car and ring his door bell.

The entire ride, Dakota dug into Najwa's skin about being his escort for the evening and how he expected her to conduct herself. Not teasing her would have been unnatural. It wasn't often that he was able to claim victory over her. Dakota and Najwa pulled in front of the Barkston Center just as many of the guests were beginning to arrive. Dakota, being the chairperson, was eager to get inside and see how everything was going. Najwa offered to drop him off at the door, but he refused. He insisted on entering on the arm of his escort. Najwa cringed but conceded as she turned in the parking lot. Instinctively, Najwa cut her car off and was almost out the door when Dakota grabbed her arm and pulled her back.

"If we are going to do this then let's do it right," Dakota insisted.

He jumped out of the car, walked to the driver's side and opened Najwa's door. He extended his hand to help Najwa to her feet. Her eyebrows raised in amazement. She reached out and it was official. This was a date.

Dakota closed the car door behind Najwa and extended his arm for her to hold as they walked along the Barkston Center pathway. Najwa clung to his muscular arm and for a moment, thought of how she must look just as Pat did when they made the infamous Thanksgiving Day entrance. But in that instant, just like Pat, she did not care. It felt too good.

Before Dakota went inside to assume his chairperson duties, he made sure Najwa was settled in the waiting area. Najwa wondered where the pompous man she picked up ten minutes earlier had disappeared.

"Can I check your coat?" He asked.

Najwa was still awe struck. "Uh …yeah…okay. "

Dakota positioned himself behind her to peel the outer layer of what would be the main attraction of the night. Dakota was gathering Najwa's coat when he finally looked up and caught the first sight of his lady for the evening. His eyes started at the neckline of the long, black dress that gently choked her from the chin down to her ankles. Unlike any other dress she owned, this one left Najwa's arms bare. It revealed her soft shoulders and defined, yet feminine muscles. Her skin was so even and silky. Her breast shadowed a stomach that was flat and hips that were full. The black, silk gloves she wore fit so well. An hourglass figure was an understatement.

"Wow," was all Dakota could manage.

"What? Najwa blushed. "You think it is too much don't you? I knew I shouldn't have let Irby talk me into buying this dress."

"Too much? No! Naj…I don't think I have ever seen you look as beautiful." He reassured her. "Here, let me take this coat but don't you go anywhere. Promise you won't come in until I come back and get you. Promise?"

"Okay," Najwa replied.

Dakota ran off to the coat check and disappeared into the ballroom.

She walked around the lobby in search of her sorors until she

209

finally found them by the entrance. Najwa was relieved to see her sands finally arrive. They were speechless, as most of the chapter was after seeing Najwa.

Gamma chapter had a table reserved so that most of them could sit together. However, Najwa would be sitting at the VIP table with Dakota. Initially, she thought of the seating arrangement as the price to pay for escorting the event chairperson. Now she did not mind at all. As all the sorors began to enter the ballroom, they looked back puzzled at Najwa who was still standing at the doorway.

They called to her. "Aren't you coming in?" They were accustomed to making their entrance together no matter what was going on.

"No you guys go ahead, I will be along in a minute," she answered.

Although Dakota made her promise to wait outside, she was beginning to think it was another one of his pranks. He probably would have her standing in the lobby for most of the evening. The gentleman routine had to be act two of getting back at her. A few minutes passed as Najwa began to second guess waiting any longer. Maybe he had gotten busy and forgot about her. She decided to just go in and sit with her sorors when Dakota snuck up behind her.

"Hey, I thought I told you to wait for me out here?"

Najwa began to fuss. "It was taking you so long. Everything is about to get started and I am the only fool still standing out here."

He put his finger over her lips. "Shh…" He stood with his other hand behind his back. "I have something for you and I got a surprise.

Close your eyes."

"What?" Najwa looked confused.

"Just close your eyes!" Dakota pleaded.

Finally she huffed and gave in to his request. She felt him lift her arm and gently hold her hand. His hands moved up her wrist and she smelled heaven.

"Okay open," he said.

Najwa slowly opened her eyes and confirmed the pleasures her nose enjoyed.

"Thank you, Dakota." Najwa said softly as she smelled the corsage made of a single rose and baby's breath. Najwa would not allow herself to believe that Dakota was being so nice for no apparent reason.

"What do you want from me? I don't have any money for you to borrow. Are you getting kicked out your house? 'Cause if you are being so nice to me 'cause you need a place to stay it is not going to work. Oh…wait...I know what it has to be. I am not covering for you with your parents over the Christmas break. Whatever it is, the answer is no!"

Dakota laughed. "Would you just be quiet and enjoy the Ball? Now the surprise. Come with me." Dakota again extended his arm for Najwa and walked to the main entrance of the ballroom.

There, all the officers of the Greek Council were lined up. One by one they were introduced to the crowd as they walked down an aisle that extended the entire length of the room.

"We don't have to walk down that aisle do we? All the way up there to the front? You didn't say anything about that. No one else has an escort walking them in. Dakota, I can't walk up there. I will be a nervous wreck!" Najwa pleaded.

"Najwa stop it. You'll be cool. You are the finest sister up in here. I am the luckiest brother and I want everyone to see how fine you are tonight." Dakota gave Najwa his puppy dog face. "If you don't go in, then I am not going in. And, I am the chairperson."

It wasn't until then that she noticed Dakota had rented a black tuxedo. He looked so handsome looking over his black butterfly bow tie.

Najwa gave in. "Come on. Let's go."

Dakota gave the signal. The lights went down in the ballroom as the last person was introduced. The violins in the orchestra floated above her head as Barry White's, "Love Theme" played from the loud speakers. The double doors swung open and the dream began.

"Ladies and gentlemen please give a big round of applause for the man who made this evening possible, Mr. Dakota Phillips who is being escorted this evening by Ms. Najwa K. Jackson." The announcer rang.

Najwa swallowed her heart and immediately clutched Dakota's arm.

"They are playing our song. Let's go." Dakota smiled larger than life as he lead the way.

The crowd gave Dakota a standing ovation for what was a historical moment for the Black students of Casperton University. The men of Omega and the women of Gamma chapter went wild applauding for their frat and soror. The men in the room whistled as they caught a glimpse of Najwa's hourglass figure.

"Right on Brother! Foxy mama!" Some of them hollered.

Carla leaned over to Lynette who was applauding and screaming Najwa's name. "Damn they look good together!"

"That's my girl!" Lynette screamed.

The local newspaper snapped pictures. Dakota treated Najwa like a bride the rest of the evening.

*She clutched the straps of her bag and walked into the night air.*

# Saturday, December 15, 1973

Twenty-four hours passed and the campus was barren. Najwa turned in her glass slippers for a plane ride to Washington D.C. Together Najwa and Dakota raced to the Casperton station and boarded the last bus for O'Hare airport. The mirror images of cornfields surrounding the bus' pathway were hypnotic and lured them both to sleep the entire ride into Chicago. Much of the same continued on the flight into Washington D.C. Each moment Najwa spent both awake and asleep recalled every detail of the previous night. The Snowflake Ball gave Najwa her most memorable college experience.

Washington D.C. welcomed Najwa with winter's first snow and all her favorites on the dinner table. No dinner at Mrs. Dixon's could match the special meal her mother prepared with love. Najwa was home. If only for a brief moment, she was home.

Against her own better judgment, Najwa hoped for signs that the evening they shared meant something to Dakota. She searched for signs that while walking down the aisle he possibly felt the same

214

tingle in his stomach as she. Perhaps he too felt the need to hold on to the last dance for just another moment. Maybe it wasn't all in her imagination that he held her especially close while the photographer took pictures at their table. She desperately wanted the answers to these questions without asking. But Dakota would not bite.

After the third day home, Najwa convinced herself to say something to her longtime friend. It was the least she could do. There was nothing she felt uncomfortable talking about with him. She had it all planned. She would go over on Christmas to wish their family happy holiday and give Dakota a special Christmas gift. She would tell him how she really felt about him. Maybe he would return the gesture by affirming that he felt he same.

Over and over Najwa recited her speech for Dakota in her brain. She had even written it down. Giving him a letter had also crossed her mind as an option. However, she didn't want Dakota to look at her as his little sister anymore. She wanted him to see the mature woman that she was. After deciding that the best approach should come straight from the heart, she ripped up the three-page confession.

Christmas Eve was the most special night for the Jackson family. Najwa's anticipation as a child started a family tradition that never left. Her mother made eggnog, apple cider, and freshly baked cookies in the shape of Christmas trees. To the sound of her father's favorite Christmas records, Najwa and her parents would each open one gift from under the tree. Afterwards, Najwa would run next door to show off her gift to Dakota and sneak a taste of his mother's gingerbread. Tonight would be no different. If things went well, she would have a talk with Dakota.

After going through their family tradition, Najwa took a deep breath and decided take the trip over to Dakota's. Twice Najwa opened her front door and closed it hesitating. The third time she finally found herself ringing her longtime neighbor's doorbell.

"Najwa sweetie!" Dakota's mother exclaimed.

"Mrs. Phillips, Merry Christmas." Najwa began her annual formalities. But this time she was so nervous she suddenly was at a loss for words. "Uh...Mrs. Phillips...I...uh...I hope I didn't interrupt."

"Najwa, what has gotten into you? For the past fifteen years or more you have popped up on my porch on Christmas Eve around this time of the night with that same bright smile and lovely little face." Mrs. Phillips laughed. "Don't you think by now that we have come to expect you?"

Najwa had to laugh at how ridiculous she must have looked and sounded. Although she felt differently about her relationship with Dakota, there was no reason to make a fool of herself. No matter the outcome of her conversation, she knew she would always have a dear and best friend in Dakota. Either way, she figured, she would still have an advantage.

Najwa went through her normal Christmas Eve routine at the Phillips house. Her first stop was over to the Christmas tree. Every year Mrs. Phillips showed off her crafty expertise with hand made Christmas ornaments, each bearing the names of family members and friends. Najwa was amazed at how they never were the same. One in particular always bore her name. Her second stop was the kitchen where the sweet smell of gingerbread cookies and cider always found its home. Tonight, however, she was surprised by a young lady sitting at the kitchen table eating a slice of gingerbread.

"Hello," Najwa said surprised.

The young woman, about the same age as Najwa, looked up. "Oh, hello. How ya doin' and Merry Christmas!" The woman's smile was wide and genuine.

Najwa immediately noticed her deep southern accent. There was no way that she was from this area. Mrs. Phillips walked into the kitchen and seemed startled herself.

"Oh my goodness, where are my manners? Maxine, this is our neighbor Najwa." Mrs. Phillips said.

The two spoke to one another again.

Mrs. Phillips turned to Najwa. "Maxine is waiting for Dakota to come downstairs. But you know how slow he is. The boy is vainer than I am!" Mrs. Phillips laughed and turned to Maxine. "Child you may never get to your date with my son."

Mrs. Phillips handed Maxine another slice of gingerbread. "Here you better eat another one of these. There is no telling when he will be ready to go!"

"Date? Date!" Najwa thought to herself. Her heart sank into her stomach and she felt sick. She had not had time to gather her thoughts or emotions when Dakota came running down the stairs.

"I'm ready to go now," Dakota hollered as he reached into the closet for his coat. He fumbled with the sleeves and finally walked into the kitchen.

"Najwa!" Dakota seemed surprised.

Najwa only hoped that what she felt at that moment did not show on her face. She was frozen.

"What's happening girl? I haven't seen you since we left school."

Najwa snapped out of her daze. She searched for the right lie. "I been just kicking back and resting. You know it will be time to get back to school sooner than we think."

Dakota felt the moment to be very strange. But he did not know why.

"Ya'll go to the same school?" Maxine asked.

"These two have gone to the same school practically all their lives. Najwa is like the daughter I never had. I don't know if we will ever be able to separate these two. They are like Siamese Twins sometimes." Mrs. Phillips laughed.

Maxine laughed. Najwa struggled to smile. Dakota pretended to be humored but was more interested in Najwa's strange behavior.

There was an awkward silence in the kitchen for a moment.

Mrs. Phillips broke the tension. "Well what time does your movie start?"

Dakota looked down at his watch. "In fifteen minutes. Actually, we better go."

Maxine rose from the table and turned to Najwa. "It was really nice meeting you."

"Huh? Uh...yeah. It was nice meeting you to." Najwa struggled.

"See you tomorrow Najwa?" Dakota asked.

"Yeah, of course. Come on by. That is if you are not too busy." Najwa replied.

Dakota did not have time to entertain the comment. But he knew his old friend was not her self at all.

To Najwa, on the other hand, everything was crystal clear. There was no reason to have any conversation with Dakota about her feelings. She was certain that their special evening at the Snowflake Ball was just another one of Dakota's dates. Najwa promised herself not to spend any time thinking of any possibility beyond a friendship. She and Dakota never spoke about the Ball the entire vacation. It was as if it never happened.

It wasn't long before Najwa's parents started on the "after college" lecture. Najwa's savior was the sociology application she turned in right before the break. Her parents were impressed as she sold them on the program she had not yet sold on herself. Najwa knew, deep in her heart, this was an easy way out of making a decision about her future. She was almost ashamed to admit that she really did not know what she wanted to do. How could her parents boast of the child they sent over 300 miles away to school for nothing? All she ever had to do was be a good girl, go to school and get a good education. That didn't require much decision making. How was she was able to make all the best decisions for Gamma chapter and not her own life?

Christmas break was starting to take on a larger meaning than just rest. Oddly, away from the university, she was forced to deal with the uncertainty of her future. This was her biggest worry and fear. She was staring all her problems in the face. There was nothing she wanted more than to just run. Najwa's mind was haunted constantly not only by her future but by her newfound feelings for Dakota. Knowing nothing else to do, or having nowhere else to run, Najwa returned to Casperton's winter plains a day early.

# Friday, January 4, 1974

Soon after her arrival, the campus newspaper printed a snap shot that captured Najwa and Dakota in an unforgettable moment at the Ball. It was the first time that Najwa could remember any Black organization of Casperton University in the social section. A small insert, "Snowflake Ball Hits the Campus in Style," described the evening. It appeared at the bottom of the page and included four sentences about the purpose of the Ball, far less than Dakota commented in his interview. There was no mention of the scholarships they raised. Nevertheless, it was an accomplishment.

Najwa took out her scissors and carefully cut along the edges of the picture and the article. She wanted to capture the memory of the evening forever. The corsage Dakota gave her was still lying on her coffee table. She took one of the lifeless buds, along with the article, and placed it in her photo album.

That same day, Dakota called Najwa asking had she seen how good he looked in the newspaper. She actually wished she had never answered the phone. She still had not resolved her feelings about him and hoped during their conversation he would mention how he felt being at the Snowflake Ball with her. As she lay across her bed dismissing Dakota's self-absorbed comments, knowing he was right, she caught the headline of another small article. She sat up. Dakota never noticed the silence as he went on about how "bad" his tuxedo looked. Najwa abruptly excused herself and focused on the article's headline. She read it aloud.

*"Female Student Expelled for Marijuana Violation"*

Najwa read the article at least four times soaking in every fact. It only mentioned that a female student in the Madison Residence Hall was expelled for drug possession. The article alluded to a surprise inspection that resulted in the discovery of marijuana in a student's room. No name was mentioned. Najwa knew immediately it was Keisha. Her heart raced. She picked up the phone anticipating Carla was on duty and could confirm her suspicion. She dialed three numbers and then slammed the receiver back on its base. If Carla were on duty, there would be no way she could confirm the success of their plan. It would be too risky. Maybe Lynette would have some news. She too had come back to the campus early to work on extra credit assignments in the lab.

Again she picked up the receiver and furiously dialed Lynette's number hoping she would be home. She clung to the article with one hand pacing the living room floor. Finally, Lynette answered.

"Lynette it's me. Have you seen the article?" Najwa continued to pace.

"Hey girl!" Lynette exclaimed.

222

"Lynette, the article, did you see it?" Najwa impatiently asked.

"Article? What article? Oh you talkin' about the picture of you and Dakota in the campus paper. Yeah I got it right here. Y'all were looking good!"

"Lynette, no. Turn to page three. Look at the article in the right corner."

Lynette reached over and grabbed her copy of the campus paper.

"Girl, you know I don't read this paper. I was only interested in seeing if the Snowflake Ball made it. Once I saw you and Dakota's picture, I never even glanced at the rest." Lynette juggled the phone and the newspaper. "Okay, wait a minute. I am turning to the page now." She read the small article aloud.

"Naj? Is this about Keisha?" Her voice lowered as if someone would overhear the conversation.

"I don't know. Have you talked to Carla?" Najwa asked.

"No. You're the only person I have talked to since I got back. Have you tried to call her?"

"I thought about it but that dorm has ears all over the place."

"So what you wanna do?" Lynette asked.

"I got to know something now. I can't wait for her to call me. I am going over there now. You in?" Najwa asked as she slid on her shoes.

"I'll be waiting by the window. Just blow and I'll come out." Lynette hung up her phone, ran to the closet and grabbed her coat.

Lynette stood by the balcony window peeping behind her curtains. Her heart was beating double time. She didn't know what to think. She was trying to get her thoughts together. She had to keep her cool. If it were Keisha then that meant their plan worked. But what if Carla got caught? What had Najwa talked her into this time?

The distinct horn of Najwa's car broke her concentration.

They were silent the entire ride. Neither knew what the other was thinking. Najwa pulled into the campus parking lot and the two made their way into Carla's dorm. Najwa slowly approached the front desk assistant and confirmed that Carla was on floor duty. The resident assistant mentioned something to the fact that due to the incident, Carla could not leave her post. They would not be allowed to her floor unless someone signed them into the building.

"Girl, they got this place locked down. This is starting to make me nervous," Lynette whispered to Najwa.

Najwa turned to the RA and began her second attempt. She could only think of the same code they used while pledging.

"Is there some way we can at least call her? Her mother called and she has a really important message that she wants me to give her," Najwa said.

The RA hesitantly handed over the house phone and allowed Najwa to call up to Carla's floor.

Najwa was relieved to finally hear her sands voice. "Carla! It's me Naj."

"Naj? Are you downstairs?" Carla asked immediately.

Najwa hoped Carla remembered their code from pledging days.

"Yeah it's me and Lynette down at the front door. Listen, your mother called and she has a really important message she wanted me to give you about your big sister."

Carla immediately caught on. "Najwa did you drive?" Carla whispered.

"Yeah, she called a few minutes ago." Najwa played along knowing Carla understood.

"Leave now and just drive around for about ten minutes. Meet me by the back door."

Najwa continued knowing the RA was listening. "Okay Carla, but are you sure you want me to call her back?"

"I got to go! Ten minutes Najwa," Carla ended.

"I'll call her back for you and let her know you will call her tomorrow. I'll just see you around campus tomorrow about ten." Najwa hung up the phone and beckoned for Lynette to follow. The two walked back to Najwa's car. She sped off.

Ten minutes later Najwa pulled around the back of the dorm. The back door crept open and Carla emerged. She ran to the car and immediately jumped inside.

"Pull off!" Carla commanded.

"You're on duty!" Najwa answered.

"Just go. Go to the old library," Carla insisted.

Najwa screeched out the back parking lot and onto the street.

Lynette turned to the back seat. "What is going on? Did you see the article? Is it about Keisha?"

"Yeah it's about Keisha alright. But just listen. I don't know if

225

we should have done this," Carla said.

"Are you in trouble Carla? Nobody suspects anything do they?" Najwa asked as she pulled around to the small vacant library lot and put her car in park.

"Najwa they've had this campus on alert since it all hit the fan. All the RA's have been on twenty-four-hour duties. They have us under close watch."

"Why?" Najwa asked.

"I heard through the grapevine, Keisha is protesting. Making a big stink with the administration. She is saying the pot was planted." Carla said.

Najwa looked at Carla through her rear view mirror. "Damn, she suspects something."

"Yes and no." Carla answered.

"What does that mean?" Najwa asked.

"She is saying that a White RA set her up. Keisha is threatening to call for a walk-out on the university. Now they are doing an all out investigation of both Keisha and all the RAs. You know this school administration doesn't want to bring any more controversy than they need."

"When did all this happen? And why didn't you tell us?" Najwa asked. She never liked surprises. "I didn't expect it to go down this quickly."

"Girl this hit the fan while we were gone. They did a hearing during the break. Hell, I just got back yesterday myself and the next thing I knew, it's all in the paper." Carla answered.

"You alright?" Najwa asked.

"Yeah I'll be fine."

Lynette finally spoke. "But what if they find out you had something to do with it?"

"Don't worry. You think I am stupid enough to do my own dirty work? I was nowhere near Keisha's room or that dorm when the mess went down. And you know they wouldn't suspect me of doing anything like that to another sister!"

"Then who put the pot in her room?" Lynette asked.

"Keisha set herself up! When I went in her room looking for our money, she already had a bag of pot and a couple of joints hid under the bed. Her floor's RA received an anonymous tip telling her exactly where she could find the stash, compliments of me."

Najwa reached over the seat and slapped Carla's hand. "That's right Carla!"

"But wait, you said you think we shouldn't have done this. Why?" Lynette interrupted.

"This is controversy. Controversy and attention we don't need." Carla explained.

"Which RA did you tip off Carla?" Najwa asked.

"The queen White girl herself, Beth O'Neal. You know she was just itching to catch a nigger in the act. I had to tip off someone who would surely blow the whistle." Carla said.

"What if they think Beth did plant the drugs? We'll be responsible for two people getting kicked out of school. I don't like this." Lynette turned and looked out the window.

"They are not going to kick Beth O'Neal out! As much money as her family gives this university! Please! And if they did it would be no big loss," Carla assured.

"Lynette, I hear you. They are going to believe Beth over Keisha. You can bet on that. In the meantime, we got to support Keisha no matter how much she lies," Najwa said.

Lynette turned back to the two. "Support her! What? Why would we support her and we just ratted her out?"

"We can't just turn our backs. That would look funny. We got to play along with her. Support her as much as possible. If she says it was planted then we got to play along. Just until it dies down. I say one month at the most." Najwa only hoped.

"Najwa, I don't want to have anything else to do with this. Two wrongs do not make a right. How do we know for sure she took our money?" Lynette asked.

"Oh Lynette stop it! She took the money!" Najwa could not believe they were revisiting this issue. "So what do you suggest we do? Go tell Keisha that Carla sold her out? Piss her off even more? It's not going to change a thing. The pot was in her room. She is still expelled AND our money is still gone. Just what would you like to do? Tell me. I am all ears." Najwa waited.

There was silence in the front seat.

"Everything is going to be okay! There is no need for us to get all worked up with each other. Najwa, Lynette and I are behind you. We are not going to leave you out there alone. You know we are tight!" Carla reached over the seat and nudged Lynette's arm.

"Right, Lynette?"

"…right," Lynette mumbled.

"Look guys I need to get back to the dorm. A girl can be in the bathroom for only so long," Carla kidded.

Najwa did not say a word as she pulled out onto the street. She dropped Carla off at her dorm. After making sure she made it in the back door safely, Najwa drove Lynette home in silence. As Lynette got out the car she looked back at Najwa. She balled her fist and raised it to her shoulder. Najwa returned the gesture. She knew that although Lynette was upset, she was still in her corner. Najwa knew Lynette just needed time. They all needed time to get over the shock.

The rest of the evening, Najwa thought over the chain of events. In a blink of an eye, she made the decision that something had to go and it was gone. It was just that simple. Everyone sought Najwa's advice. Everyone looked to her before decisions were made in chapter meetings. No one moved until Najwa arrived. No one left until she said it was time to go. She had power.

Perhaps it was her strong personality. Perhaps it was her desire to make the chapter successful by any means necessary. She wondered if it was even right to have so much power. She didn't ask for it. It was thrust into her lap. She wondered if her predecessors possessed as much power as she. The moment Carla confirmed Keisha was dismissed, Najwa's outlook changed. Everything changed. Something awoke. Najwa changed.

This power excited her with an adrenaline rush she never felt before. Yet she was frightened by the thought of how far she could take it. It was overwhelming. Her brain was working too fast. Thoughts were random and her conscience was screaming over it all. She lay on her bed trying to stop the noise of thought. She woke the next morning in the same clothes she had on the night before, in the same position but not the same person.

The Najwa everyone knew would act immediately. There would be no way that she could wait for the regular chapter meeting day to discuss a plan of action. She had to follow through as if she was just as surprised as everyone else.

"I gotta call a special meeting as soon as everyone gets back," she muttered to herself and turned over.

# SECOND SEMESTER

# Thursday, January 10, 1974

Najwa spoke to no one including Carla and Lynette in the days to come. An announcement went out to the chapter that there would be an emergency meeting at her apartment. All members of Gamma chapter arrived in Casperton with the news of Keisha's dismissal from school. It was no secret. This was the reason for Najwa's emergency meeting.

"I don't think anyone planted anything sorors." Irby dared to think aloud.

"How do we know she is telling us the truth? You know she has a tendency to stretch the facts," Diane added.

"No matter what, she is our soror. We got to support her," Candace said.

"What is this going to do to the reputation of our chapter and sorority?" Diane asked.

Gloria broke her silence. "Why is Keisha always the center of controversy?"

Berri played both sides of the fence. "How many of us have

gone to Keisha's room to smoke a joint? Who are we to be so harsh on Keisha 'cause she got caught?"

Najwa sat back in her wicker chair, crossed her legs with her fingers locked together, and listened. She knew she had to play this meeting like a fine tuned instrument. She wanted to know where each and every sorors' head was before she offered her opinion.

"Has anyone spoken to Keisha?" Najwa finally asked.

"I have," Irby answered.

"And?" Najwa asked.

"She is pissed off. This was her senior year and now she is kicked out of school. She said something about taking down anyone and everyone who had anything to do with it. She just kept talking about that RA having it in for her and that she was set up."

Najwa investigated further. "Did you ask her if she really did have the pot?"

"Yeah I asked her. She never really answered me. But I know for a fact that she did have some pot the week before the inspection. She got it from some dude in the hood. She was talking about how good it was."

"That figures. This is going to be the hottest gossip to hit the campus," Gloria said.

Najwa knew she had to bring the focus of the meeting back. "Sorors, we need to decide how we are going to act."

"The first thing everyone is going to say is 'Keisha, the member of Omega Pi Alpha.' As usual, we are going to be drug into her mess," Diane stated.

"Ladies, we need to decide if we are going to feed into the garbage or if we are going to seize this crisis as an opportunity for the chapter to rise." Najwa began to speak as if she had a plan. As she listened to her own words, she realized there might be a way out after all.

"Najwa, nobody wants to feed anything. I just don't see how we are going to make anything good come out of this," Irby commented.

"Oh, but I do soror. First, we support Keisha unconditionally." Najwa sat up for the first time during the meeting. She looked around the room into the eyes of each soror before she continued. "No matter how much Keisha lies, we must support our sister."

Lynette and Carla sat silent. Najwa, in fact, had forgotten they were even there. As she expected, they had not uttered a word since their arrival. She issued the order to rid the chapter of Keisha and now she would take the responsibility for cleaning up behind herself.

"Second, we file a formal complaint against Keisha's dismissal with the Dean's office." Najwa continued.

"A formal complaint? We don't even know if she was telling the truth. According to Irby she is guilty!" Berri exclaimed.

"Sorors, we will not say that the weed was planted. Keisha had the pot. We are protesting the fact that others have not suffered the same punishment as our soror. Had Keisha been White she would have never been kicked out of Casperton University." Najwa's confidence increased as she continued.

"As a matter of fact, let's take one organization in particular. The Epsilon's have had their Free Love Festival every semester since I have been a student at this university. What is the main course of their event ladies?"

"Marijuana," the entire room said in unison.

"Have any of those students been removed from this campus? Najwa continued.

"No," they answered again in unison.

"So then why is our soror any different? Ladies, we are not trying to get Keisha back in school. She broke the rule and expulsion is the consequence no matter how much we protest. It is written in the student handbook. We will fully acknowledge this in our complaint. But only two students this year have been expelled for possession of marijuana. Both Black.

"Everyday I walk past White fraternity row, I am damn near high by the time I get home from smelling weed. Sorors, we will demand that the same punishment extends to all who violate the rule and not just the students of color. We will let them know from here on out, we will hold them accountable for every decision that is made on this campus."

"I still don't know if I completely understand. Why make such a big deal out of an already embarrassing situation?" Berri said.

"We are going to pull every Black organization and faculty member on this campus into our campaign," Najwa answered.

"Yeah but we still are going to be the center of the gossip. How are we going to deal with that?" Berri added.

"Sorors, it is gossip if we are all a part of the story?" Najwa cleverly answered.

"She's right. We need to follow Najwa's plan. We don't have a choice," Diane said.

Lynette finally gave her approval. "Sands you got my support. If you need any help writing the formal complaint just let me know."

Carla was eager to add all she knew. "I can give several instances where White RA's have written up Black residents for minor offenses that White girls get away with everyday."

"What about the rest of you?" Najwa looked around at each member of Gamma chapter.

There was no other choice but to concede. Najwa eloquently persuaded each of them that Keisha's demise might in fact be an opportunity for Gamma Chapter to shine.

# Wednesday, January 16, 1974

After their meeting, Najwa immediately contacted the Black Greek Council president, Karen Walters. She explained that the entire Gamma Chapter would be present at the next council meeting, asking for the support of their sisters and brothers. This was an issue that affected the entire campus. As usual, Karen welcomed Najwa to address the body as long as she wanted. Najwa expressed to Karen that it was imperative that she be allowed to speak first on the agenda.

Najwa amazed herself at how it only took her an hour to prepare the letter to the administration, yet weeks for her graduate school essay. Nevertheless, she knew it was her best writing. The Greek council meeting day, Najwa prepared copies to give to all in attendance. She even had extras for the representatives to give to their chapter members. Najwa appealed to Gamma chapter that if they showed they were unified, surely they would convince the masses to join. Their battle would not only be legitimate in their own eyes, but in the eyes of the critics as well.

The entire chapter met at the campus library and walked over to the Black House as one. Seeing her sorors dressed in their sorority colors, an added touch from Lynette, gave Najwa a rush for the first time like no other. She felt like she was the general of an army. It was one thing to have arms ready for battle. But she had a group mentally unified. There had to be no other feeling like it.

As they took their symbolic walk across the campus quad, dressed in their black leather coats and red sweaters, the White students looked puzzled and even frightened. Twelve Black women all bearing a strong resemblance to Angela Davis, Kathleen Cleaver, and all other Black woman perceived as a threat to their dominance as a White race, walked across the white paved campus grounds as if they owned the world. Exactly five minutes before the Greek Council meeting was scheduled to begin, Gamma chapter walked up the old rickety stairs of the Black House with Najwa leading. For the first time all year, the room was filled with all members of the Black Greek organizations.

Heads turned and mumbling began as Gamma chapter filled what empty spaces were left.

Lynette leaned over and whispered to Najwa who did not look as surprised. "Karen must have let the other presidents know we were coming."

"News travels Lynette," she simply responded.

This was exactly what she hoped would happen. Everyone knew Keisha had been expelled. This was not so much their way of supporting, but having a front row seat in the gossip circus.

"You okay?" Lynette asked Najwa.

"I'm fine sands. This is going to be like taking candy from a baby."

Najwa walked over to Karen and thanked her for allowing her to speak. She assured she would take no longer than ten minutes. With standing room only, Najwa assumed her position until it was her turn.

Karen quickly made it through the first half of her agenda. Nothing but praises and a big round of applause was heard as Dakota was congratulated for his work on the Snowflake Ball.

Next, Najwa was given the floor. Calmly and graciously she emerged. Standing tall and firm she placed her notes and copies of her letter on the wooden podium. She looked around into each eye. As whispers went back and forth, everyone sat up to give their attention. This was the moment for which they all awaited. Silence quickly prevailed and Najwa began.

"Brothers and Sisters I thank you for allowing me the opportunity to speak before you on such short notice. But, as I explained to my dear friend and sister Karen, this is a matter that will affect all our lives. I'm not going to sugar coat anything or beat around the bush. My soror, Keisha Jones, was expelled from school over the Christmas break. I am sure all of you have heard about it. I am certain that's what you expected me talk about. Well, as you can see, every member of the Gamma chapter is here tonight and we stand on behalf of our soror.

"My chapter soror, Keisha, was expelled for having marijuana in her dorm room. Let the record show, we don't hide behind this fact. We are not ashamed of our sister or her mistake. We stand with her. But allow me to bring one thing to your attention. It says here in the updated student handbook issued to each and every student of Casperton University both White and Black that any student caught with any illegal drugs will be suspended from the university. So, I come to you this evening to say that although our soror suffered an unfortunate fate, she still suffered a clearly outlined penalty for her wrong doing."

The room was silent as a mouse with the exception of the few who whispered back and forth. Najwa looked up from her written speech and continued as if she were speaking to each person personally.

"How many of you smoked a joint before you came here tonight? How many of you got a little nip of Crown sitting in your window for that cold night? How many of you still have that old copy of the first midterm that Mr. Simon gives every fall semester since I've been at this school?"

Chuckles came from around the room as those present showed their own guilt.

"And how many of you continue to be guilty just because everyone else is doing it and getting away with it? If that's what you think then you are just as stupid as they play us to be." The chuckles stopped and all were captured by Najwa's conviction. Najwa looked at Dakota and mercilessly used him as a prop in her best stage performance.

"Brother did you think just because you just chaired the biggest and blackest social event on this campus that they now look at us as dignified enough to dine at the President's award banquet?" She plucked another from the crowd. "Sister, you have been on the Dean's list since you have been at this school. When was the last time a professor gave you a nasty look or even ignored you 'cause your opinion didn't matter in his class?"

"Humph...just the other day." The senior answered. Others nodded their heads.

Najwa paused and shook her head.

"Just as my sorors and I walked down the sidewalk of this campus together we received looks that I can't even describe to you. You know, I am beginning to think, maybe taking a seat on the CU Fraternal Council was a bad move. This university needed a way for us to forget where we really stand. I am beginning to think that this was their way of making us believe we mattered. And we fell for it. Ever since, we have begun to think that our grass is just as green on this side and that we actually are ahead. I know this because most of you came here today to ridicule and to fuel the gossip of the plight of OUR sister.

"The Brothers and Sisters I knew on this council last year would have never done this. The Brothers and Sisters I knew not only rejoiced in each other's success but we stuck together in the trying times. Somewhere along the way we forgot that we are soldiers in a battle. Whose side are you on?"

Najwa paused again.

"If you think this situation is Keisha's problem, you are sadly mistaken. Frankly, we don't know who will be next. As a matter of fact, you can be sure it won't be Sally or Mary Sue or Becky down at the Tri Delta sorority house."

Najwa held up the school handbook.

"Remember, I said to you that this handbook is issued to all who enroll in this…great institution. But not everyone is governed or judged by this book. We've lost two Black students…" Najwa pointed over to the men of Kappa who were nodding their heads in agreement. "And a chapter on this council this year alone. No one has said a thing. I am here because this nonsense must stop right here! Right now! Today!"

"That's right Najwa! It has to stop. She's right!" Voices broke the silence.

"We are prepared to go to the administration right now, today. We are not going to demand that Keisha is readmitted, but we will demand that everyone else on this campus is judged and penalized by the same standards. We need you to take this stand with us. I tell you, the battle was not over when we took that money and had a Snowflake Ball. I'm here to tell you, it had just begun."

Najwa was abruptly interrupted as the crowd erupted in applause and a standing ovation. The members of Gamma chapter continued to stand even after the applause stopped.

"I have here in my hand a letter we will be delivering to the administration building tomorrow morning as soon as that annoying campus clock rings 9:00a.m. I want this letter to be signed by every individual in this room tonight. Do I have your support?"

Not only did Najwa receive the support of the entire Black Greek Council, but of each individual member of the Greek organization. Signed copies of her letter went in the mailboxes of every Black student. Before the third week of spring semester there was already a petition circulating throughout the campus calling for a review of not only the treatment of Keisha and the young freshman arrested at the Kappa Land party, but the decision made against every Black student in the past year.

Omega Pi Alpha was at the wheel of the driving force. Najwa's plan worked. As a sign of solidarity, the Black Greek Council withdrew itself from the White Greek Council. Until fair treatment was given to all students on the campus, the council contended that it would not be a part of any university affiliations. The Black Greek Council forfeited all future funds they would be receiving for their affiliation, changing the tides abruptly and calling it "hush money."

The campus' black newspaper, Tiger Pride, jumped on the story and pounced the campus administration, citing harsh judgments against Blacks as far back as the early sixties. For the first time in the year, the Black campus community banned together for a cause. Unbeknownst to them, the cause was to save the face of Gamma chapter. Najwa sat back and watched as her little spark ignited into a blazing forest fire that rolled and grew bigger and bigger by the days. The mood on the campus was tense. Anything could start a riot. This was the biggest fear of the campus administration. Meanwhile, Omega Pi Alpha looked like the leaders of a legitimate protest.

Najwa never anticipated the attention it brought her. The chapter believed in her decisions, the Black Greek Council followed her lead, and the Black campus community saw a leader. Over the next days, she was asked to speak at a rally meeting. The regional officers of Omega Pi Alpha received word of the battle Gamma chapter was leading and sent letters to the university offices. Support from the surrounding Omega Pi Alpha chapters poured in. Secretly, Najwa was riding the waves just as blindly as the next person. Through it all, she acted as if she was in total control of every carefully calculated move.

Everyday Najwa seemed to resemble the local activist as opposed to the actual student that she was. The campus administration was not happy at all by the rising controversy. They responded swiftly with a rebuttal of any wrong doings. Town hall meetings were held to discuss the mood of the campus. The credibility of the Black Greek Council was questioned as well as their decision to pull out of the White council. The larger campus newspaper accused them of fueling the race problems and not wanting to make a change. Everyone was scrutinized and examined with a fine-tooth comb including Gamma chapter.

Being an English major, Najwa was not a stranger to writing. Since her first day on the campus, Najwa kept a journal of daily experiences where she noted anything that touched her mind. Somehow this all played into the scheme of things as well. Najwa was asked to rebut the newspaper with her own article in the Tiger

Pride. Her article, proving a success, quickly became a permanent addition to the newspaper.

Initially, when asked to join the writing staff, she was reluctant. The first and biggest reminder was of her ex-boyfriend Paul. Although he encouraged her to express herself with a pen freely, much of Tiger Pride still smelled of Paul. He still was in contact with the editor and sent correspondence to be printed in the paper from time to time. But Najwa knew she had to get past that phase of her growth. She had to move on. More importantly, she had to keep up her trusted status in the struggle. She had to follow her hero script to the end.

Her first article, addressing the university and the unfair interpretation of rules, received rave reviews from the Black student body. In the next two weeks, Najwa dished out two more articles that were just as powerful, but this time not focusing on the university administration. She justified that the university system was exposed. Now her writings would move on to the more noteworthy and positive aspects of the Black Casperton community. Najwa's next two articles focused on landmarks of the Casperton community, the community center, and everyone's favorite, Mrs. Dixon.

Not amused and obviously threatened, the university responded swiftly to the supporters of Gamma chapter's cause. The Delta's became the next casualty in the war against the administration. Surely their demise stemmed from the petitions they helped circulate. Citing several fire code violations, the chapter was placed on probation for the remainder of the semester for lighting candles in a Barkston Center room. Another infraction and the chapter would be suspended indefinitely. Though a violation petty in nature, it was nonetheless an effective way of putting all pawns into place. The administration was on a mission to silence the voices that made them look like fools.

Najwa didn't know how Omega Pi Alpha would be targeted, but she knew it was coming soon and they would need to be ready. Carla barely survived the scrutiny she faced from the RA's for her involvement in the protests. She received the silent treatment, odd working hours, and the dirty looks from other RA's who felt an enemy infiltrated their secret society. Nevertheless, she carried on her duties. Najwa, Lynette and Carla hardly talked about the situation at all. Everyone was just barely making it. They were too overwhelmed by their own problems as a result of Keisha's dismissal.

Najwa could not ignore the fact that the chapter was moving into the most intensive and important phase of the year, pledge period. The added pressure made life no easier for the chapter programs. At the first official chapter meeting of the semester, Lynette recommended that they step up their pledging calendar immediately. There was entirely too much pressure from the campus administration. The sooner the pledges were initiated into the sorority, the better.

Far too occupied with both her studies and the pledges, Lynette tried not to get involved with the rally behind Keisha's cause. Making sure she passed her classes while passing the traditions of the organization to the pledges, took enough of her time. Najwa's plan was too far over her head to get involved.

*The deed was the first thing he owned after becoming a free man in America. It was a reminder of the promise she made to the Negro citizens of Casperton. She was also aware of the White man's history of stealing land from their rightful owners. The most important reason was mailing the deed to her was for safekeeping.*

# Tuesday, February 5, 1974

Najwa had completely forgotten about the graduate teachers program for which she applied over the break. She turned in the application at the end of the semester and never looked back. She arrived home late one evening from a long stay in the library writing a paper for her English class, to find a brown legal envelope in her mailbox. Her first reaction was that it had to be something from the sorority. As president, she received mailings from their regional director on a monthly basis. Now that the news of their battle hit the sorority grapevine, she was receiving even more than usual. This envelope was different. She was surprised to see it was from the Dean of the Graduate Sociology Department. Najwa was invited to interview for a spot in the program.

After reading the entire letter again, she noted the time of the interview and threw it on the coffee table. No excitement or nervous feelings. The thought of having no plan after graduation was unsettling. But, she was still not convinced that social work was her calling. Nevertheless, she would give it a try. In her mind, the interview was better than nothing

The day of the interview crept up on Najwa like a thief in the night. Had it not been for her mother mentioning it during their now bi-weekly discussions she would not have shown up at all. Najwa ran home from her morning class and changed into her tweed, two-piece, brown suit with the skirt and her knee high boots.

She entered the office of the graduate department exactly ten minutes early as she did for every appointment. Just because she was not excited was no reason to not make an impression. Najwa had actually prepared by talking to a few sorors who were Sociology majors to see what type of questions she may have to answer. She even took the time to jot down some ideas for her interview. Her interest perked slightly. For Najwa, that was a bright sign.

Najwa gave her name to the student chewing gum and reading a magazine at the reception desk. She sat in the chairs in the lobby and began reading the Sociology department newsletter. She was slightly impressed. This literature was different from what she read while filling out her application. Moments later a short, stout, cocoa brown woman emerged from the hallway.

"Najwa Jackson? Are you Ms. Jackson?" The woman asked.

Najwa turned swiftly, startled by her voice. "Yes, I am Najwa Jackson."

"Ms. Jackson, hello my name is Professor Helen Baker. I will be interviewing you this afternoon. Come with me to my office." The stout woman turned and waddled down the hall to an open office door.

Najwa was taken aback by the fact that she was interviewing with a sister. A sister she had never seen on campus before today. Nevertheless, she was a sister.

"Wow. This may not be so bad after all." Najwa whispered to herself. She hurried down the hall, walked into the office and sat behind a table facing the mystery woman.

"I am sorry Professor Baker, but are you new here? I just ask because I've never seen you on campus." Najwa had to know.

"You could say I am new. I only come in for special interviews for the graduate program." Professor Baker winked at Najwa.

Immediately, Najwa knew what she meant.

"Actually, I teach the offsite class and from time to time I am asked to conduct interviews for prospective candidates," Professor Baker replied as she continued to read Najwa's application.

"I see. Well that would explain…" Najwa began before she was interrupted.

"Explain why you've never seen me on the campus?" Professor Baker looked over her glasses at Najwa and smiled, acknowledging her surprise to see a Black woman interviewing her for a graduate position. "Yes I am pretty much hidden and tucked away."

Najwa returned the smile but maintained professionalism.

"Ms. Jackson I have read over your essay. Very impressive. I have also read your articles in the Tiger Pride. Very interesting."

"Uh oh, this woman knows a lot about me, maybe too much. This is not going to be a cinch after all," Najwa thought.

"I have looked over your credentials and recommendations

from the good people over at the Casperton Community Center. I think you would be an asset to the Sociology program." Professor Baker looked Najwa straight in the eye. "So tell me. Am I correct?"

Najwa took a deep breath and there was no turning back. She erased all she had rehearsed the night before. She knew she would need to take a different approach, an honest one. After an hour of interviewing, Najwa was probably more impressed with the program than she was during the entire application phase. Najwa left the interview feeling as if she knew Professor Baker for years, and hoping that this woman would possibly be assigned as her mentor during the first year.

Professor Baker was equally impressed with Najwa's performance. She suggested that Najwa come to one of the field sites to get a feel for what she may experience if accepted. By the next week Najwa arranged her visit. In between class and work, Najwa rushed to the far side of the Black community where Ms. Baker had an office in the Casperton Women's Mental Health Center.

On Najwa's first visit, she discovered that it actually was much better than the Casperton Community Center in the impoverished area. It was a privately funded adult social center that had access to more manpower and monetary resources. So impressed, Najwa returned to volunteer her services on a permanent basis. Professor Baker assured Najwa that a recommendation for her admission would go to the board. There was hope and a light flickered at the end of the tunnel for Najwa's future.

# Wednesday, February 6, 1974

The pledges were meeting with the chapter at least three days a week. One of those days was always spent in the campus cafeteria for "meal time" with the chapter. It seemed to be more of a spectator time than a mealtime. Yet it was the tradition of the Black Greeks on the campus for years. Every Wednesday the pledges of the respective organizations would march into the cafeteria dressed alike and at full attention. At designated tables, they sat silent and unmoved by the general population. A stampede could come through the cafeteria and not one pledge would move or break their silence unless instructed by their Dean. This Wednesday would be the first that Gamma chapter would have their pledges on display.

Their clothes matched down to the stitch. In a straight line, the Immortals walked into the cafeteria wearing black berets, black sunglasses, red sweaters, and black mini skirts that came right to the exact point on each woman. Each carried a black shoulder bag over their left shoulder. Held in the right hand of the first pledge was an hourglass passed from one line to the next. As soon as they sat at the corner table designated for Gamma chapter, the hourglass was flipped. The pledges had exactly until the last grain of sand dropped, to greet their big sisters, other Greeks, and manage to eat. No matter where they were in their meal, by the end of the hour, they would all stand at the signal from their head pledge and recite the same phrase each week.

"Like life, time is precious and there are miles to go before we sleep. Through the sands of time our love will transcend all. We will uphold the promise whispered on that fateful day. We shall stand tall. Until next time big sisters, we most humbly leave thee."

They turned like disciplined soldiers and marched out of the cafeteria just as they had come in exactly an hour earlier. The show was over. The spectators went about their normal business.

Najwa leaned over Lynette's shoulder. "I am impressed. It seemed like they weren't ever going to get that greeting right last night."

"Tell me about it! I think I was reciting that mess in my sleep, we went over it so many times," Lynette replied as she watched the girls march out the cafeteria and onto the distant campus hills.

"So are we meeting Friday?" Najwa asked.

"Yeah. The sorors from Bradley University are coming up to meet the girls. I told them it would be fine. The pledges need a challenge. They know us too well. We need some new blood in here to put them on edge."

"That's cool. I'll be glad to see my girls from Theta Epsilon anyway," Najwa said referring to the Omega Pi Alpha members from the Bradley campus located a little over an hour away. She and Lynette sat back down to finish their lunch.

Carla popped around the corner with several books in her hands five minutes after the spectacle ended.

"Hey sands! I guess I missed the girls, huh?"

"My girl! Sit down and take a load off. You carrying the world!" Najwa kidded. She was simply excited that she and her sands were together for once outside of meetings.

"I would have been here earlier but I have some really crazy hours at the dorm. I just got off." Carla huffed, laid down her bag and dropped the books to the table in exhaustion. She pulled up a chair after she waved to her chapter sorors.

"They still trying to wear you down sister? Hang in there Carla. This is going to be over in less than four months. We will be outta here!" Najwa said. It seemed as if everyone was being punished for their part in the circulation of the petitions.

"Yeah, hang in there. We are all taking some pressure." Lynette added.

"I know, I know. Now you know they can't wear me out. They are doing a damn good job at trying, but I am cool. I almost went off on the head RA yesterday. But I had to stop and tell myself to keep my cool. So where you been Najwa? You around here being the Angela Davis of the campus. Your afro has even gotten a little bigger!" Carla kidded.

"Ha ha very funny. I see you are tired but you still have your sense of humor. I am not enjoying this spotlight at all." Najwa was slightly embarrassed.

"Yeah right! You love it Naj. Who do you think you are

kidding? I am surprised you haven't hired a bodyguard to escort you to class." Carla continued to tease Najwa. "You are causing a raucous on this campus."

"Aw come on Najwa, you mean to tell me you aren't enjoying being the leader of the campus movement," Lynette smirked.

"I never planned to be the leader of any campus movement," Najwa mocked Lynette. "You all know very well why I have done what I have. This all started as something totally different and now look...."

"Oh stop jiving Najwa, you love it!" Lynette interrupted.

"Are you joking or are you serious? I know we haven't talked much since all this started but I sense hostility." Najwa never bought into the humor. Perhaps it was her newfound paranoia but she genuinely felt there was more to Lynette's statement.

"Ladies, ladies. Look I deal with enough bickering from day to day with the other RA's. Cool it. I just want to sit and have lunch with my favorite sorors. Okay?" Carla attempted to stop the ensuing argument.

"There is no hostility. I was just asking a sincere question that everybody is thinking but don't have the courage to ask," Lynette said.

"Everybody? What are you talking about? What questions Lynette? Tell me. I want to know." Najwa calmed herself. She felt she was heading toward the root of the problem.

"Najwa look..., the chapter is talking about all the attention you been getting lately that's all." Lynette revealed.

"You mean all the attention Omega Pi Alpha has been getting?" Najwa asked.

"No. I said what I meant Najwa." Lynette did not back down.

"Lynette, I am the voice of this chapter. I thought the concerns I expressed were what the chapter wanted me to," Najwa said.

"No, you are expressing what YOU thought should be the chapter's concern. Remember? Make this work to our advantage." Lynette answered mocking Najwa's own statement.

Carla looked on quietly.

"Whoa, wait a minute Lynette. I was only trying to get us out of a mess that was about to blow up in our faces."

"And who's bright idea was it to get Keisha expelled in the first place?" Lynette asked.

"Now that's not fair Lynette." Carla finally joined the debate.

"Lynette if I recall correctly, we all agreed about the Keisha thing. It wasn't just my idea or my doing. Remember?" Najwa looked around at the blank expressions. "You know I am really sick of this bull. Why don't you just come out and say what it is you have to say Lynette? I get the feeling you are trying to imply that I planned all this so that I could take center stage. You know good and well that is not the case." Najwa argued.

Lynette suddenly became mindful of the fact that they were in the school cafeteria and any display would bring attention. "Najwa calm down. It just seems like…,"Lynette could not finish before Najwa interrupted.

"No you calm down!" Najwa was past angry. "Everyone has

come to me with problems from personal to chapter-related and I have been there. You all look to Najwa for all the answers. You ask Najwa what to do for everything. The chapter won't eat, sleep, pee, or make a decision unless Najwa says it is cool. But its cool cause Gamma chapter is on top.

"I wake up and go to sleep taking care of something having to do with Gamma chapter. I live with the pressure on my back that I...no, WE have sparked one of the biggest controversies on this campus for the sake of saving the face of Omega Pi Alpha. Well guess what, Najwa doesn't even have her own life in order. And you think I love this?"

"Najwa, we all feel the pressure. Trust me I have been catching some real hell back at the dorms. I haven't given myself a manicure in two weeks!" Carla said with a serious look on her face.

Najwa burst into laughter. Lynette laughed equally as hard as Carla looked puzzled. Her antics were just what the three needed to take away the tension.

"I don't see what is so funny. You all know how much my hair and nails mean to me." Carla replied.

"Girl you are a mess. Thanks, I needed that laugh." Lynette turned to her sands and continued. "Najwa, I know you did not plan for this to happen this way. It's just that things are not like they used to be. This is not fun anymore. Remember the days when we had fun on this campus? Whatever happened to that?"

"You started spending your life in the library and with the pledges, Carla got sentenced to dorm duties and me...well...I became the savior of the campus." Najwa stared out the window as her mind drifted.

"Since we are being honest, Najwa, no one ever knows if you are coming or going anymore. It's like you are becoming some invisible voice. I was surprised to even see you today. It's been almost a month now and the only times we ever see you are chapter meetings, or when you are doing something that has to do with our complaints to the administration. Where have you been? What's going on?" Carla asked.

"So now you speak up, huh? Sands I just got a lot of pressure on me right now and the more I stay out of sight, the less I bring on myself. You may not dig where I am coming from right now. But I am cool sands. I'm cool."

Najwa paused for a long period leaving silence between the three before she emerged from her distant world.

"Look sands, I need to split. I need to go and work on my article for next week's Tiger Pride. Let's get together tomorrow and eat. We can finish talking then. We can do it at my place."

Najwa made her exit just as a Black student came up to her to talk about the status of their protest. Najwa politely excused herself after she assured the sister there would be a meeting in the Black House the following week.

"I thought we agreed to talk to her about this differently Lynette? Not make her defensive. We bombed on that one," Carla said as Najwa walked out the cafeteria doorway.

Thursday passed and the three never had the dinner Najwa

promised. Najwa did, however make mental note of the fact that others thought she was distant. It did not help that she had not attended the chapter's volunteer project in two weeks. She also realized that she had not spent any time with her personal, Irby, since the Thanksgiving break. One thing was certain, if her sands noticed and thought something was wrong, then everyone else knew too.

The last thing she wanted was to fall out of favor with the chapter. There lied her major support base. Without them, she was nothing. Najwa honestly did not know what she was feeling. Although, every word she said over the past month was genuine, she could not get past the reason all this came into being.

Perhaps, it was her guilt. She was angry with herself. She was angry with Keisha. She was angry at the administration. She was angry with Dakota for not noticing she was angry. She wondered if it was all worth it. Their solution to a very minor problem was turning into a situation that affected many lives. Lynette was right. She wasn't uncomfortable at all by the attention. The attention and power gave her a rush but it was not fun. It was a feeling she could not describe. In the blink of an eye, she not only was the president of Gamma chapter but commander in chief of every Black campus organization. The students were empowered by the words in her weekly column. Lynette was right, in an odd and painful way, she loved it.

# Friday, February 8, 1974

"Greetings Big Sisters of Theta Epsilon Chapter!" The pledges said in unison as members of Omega Pi Alpha from the Bradley campus walked into Lynette's apartment.

"What's happening Sorors?"

They all walked around the pledges as if they were invisible hugging the members of Gamma chapter.

"Come on in! You know we glad to see y'all." Lynette welcomed her sorors. "We just talked to the Lambda chapter sorors and they are on their way down here too!" They were all very familiar and often road tripped to other schools with one another.

Most of the members of Gamma chapter had attended an earlier party hosted by Dakota's fraternity. With the exception of Najwa, close to twenty sorority sisters and all the pledges crammed in the small living room space of Lynette's apartment.

Earlier, the pledges had two assignments: Move furniture to make room for everyone and provide a meal from Mel's.

Lynette's doorbell rang a second time. "Hey one of you get the door." Lynette ordered the pledges from the kitchen.

Two of the pledges ran to the door, climbing over all the big sisters sitting throughout the room. Lynette's attention was directed to the kitchen where she was kidding with sorors and making drinks for her guests. She heard the pledges greeting loudly.

"Greetings Big Sister Berri Matthews. Greetings Big Sister Keisha Foxy Mama Jones! Greetings Big Sister Donna Davis"

Lynette dropped the ice cubes out of the frozen metal tray she held and jerked her entire body around. Not only Donna but Keisha too? No one heard anything from Keisha since the Christmas break nor had she returned any phone calls. Donna had only been a distant figure since the Thanksgiving basket giveaway.

Keisha's annoying voice pierced through the noise of the room. "That's right! Keisha is here! That's right Keisha is back!"

The visiting sorors immediately stood to hug their soror. However, with the women of Gamma chapter, there were mixed feelings clouding the room. They masked their surprise and hugged their long lost soror. Showing any signs of dissention would be unthinkable, especially in front of another chapter.

"What the hell are they doing here?" Lynette whispered to Carla.

Lynette was more concerned with Keisha's appearance. For over a month, they fought a battle, so it seemed, on behalf of the soror they had not seen.

"Lynette, for the first time in four years, I don't have anything to say. I mean I really have no idea what to say right now." Carla whispered through the phony grin on her face before she walked out to hug Keisha and Donna. She didn't want for one minute to look stranger than she felt at that moment.

As soon as she thought no one was looking, Carla grabbed Irby and took her into Lynette's bedroom. She closed the door.

"What is Keisha doing here?"

"Carla, I have no idea at all. I am just as surprised as you. I have not talked to that girl since the break," Irby confessed.

"Obviously, Berri had to have known she was coming in town. Did Berri say anything to you?"

Irby shook her head and sat on Lynette's bed. "Not a word."

"When Najwa gets here she is going to have a fit. I don't know who she is going to be more upset about, Donna, Keisha or Berri for even bringing them. Honestly, I don't want to be here when she gets here."

"Tell me about it. I know how Najwa feels about both Keisha and Donna. But what can we do about it? They're here now. We can't hide them. You know Najwa is going to find out either way it goes." Irby answered.

"Somebody has got to stop Najwa before she comes in this apartment. If she comes in and sees Keisha and Donna without any warning she is going to go ballistic."

"Maybe you should watch for her out the window and meet her at the stairs," Irby suggested.

"That's what I'll have to do." Carla paused. "Of all nights, why did they pick tonight to show up? We have visitors and …this is just a mess!"

Carla gathered herself and walked back into the living room as if the conversation never took place. She positioned herself by the window. Finally after announcing that she needed a little air, Carla walked down to apartment complex entrance and began pacing.

Like clockwork, Najwa turned into the parking lot entrance the exact time she said she would. Carla took a deep breath and walked over before Najwa could get out.

"Hey girl, what's happening? The sorors here yet?" Najwa asked as she eagerly climbed out her car.

"You in a good mood sands?" Carla asked.

"Pretty much. I'm a little tired though. Why?" Najwa asked suspiciously.

"When I tell you who is in that apartment, you would want to be in a real good mood."

"Who Carla?" Najwa closed her car door and waited.

"I need you to keep in mind that we have visitors and we need to all just play it cool."

"Who Carla?" Najwa asked again.

"Remember sands, play it cool 'til the night is over." Carla emphasized.

Najwa motioned for Carla to reveal the identity of the mystery guest.

"Donna," Carla blurted and waited for Najwa's reaction. She wanted to save the best for last.

"What? She just showed up out of nowhere?" Najwa asked preparing herself for the entire situation.

"Yeah she just showed up with Berri of course," Carla added.

"You know what, I'm not surprised. I knew she would turn up sooner or later."

Najwa surprised Carla. "You are taking this much better than I thought girl."

"I said I was not surprised, I didn't say I wasn't pissed off. Well we can't stand out here out all night. Come on let's go in. This is going to be an interesting night to say the least." Najwa began to walk away.

Carla grabbed her sands' arm. "Wait Najwa, there is one more person you need to know about before you go up."

"Who?"

"Keisha," Carla blurted.

"Kei..." was all Najwa said before she jerked away from Carla and made her way to the building courtyard.

"Najwa remember visitors are here!" Carla shouted.

Najwa stopped and took a deep breath. "I will be calm. I am Najwa Jackson and I must stay cool." She muttered to herself as she tried to lower her blood pressure.

Her affirmation must have worked as she managed to save face all night. It was all she could do to not invite Keisha or Donna outside for a long talk. But she knew that this was not the time nor was it the place. More so than with their unexpected guests, Najwa was interested in speaking to Berri. What exactly was Berri thinking by surprising everyone with an appearance by Keisha? She wondered if her soror really did have bad judgment in the company she kept or was she intentionally creating obstacles.

Keisha was a whole different situation altogether. Perhaps, Najwa delayed her comments on their surprise guests out of her own guilt in Keisha's situation. Who was wrong? Who was right? The web of the year was so tangled now that even Najwa was lost. .

Around three o'clock that morning Lynette dismissed the pledges and the visiting sorors decided to stay the night. The festivities were over at least for this one evening. Escorted by their assistant dean Candace, the pledges were on their way back to the dorms for a much needed night's sleep. They were expected to be at Lynette's the next morning with breakfast and then the chapter's public service. As everyone began to leave, Lynette beckoned for Najwa.

"So are you going to say anything?" Lynette asked as she slightly closed the bedroom door.

"No. This is not the right time. There are too many outsiders here," Najwa replied frustrated.

"I can't believe she pranced in here like nothing happened." Lynette was appalled.

"Which one of them, Donna or Keisha? It was almost as if Keisha had nothing to be sorry about. Like she knew," Najwa said emotionless. "She knows that she is sitting in the best seat in the house. She knows we are playing a game. And...she knows that she never has to make another move 'cause we are fighting on both sides, hers and ours. It's feels like...I feel like I beat myself at the game this time."

"This is crazy! This is too much for me to even comprehend right now Najwa." Lynette sat on the bed looking to Najwa for answers. "So what are you going to do?"

"I am going to take care of Ms. Berri Matthews. That's what I am going to do. It was bad enough that she brought Donna out here. Keisha was a personal punch right in my stomach."

"Look, you better go. The Lambda and Theta E sorors are waiting. Four of them are staying here tonight and I think the rest are going over to your place." Lynette started pulling out extra blankets from her closet. "You cool with that?"

"Yeah I'm cool with it. I'm splittin'. I'll talk to you in the morning."

A few of the Gamma sorors remained in the living room talking to the visiting sorors reminiscing on old times.

"Keisha, Berri, and Donna left without saying goodbye?" Najwa sarcastically remarked.

*So deeply contained in thoughts of the future and the father she adored, a smile eased across her face. Sadie never heard the footsteps of the man behind her.*

# Monday, February 12, 1974

The weekend passed and the visiting sorors road tripped back to their schools. Keisha returned home. Donna again slipped into her state of nonexistence. Najwa felt it ironic that in the same week her sands confronted her, a member of Gamma chapter defied her authority. She knew that there would be more pressure thrown her way. But she also knew that there weren't many brave enough to tread those waters except those closest to her such as Irby.

Irby stopped and looked as the pledges studied on Najwa's living room floor. "Najwa, can I ask you a question?"

It was their turn to oversee the pledges study hour and help them organize a fundraising event for the chapter. Irby motioned for Najwa to follow her into the bedroom.

"Go ahead," Najwa said as she started picking up some laundry thrown on the floor.

Irby stared. "I need you to be honest with me."

"Have I ever lied to you before?" Najwa wondered where Irby was going with her questioning. She never stopped folding clothes.

"No you haven't. And now I don't know if I even want to know the answer." Irby stated.

"Then maybe you shouldn't ask," Najwa replied.

Irby hesitated then looked Najwa directly in the eye. "Did you have anything to do with Keisha getting kicked out of school?"

Najwa returned the stare. "You have wanted to ask me that for a while haven't you?"

"As a matter of fact, I have," Irby answered.

"So do others share your suspicion?"

"I don't know. Most of the chapter knew how you felt about her. But then again, no one knew about the night at Kappa Land."

"And a lot of people, including you, don't know what I know."

"What do you mean?" Irby asked hesitantly.

"Irby let me set a little hypothetical scenario. Would you be asking me this question if...lets say...Keisha had gotten pregnant that night...and...stolen the chapter's money to have an abortion?" Najwa watched as Irby's expression went from concern to appall.

"No," Irby muttered.

"So now what was it you asked me earlier Irby?"

"Nothing," Irby replied.

Irby was speechless. However, silence was not what Najwa wanted. She needed to know that she still had both Irby and the chapter behind her. Besides Carla and Lynette, Irby was the next person that Najwa trusted the most.

"Irby I know you aren't the only person wondering. I just need you to trust me. Everything is under control. You still trust me

Irby?"

"I trust you. I never stopped. I have wondered what you were thinking from time to time. But I still trust you."

"What about the rest of the chapter?" Najwa asked.

"Are you kidding? They think you are the next best thing to sliced bread." Irby laughed for the first time.

"Sliced bread?" Najwa finally laughed. "Yeah, right! Really Irby, I don't want anyone to think that I am getting beside myself. I don't want anyone for a minute to think I am power tripping."

"Najwa are you crazy? Nobody wants to be in your position right now. We were talking about it the other day. The sorors will do anything it takes to support you. Anything to take the pressure off of them. Nobody wants to lead this campus."

Najwa asked the ultimate question . "Would they be willing to take a fall with me? Because you know this is where this all could lead."

"Right now if you lead them into the Red Sea, everyone would follow, including Berri Matthews. That's just how much they believe in everything you have done," Irby replied.

"Oh so now I am Moses! Whew! Irby you sure know how to make me feel good." Najwa laughed. She regained her composure to ask one final and decisive question.

"But Irby is it 'cause they truly believe in me or is it fear?"

"It's a little of both. They believe that nobody else is going to step to the plate the way you have and they fear having to take your place if you were to disappear. Najwa, the bottom line is that they don't have any other choice."

# Thursday, February 15, 1974

The only sign Najwa saw of Omega Pi Alpha were through the pledges. Every other morning two were assigned to bring her a copy of the newspaper, orange juice, and a thought for the day. Carla and Lynette were right. Najwa had become a distant figure. She would have continued to fool herself into thinking otherwise had it not been for a note given to her by one of the pledges who hunted her down.

*"Najwa, I need to get together with you on the Founders Weekend celebration. Can you meet me in the library tomorrow? – Berri "*

Najwa had not seen or talked to Berri since the night at Lynette's. All attempts she made to contact Berri were avoided. She found it quite funny that now Berri was asking to meet with her about the annual Founders Weekend celebration. Every year the sorors of Gamma chapter celebrated the founding of their sorority with a weekend of activities that their alumnae and other sorors traveled to Casperton to participate. The largest portion of the vice president's duties included planning the entire weekend. Being a neophyte, Berri had absolutely no clue what she was to do. Najwa knew she would hear from her sooner or later.

Najwa pulled into the library parking lot earlier than her planned meeting. She sat and listened to her car radio for a moment. "Seven days and still no new leads in the kidnapping of Patti Hearst," the reporter said. Najwa cut off her car.

"Humph, what they will do for a rich, White girl," she smirked.

As she entered the front of the library, Najwa noticed Berri standing by the check-out desk waiting patiently. Immediately, after catching a glimpse of Najwa she smiled and began to wave frantically.

"Najwa! Hey soror you made it."

"I'm here. Did you think I wasn't coming?" Najwa smirked.

"Oh, I am just happy to see you. Now you can help me with the Founders stuff." Berri began pulling out notes from her canvas bag.

"Well don't you want to go somewhere and sit down in private? We have a lot to talk about." Najwa guided Berri over to a wooden table tucked behind the last set of bookshelves. This was actually Najwa's hiding place while pledging. Often she returned to take advantage of its exclusivity to study.

"So what do you need help with Berri? We went over every thing at the last chapter meeting. You should have everything almost together by now." Najwa looked at her soror trying not to show her dislike for her.

"I just want to make absolutely sure that I have every "I" dotted and "T" crossed. This is the one event that I get to chair during the

year and I want to make sure everything is right." Berri continued
organizing pages of notes spread across the entire table."

"I see," Najwa said.

Meticulously, Berri revisited every detail of the Founders
celebration listening for Najwa's approval. Najwa thought it was a
shame that they would have such a productive meeting and she
would still need to tell her off for bringing Keisha back on the
campus. Najwa even thought for a minute that this was Berri's way
of taking Najwa's mind off of the fact that she was still in the
doghouse. Berri finally went over the last detail of the weekend after
over forty-five minutes. Najwa knew this was her opportunity.

"Look, I am going to cut to the point. Just where was your mind
last week Berri K. Matthews? How could you just bring Keisha to
Lynette's house like nothing ever happened?"

"Najwa I didn't think I did anything wrong." Berri's eyes
widened as she tried to explain. "Keisha called me and said she was
coming in town for a party and wanted to know what was going on."

"And that's it?" Najwa waited for Berri to offer more
information.

"She asked if she could stay with me. She is my sands Najwa, I
couldn't just leave her hanging. If I had said no, she would have
known something was wrong."

"Then you should have called your good ole Dean Donna and
you both could have stayed at her house!" Najwa snapped.

"So is this is about Donna too? Look they are both sorors
regardless of how you feel about them. Are you saying that they had

no right to be there? They were made in this chapter too!" Berri began gathering her notes and shoving them into her bag. "Keisha was right, you are power hungry." Berri mumbled under her breath as she picked up the last sheet of paper.

Najwa stood and moved closer. "What did you say?"

"Nothing Najwa just forget it. If I was wrong then I apologize." Berri replied looking up to Najwa's towering frame.

"No. What did you say Berri? Did I hear Keisha's name come out your mouth? First Donna and now Keisha, the two most trifling members of Gamma chapter! Don't ever put that woman's name in any sentence about me," Najwa smirked.

"Why do you have to come down on everyone Najwa? Do you think you are all that?" Berri fussed.

"When you compare me to her…then yes I guess I do think I am all that."

"Just what have they done to you Najwa? I don't understand where you are coming from these days."

"Berri are you an idiot or are you just trying make me think you are? I won't even begin to get on the problems Keisha has caused. Trust me, they are bigger than you will ever know!"

"You have made your point Najwa. I am leaving." Berri picked up her bag and threw it over her shoulder.

Najwa immediately jumped in her pathway. Pointing her long finger in Berri's face, Najwa was so angry her teeth clinched. She took a quick moment before she could speak. It was all she could muster to not rip Berri's head off.

"Berri Matthews, don't you ever as long as you are Black and a student on this campus, bring Keisha around anything Gamma chapter has. I am having a good year and you are seriously messing with my groove. I don't like when anybody tries to break my groove. Now I don't know what it is she's told you. And you are entitled to your opinion of me. But don't let them make you write a check with your mouth that your behind can't cash. When Keisha goes back home it's just you and me. I doubt very seriously that she has your back. You keep that in mind." Najwa poked Berri's forehead with her forefinger and smiled.

"You got that Berri?" Najwa waited.

"Yeah I got it." Berri said as she shuffled away.

Najwa remembered the days when Berri was on line and how she made her months a living hell. She hoped that Berri remembered those moments as well. Najwa wanted there to be no doubt in Berri's mind whatsoever whose team she needed to be on.

*A glimmer sparkled from the tip of his cane and against the moonlight. His steps had echoed hers since her journey began. He had watched as she waved goodbye to the Irishman in the hotel.*

# Tuesday, February 19, 1974

"Najwa!" Najwa heard her name being yelled from across the campus yard. She knew immediately who it was. She successfully avoided spending any extended periods of time in his company for over month.

"Najwa!" Dakota hollered again as he rushed over to her. "Wait up!"

"Dakota, hey," Najwa returned with half the enthusiasm.

"Where you been girl?" Dakota asked as he hurried to stop her. "Girl I have been trying to talk to you for a couple of weeks. No one told you I been looking for you?"

"I've been around. And no I haven't gotten any message from you." Najwa was lying. She had, in fact received each of his messages he sent through Lynette, Irby, and even one of the pledges.

"Well, I got you here now. So what's happening? We haven't hung out since the break."

"You know how it is Dakota." Najwa continued to be short with him, never once looking him in the eye. "Just busy, that's all."

"Never too busy for me!" He playfully snapped back.

"I guess there is a first time for everything, huh?"

"Is there something wrong Najwa?"

"Wrong? No, not at all Dakota. I just have a lot on my mind." There was no way Najwa could bring herself to tell Dakota how she felt.

"Listen, I want to spend some time with you. I see you passing on the campus and we haven't had a conversation over five minutes in almost a month."

"I'm here anytime you get ready. Not going anywhere until June." She sarcastically replied. Najwa was not going to take the lead. There would be no way she would set herself up for the evident heartbreak.

"How 'bout right now? Let's do something," Dakota insisted.

Najwa was not expecting him to be so direct. "Now?" She answered.

"Don't tell me you have a meeting to go to."

"Actually no I don't. I need to go home and get some studying done." Najwa stopped and looked at him strangely. "What is wrong with you? You are smiling too much. What do you have up your sleeve?"

"There is nothing wrong with me. Can't I just be happy to see you Najwa?"

"No."

"Fine! You are looking at the newest engineer of Potter Electrical. My father called and told me last week."

"What? You got a job? Already?" Najwa looked stunned.

"That's why I have been looking for you. I wanted you to be the first person to know. I start as soon as I graduate."

Najwa still had a stunned look on her face. "Wow."

"Well aren't you happy for me? You look like I said something wrong."

"Oh no Dakota, I think that is really great." Najwa attempted to save face as she hugged Dakota to make up for her less than enthusiastic reaction. "I am happy for you, really."

"Najwa are you mad at me about something?"

Dakota waited. Najwa was surprised. He knew her even better than she thought.

"Come on let's walk." Dakota put his arm around her shoulder and lead her off unto the pathway of the campus quad.

Najwa did not resist. Finally, she broke her silence. "Why would I be mad at you Dakota?"

"Najwa you haven't really spoken to me since the break. I noticed the change when I got back. And, you can't tell me its 'cause of all this Keisha drama."

"So you think there is something else?"

Dakota suspected he had done something that initiated Najwa's strange behavior towards him. He pondered the possibilities for over a month and had only come up with one thing.

"Does it have something to do with the Christmas break? I know I kind of disappeared. But I had some things on my mind that I needed to get right."

He wanted to tell Najwa the truth. She was his best friend and until now he never realized that he had never told her.

"Look it is too cold out here for me. Let's go inside somewhere and get something to eat."

"I'm not hungry," Najwa snapped.

"Come on girl, you always hungry!" Dakota's smile began to melt Najwa's cold attitude.

Najwa wanted no more of the small talk. She wanted to know exactly where Dakota's mind was. "Things, like what Dakota?"

"You tell me the real reason why you've been avoiding me and I will tell you what things," Dakota replied.

"Let's start with the dance!" Najwa exclaimed.

"The dance? I thought you had a good time." Dakota looked confused. "You were on cloud nine when we left."

"I did have a good time!" Najwa answered.

He stopped walking and turned to her. "So what is your problem?" Dakota hollered back.

"THAT is the problem Dakota! I wasn't going to say anything cause I knew you would not understand."

Dakota's brow raised and a light bulb turned on inside his head. "So did you think that I didn't have a good time with you Naj?" Dakota gently asked.

"I didn't know and I really couldn't tell."

"Why are you being so silly? I had a great time." Dakota reached out and rubbed Najwa's shoulders. "Listen I am sorry if I didn't tell you sooner. As a matter of fact, I had a better time than you think.

But then again, I wasn't too sure about you either."

Dakota had never been more sincere with Najwa than now.

"Did you ever stop to think, maybe THAT was the reason why I hadn't said anything to you?"

"No Dakota, I never thought that," Najwa replied looking in his eyes for the first time in weeks. "Why would I think that? If you were thinking about me and the good time you had then what was up with the date?"

Najwa promised herself she would never bring up the date. The last thing she wanted was to sound jealous.

"The date? What date Najwa?" Dakota was genuinely confused. He struggled to understand what Najwa was referring to.

"Come on Dakota, your southern belle. Christmas Eve? Or do you have so many dates that they all blur together?"

"So that's what this is really all about?" Dakota shook his head. "Najwa, if you only knew the story on that one."

"Well…I'm listening."

"I can't believe you are acting like this Najwa. This is so unlike you."

"Dakota, look you don't have to explain. You don't owe me anything," Najwa said and started walking away.

"Najwa! Wait a minute. If you would stop being so impossible you would see it was not what you thought it was!"

Dakota suddenly realized how this whole conversation sounded like a lover's spat. Never had he and Najwa gone through any situation remotely similar. Nevertheless, he wanted to clear the air.

Najwa's friendship meant more to him than any date he had encountered yet.

Dakota caught up to Najwa and grabbed her arm.

"Najwa, listen to me! I had just met that girl. My dad set that date up."

"Oh yeah Dakota, that's original. Use your father for your pitiful excuses." Najwa tried to snatch her arm away but the attempt was worthless.

"Would you just shut up and listen for once! My dad set that date up as a favor. Maxine is the niece of his supervisor. She was in town for the holidays. Her uncle felt like she needed to be around people her age. So my dad suggested that I take the girl on a date. That is all that was Najwa!"

"So is that how you got the job?" Najwa sarcastically asked.

Dakota released Najwa's arm from his clutch.

"Najwa, you asked me what the date was about and I told you. How much are you going to try to make me suffer about this?"

Najwa was relieved. She believed every bit of Dakota's story. She was also embarrassed and hurt.

"Dakota.... I just...."

Dakota interrupted. "Look, it's okay. I should have told you while we were still at home. But like I said I have just had a lot of things on my mind that I needed to sort out."

Najwa wanted to tell Dakota about her plans to tell him over the break how she felt. But she could not form the words. She had already made a fool of herself. Rejection was not something she could handle now.

"I am wrong for making you explain. Really, let's just forget it and move on."

"But Najwa, there are some things that I really need to get off my chest and I...."

Najwa interrupted. She anticipated what he would say with great fear.

"Dakota, please don't. I just can't deal with this right now. I am so sorry for acting the way I have. I was a fool, I will admit that. But please, I don't want to talk about this right now. I have so much on my mind. I just can't take anything more."

Dakota wanted to talk to Najwa. He too had spent the Christmas break contemplating revealing his feelings to Najwa. He wanted to confess that she was the best friend he ever had. He wanted to share with her how good it felt to make her happy at the Snowflake Ball and how he wanted to continue to make her feel that same way every day that he could. But he respected her wishes and decided that it would just have to wait another day.

"Listen Najwa, I am sorry if I didn't tell you sooner. But you just don't know how happy I was at that Snowflake Ball." This was all Dakota would be able to confide in her for now. He knew the time would come when Najwa would know all that he felt for her.

"Is all forgiven? Can I get a hug?" Dakota asked. Before she could respond, he drew her into his arms and held her closer than he had ever.

"So can we get something to eat now?" He asked.

Najwa gave in. "Your treat right."

Dakota smiled. "What ever you want."

*The blows were fierce and continuous. Sadie's world turned black. Her body slammed to the damp dirt. Her fingers clutched unsuccessfully to the bag he snatched from her grip. She never heard the laugh as he tossed it over in the dirt. Nor did she feel the weight of his body on top of her. Her pain blended into the deepest part of the night.*

# Thursday, March 7, 1974

The time flew by as Gamma chapter found themselves embarking on their annual trip to one of the many Omega Pi Alpha sorority meetings. This time it was their Regional Cluster meeting in Chicago. This year it would be held in March, a month earlier, and all chapters from the four states within their region were expected to be in attendance.

Najwa and her sorors arrived in Chicago the night before the main session. Pooling their resources, they were able to get the sorors from a neighboring chapter to share the cost of a hotel room. The comfort level of over ten women in a double room was not the best, but it was a place to bathe and sleep nevertheless. It would not be the first time they traveled in a crowd, so they were used to it. For some odd reason, which Najwa never understood, they loved traveling this way. The bigger the group, it seemed the more fun they had.

The university usually picked up the cost of the delegate for the regional cluster meetings. However, that support was questionable

284

this year. Najwa was prepared to foot the cost thanks to her part-time job. There was no way that she would miss an opportunity to actually speak on the floor of the meetings. Unlike the previous year, this time she would be attending as a voting delegate for Gamma chapter. An honor bestowed on all presidents of each Omega Pi Alpha chapter.

Najwa lay on the hotel bed as she read over the weekend long list of meetings she was required to attend. She wanted to make sure she made it to the most interesting ones. To miss a moment of the sorority's politics would make the trip worthless.

Soaking in as much as possible in her last year as an undergraduate member of the sorority was her top priority. More importantly, she wanted to visit the campus of the historical university where it all began. She wanted to see the tree that was planted in memory of her beloved founder. She wanted to walk the halls that these elite women walked. She wanted to see the shores where Sadie's life was drained and washed away like the tide.

Najwa made a visit to the offices of the Daily Defense, the oldest Black newspaper, in hope that she could find anything on the sorority pioneers, particularly Sadie. Because Sadie succumbed to such a violent death, she hoped for an article that would bring the story to life for her. She wanted to read and soak in every detail of this woman she was now obsessed with. Having worked in the courthouse in Casperton, she knew that if she phoned ahead and was nice to the archives person, perhaps they could have the articles that she needed already pulled. As delegate for the chapter, she knew that her time would be limited. Combing thousands of articles would not be an option.

Sure enough, Najwa called ahead and made friends with a voice by the name of Hubert in the archives department. He assured that for someone with a voice as sweet as Najwa's, he would make up an article if he couldn't find anything. Najwa arrived bright and early to find that her new friend in fact, found several articles on the sorority and their activities in the Chicago area. The years revealed one-sentence captions to headlines and feature stories in the social section. Scholarship balls and other community work of the sorority were highlighted in several of the dated findings.

But, what interested Najwa the most was buried at the bottom. Najwa was silent as she read the article that told of the unfortunate and beastly murder of the young, promising university student. A chill raced up her spine as she read the sordid details. The vivid accounts from the friends of Sadie were recorded for prosterity. The Omega Pi Alpha founders told of how they found Sadie on the shores clinging to life. Najwa felt her spirit sink and her heart grew heavy as she thought of the pain and the courage of Sadie. Her eyes became watery as she thought of the commitment to the promise in Sadie's death.

Najwa had what she wanted. For now, her search was over. She recovered virtually all that she could on the life of her founder. She found a record of her birth now she had the story of her death. She had seen the introduction and the abrupt ending. Never had the history books of her sorority described the death of their soror in the manner of this ancient article. It dissected every inch of the tragedy. A second article, written a week after Sadie's death, criticized the police for not making an honest attempt to find the animal that would have committed such a crime.

"Anyone capable of such a crime is no better than a Chicago Jack the Ripper," the article declared.

The victim, the newspaper stated, "was a credit to her race." Anger filled Najwa's heart as she read that the police ruled Sadie's death an accidental drowning.

"What would it take to get a copy of these articles today my good friend Hubert?" Najwa flirted.

The heavy, dark skinned sweaty man threw his hands up. "That's impossible! There is no way I will be able to get that for you today."

"Aw come on Hubert, this is a newspaper. Surely you can get me something," Najwa replied.

After flirting for ten minutes, she received a promise of a copy by the end of the working day. Najwa hugged the smiling man and kissed him on the cheek. Running out of the newspaper office she raced to catch the second half of the morning workshops.

Right before five, Najwa returned with pastries from the hotel as a gift to her new friend Hubert. He smiled from ear to ear as Najwa handed him the small bag and took her prized possessions.

That same evening, just as night fell, Nawja and the entire chapter took a trip to the founding university campus. They wanted to see where it all began and where it all ended. They wanted to see the tree that was planted by their founders for Sadie.

As they walked the old cobble stone campus pathway, they marveled as they looked at the Ivy covered buildings. They thought of how old the tall structures may have been and how they may have looked when their founders walked the same pathway. As the sun fell, a bit of light peeked through the many trees that lined the walk. The campus was peaceful yet the voices of age whispered to them as they searched for the spot.

Finally, before them stood an old and tall tree. The sturdy body had branches that ascended high into the heavens and leaned slightly to the side. Over seventy-two years old, it was full of life. Beneath the tree at the point where its roots slightly peeked out of the ground was a small metal plaque mounted by bolts in each corner on a stone. The inscription was scratched and almost faded but still legible.

Lynette leaned over and read aloud.

"In the beginning, there was a spirit. The truth shall prevail, our love will transcend and the spirit will never die. In Memory of Sadie M. Wesley - 1901."

Gamma chapter stood around the old tree looking at it as if it were Sadie herself. Robin adjusted the flashcubes on top of her camera and motioned for everyone to squeeze together for a picture. It was the first picture that the chapter had taken with one another since the Snowflake Ball.

They had been so wrapped up in the pledges, the controversy with Keisha, and the daily frustration with the university, that they had not enjoyed one another as they did at the beginning of the year.

Underneath that tree, for the first time since the Black Greek Council meeting, they were one. They were bonded by a concept that was perhaps larger than they had ever imagined. Underneath this tree they felt it stronger than they ever had before. No one uttered more than a couple words during the entire time they spent touching, rubbing and hugging the tree and the worn metal plate. It was as if it would have been disrespectful to disrupt the peacefulness.

# Thursday March 14, 1974

"Hi mom. When we got back from Chicago I was just so exhausted. I really meant to call. But it just...."

Najwa tried desperately to explain to her mother who regularly addressed her annoyance with the lack of communication between them.

"I know it just slipped your mind. You know, one day you will wake up and realize how important your family is honey," Najwa's mother interjected.

Najwa made a vow to herself to avoid arguing at all cost. "Ma, please...." She quickly changed the subject. "Hey, did I tell you about how I have been helping Professor Baker down at the Women's Center?"

"You told me that you had gone down there a couple of times but I thought that was just for your interview."

"At first that was the case. But I liked it so much that I have been volunteering on my spare time. Ma I really like it."

"Spare time? Honey it doesn't sound like you have much spare time at all. I don't want you to over do things. You know how you can over-extend yourself."

Najwa sighed in frustration. She hoped that her mother would pick up on the fact that she actually found something unrelated to her sorority that kept her interest. Volunteering with the program brought a ray of hope and possibly direction. The thought of staying at the Casperton University for another two years wasn't as painful as long as she focused on the lives she could touch in the community.

"Ma, I am not over-extending myself. I think I am really going to like this graduate program," she hinted.

"Like it? Well that's a change. You haven't even been accepted yet and you are already singing praises. That Professor Baker must be really something. You have really taken to that center. Anything that would make you want to stay at Casperton University must be something." Mrs. Jackson knew her daughter's frustration with the university.

"I know. It feels strange Ma. I finally found something that I really enjoy. And I met another student there who said that I was a sure fit. He said that Professor Baker really likes what she sees. Isn't that something Ma?"

"That is wonderful sweetheart! What about all the troubles you girls were having with the administration? That last article you mailed home to us was not a very pleasant one honey. Maybe you should watch your tone. I don't want you to get kicked out of there sweetie."

Najwa was raised in a house of protest. Only ten years had passed since she marched on Washington with her mother clutching to her with one hand, and a protest sign with the other. It was 1974 and the nonviolent protests were now an endangered species. This was what she knew her mother feared the most.

"Ma, I thought it was you and daddy who told me to always speak my mind whenever I had the chance? Wasn't it you who told me that I had to stand for something?"

"We did honey but you have to choose your battles wisely. There is a time and a place for everything. We have come a long way and even further to go. You are not going to solve all your campus problems in a year." Mrs. Jackson replied.

"At least we have made them take notice. They know now that we will not tolerate this treatment."

"Najwa, all I am saying is that your article was a little harsh. Next time just tone it down a little sweetie."

"Harsh? Ma these racist bastards weren't worried about harsh when they kicked two Black students out and suspended two Black organizations off the yard!"

"And they wont be worried about harsh when they kick you out either. And watch your language!" Mrs. Jackson snapped.

"I am sorry. I understand Ma. I really do. But I haven't done anything wrong. I am just expressing my freedom of speech."

"Be careful. I know what these people can do. And I know how they have a way of hushing a mouth that speaks words they don't want to hear. Besides…maybe it is our own fault for letting you listen by the door of those kitchen meetings we had with the rights workers." Mrs. Jackson kidded.

"Maybe so Ma. Maybe so." Najwa was a chip off her mother and father's block. She felt she was only emulating what she was taught. However, the tide was rolling slightly different now and the voices were stronger, louder, and angrier than ever.

# Monday, April 1, 1974

Najwa knew her mother's words had to be a revelation. Two weeks after their talk, Najwa walked to her mailbox in the Black House to find a note from the student editor of the Tiger Pride newspaper.

She read the scribbled note aloud. "Najwa, I need to see you as soon as possible. I will be in my office everyday this week."

"As soon as possible," she thought.

She folded the note, shoved it into her purse, and gathered up the rest of the chapter mail. She turned and walked up the stairs to the Tiger Pride office. The door was already open. Sitting in the corner of the small office was the editor. Najwa walked in and stood silently.

"Well if it isn't the infamous Najwa K. Jackson! Close the door and sit down we have a lot to talk about. You, my sister...have ruffled the feathers of some important people."

"Tell me something I don't know and I will be surprised," Najwa replied as she turned and shut the door.

Half an hour passed and Najwa was still not moved by the call from the Dean of Students. She listened intently as the editor told of the administration's displeasure with her weekly commentary. Either Najwa's article is pulled from the Tiger Pride or funding for printing of the paper would be reduced or even pulled. The choice was theirs to make.

Najwa looked at her editor. "This is an April Fools joke right?"

"I wish it were," he laughed.

"Their tactics don't surprise me at all. This ain't cool at all. So you're pulling my article?" Najwa asked.

"That never entered my mind Najwa," he quickly answered.

"Hey, I don't want the Pride to suffer. This paper is the pulse of the Black campus. I don't want to see it gone."

"Najwa we have means to get that paper printed. I have already made phone calls. I just want you to be aware of what we are against."

"I know…silence the voice so the people won't hear the message. Then the message dies. I am familiar with that one."

"I need you to be accountable for every word you write. I want you to understand and be accountable for everything you say and do from here on out."

"You've never had to worry about that! I have backed each and every one of my articles up with facts and actions. This is a war. In every war there are casualties. I just don't want the Pride to be a casualty. I will take the fall first," Najwa promised.

She gathered up her things and assured the editor her next article would be on his desk by the end of the week. Now she had even more weight thrown on her shoulders. Najwa was furious that the Tiger Pride was the next target.

"Hello there Ms. Najwa Jackson. I know you weren't going to just walk in here and not speak!" The motherly voice called from the side office and broke Najwa's thought.

"Hello Mrs. Dixon. You know I wouldn't do that to you. I was going to come in and say hello right after I ran upstairs. I just had a meeting with the Pride editor and I am not too happy," Najwa stated.

"Oh say no more. I took the call about that myself," Mrs. Dixon replied. "Oh baby, the Dean of Students called over here yesterday about your last article. I don't think he was too pleased."

"That's good Mrs. Dixon. I wrote it so they would take notice."

"That is certainly what you did baby. The last time the Dean of Students called over here was...well, come to think of it, I don't think he has ever called," Mrs. Dixon declared.

Najwa managed to crack a smile behind her anger. She knew the administration was trying to use scare tactics. However, this latest incident did nothing but make her even more eager to find a topic for her next article. Najwa enjoyed shocking the campus every week with her controversial antics. Initially, she struggled to find an idea that would keep the energy of the campus at a pique. This time she knew exactly what direction she would take.

"Mrs. Dixon, can I ask you a question?"

"Sure baby."

"Let's say you owned some land in Casperton. How would I go

about finding out where it was located?" Najwa asked.

"Well I suppose you could just ask me." Mrs. Dixon kidded.

Najwa laughed and continued. "I know that Mrs. Dixon! But what if you were dead and had no one to pass the property on to?"

"I suppose you could look through the deed records under my name. That's if Casperton hadn't already auctioned off the land. Why do you ask?" Mrs. Dixon replied.

"I am doing some research for a class I am taking. Research on land in Casperton in the early 1900s for a geography class." Najwa lied. "But wouldn't there be a record of the auction?" She continued.

"Yes there should be. Are you looking for any land in particular baby?" Mrs. Dixon asked.

"Well sort of. This would have been land owned by a Black family in Casperton," Najwa added.

"Oh that's easy. Why didn't you say that from the beginning? All the land owned by the Negro citizens of Casperton was in one location."

"Really? Where was that?" Najwa asked.

"Right by the university. As a matter of fact, it was all on the campus grounds. When I moved here they were in the process of moving the last families off the property. This was prime property back then," Mrs. Dixon offered.

"But why would they just give up their land like that Mrs. Dixon?"

"Give it up? Baby a lot of them were forced off their land. Some were given a little money to last them for a little while. And

297

others…well…they had no choice. It all started with that Barkston man."

"Not him again. I never knew how much influence that man had on this town 'til this year," Najwa said.

"Baby he WAS this town. He wasn't born here. Came from…I think…Chicago in 1903. But he raised this town to what it is today. He had the deed to the first piece of land. Don't know how he got it. But he is the one who had the first piece of land and started buying everyone out and moving all the Negroes to the other side of town. A part of Casperton no one really cared about."

"The west side?" Najwa already knew.

"Yes. The west side of the town. You know that the Black House belonged to the last Negro family on the old land. The Cotton family was the only family able to hold out. The sons of the Cotton's moved away and donated the house to the university on the condition that it would be used for Negro's attending the university in some way."

"So Mrs. Dixon, any Black family who may have had land lost it to Barkston?"

"That's not what they called it at the time. But baby…that's what happened." Mrs. Dixon shook her head.

"Thanks Mrs. Dixon. I think I am going to go get some work done now," she said knowing Mrs. Dixon would continue on as long as she was given the opportunity.

Najwa walked over to the library with a million thoughts roaming her mind. She thought of the right words in her article to sustain the fighting spirit ignited in the students just a little longer.

All she could think of was the fact that this was all because of Keisha. Sadly, no one on the campus would even care about fighting the university had it not been for Keisha's promiscuity. There would be no petitions circulating, or articles written. No one would care how the university treated the Black students - not even the Black students themselves. Nevertheless, Najwa had to continue with the façade.

In her mind, it was confirmed that the Barkston Center namesake would be the victim of her next article. As she sat in her favorite obscure corner table, she looked back over a few notes she had jotted from previous conversations with Mrs. Dixon about Barkston and his influence over the university.

"More," she muttered.

Najwa read the Chicago article again and again until she literally memorized every word. From it she learned that Sadie's parents were landowners in the Casperton area. She figured this land had to be part of the land that the university sat upon. Again, she dissected every word of the articles until she could feel the breeze of the night air of Sadie's murder.

"There has to be more to this than what I am seeing. I feel something deep inside just pulling me towards it but I can't quite put my finger on it."

# Tuesday April 23, 1974

Now Najwa was hunting down Dakota as he had hunted her. She desperately needed to talk to her old friend. Although they were never able to be completely honest enough with one another during their last talk to resolve anything, she still relied on his advice. The threats against the Tiger Pride weighed heavy on her mind. Najwa had submitted and printed two more controversial articles. However, before she was to turn in her most devastating article, she needed to be absolutely sure.

*Dakota, I need to talk to you. Can you come by my place this evening? Call me. I'll be home until ten. Najwa.*

She placed the scribbled note under the door of Dakota's room.

The brothers must have let her in while he was away at class, Dakota thought. The timing of Najwa's note was perfect. He had some spare time and wanted to see her.

"Let me in girl!" Dakota hollered as he pounded on Najwa's door in a playful manner.

"Just wait a minute! I am coming!" Najwa yelled back as she ran from her bedroom.

The last "playful" scene Dakota made caused Najwa's neighbors to call the police and report a violent Negro in the hallway. Najwa opened the door to find her best friend's smile larger than life.

"Come in silly! Don't bring your loud mouth into my peaceful building causing trouble," Najwa kidded.

"Trouble? Never! How's my favorite?" Dakota beamed.

Najwa sat on the couch. "I'm alright. I needed to talk to you about something. I need your opinion."

"Hey, whatever you need." Dakota sat next to Najwa on the couch.

Najwa finally shared with Dakota her conversation with the editor of the Tiger Pride. He was the first and only person Najwa had confided.

"Are they pulling your articles?" Dakota asked after listening very intently.

"No," Najwa replied.

"Are you going to tone them down?"

"Hell no," Najwa snapped.

"So what do you need my advice for? Seems to me you made up your mind."

"Do you think I am wrong? If for some reason that paper loses it's funding and can't survive, I will never let myself live it down. I can't be responsible for that."

"But Najwa, would you really be responsible? You are just speaking the truth in your articles. That's what the Pride has always been about. Are you going to stop hippin' this campus to what's going on?" Dakota asked.

"No, of course not. I would pull the column myself before I stop speaking my mind. And that's not going to happen anytime soon."

"Then you are only doing what you are supposed to do. It is not your fault other people can't deal with that. You took a stand and if you sit down now...the whole movement on this campus would take a seat right next to you. Is that what you want?"

"I want to graduate. I want to get a job. I want to have a career to look forward to. That's what I want Dakota. I don't want to have to make choices like this."

Najwa stood and began pacing.

"I wouldn't want to be in your shoes right now. This is a hard decision to make. I don't know anyone better to be faced with this choice though. Najwa I know you aren't doubting yourself cause your ego is about as big as your watermelon head."

"Ha ha...very funny." She continued to pace.

"If your problem is support, hey, I am here. Your sorors are here too. Not to mention, all the Black campus organizations are singing songs of praises for Najwa. You a bad sister Najwa! Everything will be fine. There is no way we will let the Pride be eliminated. Too many of our alumni built their futures through the Pride. They would not see it die. Do you think if they ever stopped to think about what the administration said or stopped speaking the truth, that paper would still be alive today?"

"No, it wouldn't. It would not Dakota. Thanks, I needed that reminder."

Najwa made her decision in that second.

# Thursday, May 16, 1974

Najwa was exhausted from the chapter's public service and then volunteering at the Women's Center. She still had not been able to catch her second wind. That day she promised Carla and Lynette a girl's night to talk about some things. They all agreed that they were long overdue to bond. In anticipation of their dinner, Najwa decided to take a much needed break from both her classes and work. She didn't want to have one excuse for missing this valuable time with her sands.

Enjoying her time alone, the morning consisted of cereal, cartoons, and then her soap operas. Following the same routine for over two weeks in anticipation of her letter from the graduate program, Najwa went down to pick up her mail.

Feverishly, she thumbed through several letters. Neatly rubber banded at the end of the stack she saw the return address of the Casperton University School of Sociology. The long anticipated letter was in her hands. Her heart raced as she brought the mail along with the letter upstairs to her apartment. Too frightened to the break seal of her fate, she sat down in her wicker chair and stared at the envelope. She turned on the television and pretended to be concerned with the afternoon movie. Finally, unable to put herself through much more torture she picked up the envelope and opened it. She read the first sentence aloud.

"Although we were very impressed with your qualifications and recent accomplishments, we regret to inform you that you were not admitted into the Casperton University Graduate School of Sociology."

"What?" If she had not opened the letter herself no one could have ever convinced her she was rejected.

"Damn!" She cried over the noise of the television. "Damn! Those bastards!"

She was finally a casualty in the war against the administration. Why she never saw it coming this way was a mystery. Her choices were down to none. Her heart sank as she thought of the failure she was handed on a university silver platter. She could not take much more. Control was slipping slowly from her grasp and she knew not how to regain the momentum.

Najwa felt an unimaginable rage. The anger and temper she managed to control for over eighteen years unleashed and forced her to pick up a glass sitting on the coffee table. She violently threw it across the room. The glass crashed against her front door, shattered, and flew in all directions. Water raced down to the carpeted floor just as the tears streamed down Najwa's face.

She rocked furiously as she held herself.

"I can't take this any longer!" She sobbed.

Najwa felt her sanity slipping away. Never had she lost control of her emotions. She tried to calm herself. The more she tried the more the tears fell and the more her emotions floated back and forth. She didn't know whether to feel sorry for herself or angry with the university.

"Those dirty bastards! They finally got me! Najwa why were you so stupid?"

She felt as if she had left herself vulnerable to a surprise attack. At the same time she tried to console herself that she really didn't want to be in the program anyway.

It hit her all at once. Her childhood fears, her sheltered life, no direction for her future, the administration, the fear of a relationship with Dakota, failing the chapter and disappointing the alumnae by proving their worst fears of her leadership abilities all crushed her world. If she didn't get out the house she knew she would make herself sick thinking about it all.

Najwa picked up her keys, coat, and scarf. Every apartment on her floor shook as she slammed the door. She jumped inside Panther and drove. She stopped along the side of the street and cried. Then she drove some more. She had no idea why, all of a sudden she felt so hopeless. Perhaps she always felt this way. This was the first time she ever confronted her feelings face to face.

She thought over all she had done wrong and how she could have changed her fate in some way or another. She thought where she would be had she not pledged. Had it not been for her membership in Omega Pi Alpha, the women who meant so much to her life would not be present. Then again, had it not been for Gamma chapter perhaps she and Paul would still be together today. Had it not been for Keisha, there would be no war on the administration. Had it not been for the chapter's war, she would not have her column, nor would she have the power on the campus that she enjoyed. The only resolution that she came to after driving over 40 miles away from the campus, was that she was in control of all the right things but herself. Somewhere in the midst of helping her sorors, saving the chapter, and being everything to everyone, she lost the most important thing, herself.

She could cry no more. She was beginning to disgust herself. Her self-pity was sickening. Never had she sunk so low. Her lids were beginning to grow tired. Sixty miles out of Casperton, in the middle of the star lit night, surrounded by fields of black, she decided to turn around and head back to the university. No matter how far she drove, or how much she drained her soul, she had to return to reality and face the next months left at the university. She decided, no matter how bad things got, she would not feel sorry for herself, nor would she apologize. She made her bed and she was prepared to lie in it. No matter what the expense. It was simple. She would have the last word.

Two hours passed and the car engine was almost as hot as Najwa as she pulled into Mrs. Dixon's parking space outside the Black House around 8:30pm. Najwa stormed into the small office and only home of the Tiger Pride.

"They want to play games well, I will play games," she mumbled.

Najwa pulled her journal from her bag and sat behind the old rickety typewriter and furiously began to type.

"Najwa!" A voice called moments later.

She did not answer. Her fingers beat the keys of the typewriter as the arms began to tangle. The carriage popped as if it were begging for mercy. A loud "ding" sounded when Najwa reached the end of every line. She shoved the carriage back to the beginning and began the abuse all over. She sensed someone standing behind her but was so engrossed in her typing that she never turned to see her visitor.

"Naj!" Dakota hollered again.

"I heard you the first time! I'm busy!" She hollered back without breaking her rhythm.

"What in the world is wrong with you?" Dakota snapped back at Najwa.

"If you haven't noticed, I am writing. Now can you please leave?"

Najwa kept typing. Dakota grabbed her hands away from the typewriter.

"No! I am not going to leave until you tell me what is wrong with you. Have you lost your mind or something?"

"Dakota you are a big man but right about now…the way I am feeling…I will bust you in your jaw if you don't let my hands go. I am not in the mood to play with you." Najwa tried unsuccessfully to jerk away from Dakota's grip.

Dakota stood firm. "No. I am not letting you go. You are going to calm down and act like you have a brain and tell me what is going on."

Najwa knew he would follow through. She settled herself back in her seat and looked at him again as he held to her wrists.

"Ok I am calm. Would you let me go now?"

"Yeah. Now what the hell is wrong with you? Lynette and Carla have been looking all over this campus for you. You had them worried when you didn't show up for dinner." Dakota released her wrists from his grip and sat across from her.

Najwa had completely forgotten about the planned dinner between she and her sands. With the arrival of the letter she had not given food or anything else a second thought.

"I didn't get accepted into the graduate program. Simple as that," she finally said.

"What!" Dakota looked puzzled. "Why?"

"All the letter said was that my application was great but hey...we don't want you. Both you and I know what that is all about. Najwa Jackson get your Black, militant ass off this campus. That is what it should have said."

"Damn girl. You had that program wrapped up. You had a recommendation from Professor Baker! What happened?"

"Dakota, I haven't even spoken to her yet. I got my stuff and split as soon as I read the letter. I been driving all over the state of Illinois. But I got something for them all." She focused her attention back on the article and began to type like a mad woman. Dakota sat with his mouth wide open in disbelief.

"Wait, you are going to appeal aren't you. Can you? Maybe Professor Baker can do something. It has to be a mistake."

"Are you crazy. There is no way I am appealing. It was no mistake Dakota. They want me out of here as soon as possible and that is what they are going to get."

"You can't just quit now. What happened to the fighter that has reigned this campus all semester? You deserve to be in that graduate school just as much as the next person."

"Dakota, even if I were to fight and get accepted they would make my life a living hell."

"That has never stopped you before. What are you going to tell your parents?"

"The truth! What else would I tell them? I did nothing wrong."

Dakota knew that Najwa's mind was made. Fighting her was useless.

She began furiously typing again.

"What are you typing?" Dakota looked over the carriage.

"My article for the next Pride."

"Your article for the next…Najwa when are you going to stop and get your own situation together for once? Seriously, baby what is wrong with you? I don't understand what is going on with you. I don't know who you are anymore." Dakota pleaded with Najwa.

Najwa stopped typing and looked at Dakota in disbelief.

"You just sat here and tried to revive the Najwa who was saving the campus and now you are lecturing me about saving myself. Make up your mind what you want! You have everything perfect Mr. Phillips. You have your life in order. You know where you will be next year. You are completely in control of everything…your career, your classes, and your little love flings. I don't have it like that. So to answer your question, I can't get my own situation together 'cause I am too busy getting everyone else's situation together! Now please leave!" Najwa continued typing.

"Najwa…I'm sorry. I didn't know this was getting to you this much. In all our years, I've never seen you like this. I'll leave but come by my place tonight when you finish your article."

"There's no need to apologize. I'll be fine. Can you tell Carla and Lynette that I am fine? And don't tell them about the letter. Now leave. Please." Najwa started thumbing through her notes.

Dakota stood and watched. He hesitated.

"Dakota, I promise, I will come by your place and we will talk. I just need to finish what I am doing."

Dakota turned and slowly walked down the stairs thinking of nothing but Najwa.

An hour later, Najwa knocked on Dakota's door. She felt horrible about the way she treated him earlier and felt an apology was in order. He was not the cause of her situation. In fact, he tried to help Najwa throughout her four years and she knew without him, she would have been back home after her first year. She needed to see the friendly face and comfort she always found in her good friend.

Finally, the door opened. Dakota's face lit at the sight of Najwa.

"Hey. Come on in," he said in a soft but strong voice.

Najwa walked into the unusually quiet house. However, she welcomed the silence. She didn't need the confusion of a lot of people running around this night.

"Where's Ron and Kenny?" She asked.

"Oh they're out with the rest of the brothers. They went down to Bradley University for the night. The Bros have a line and well, you know the rest," Dakota quickly ended.

"So why didn't you go? I hope I didn't keep you from going with them."

Najwa walked over to the couch and sunk down into the soft cushion.

"Don't worry about it. I've got plenty time to go down there. Besides, I've been thinking about you all day even before I saw you at the Black House. I am worried about you girl."

Dakota positioned himself on the couch next to Najwa.

"Please don't start Dakota. I don't want to talk about all that anymore. I'm sorry for going off on you like that. But please, let's not talk about it."

Najwa quickly changed the subject. "What about your female friends? I'm surprised none of them have you tied up tonight."

"No, I haven't been tied up much at all Najwa. I have had one person on my mind lately."

Najwa needed a diversion from Dakota's statement. The aroma from the kitchen provided the best distraction. "What's going on in there? What you cooking?" She asked.

"I just threw a little something together 'cause I knew you would be coming by. Hey, don't try to change the subject."

"Dakota, please, I don't need...."

Dakota placed his fingers over Najwa's mouth silencing her.

"Najwa just listen to me. I wanted to do something for you tonight. I just want you to relax and take your mind off everything. We are going to work through this situation. I promise. Now I know you are hungry so just be quiet and let me get you something."

"Did my mother put you up to this? She had to have put you up to this. 'Cause there is no way that your tack head could be so thoughtful. Not after the way I treated you today." Najwa kidded trying not to think of any of her problems.

"Oh, my tack head?" Dakota laughed.

"No your mother did not put me up to this. Although, I know for a fact that she is just as worried about you. You know I promised her I would take care of you while we were gone. Consider this our pre-graduation dinner celebration, Okay? After you eat maybe we can talk, if you feel like it. But for now, just relax." Dakota stood from the couch, put his favorite album on the turntable, and then walked to the kitchen.

Najwa realized for the first time that she had never seen Dakota cook without music playing. It seemed, the better the record, the better the meal. The Isley Brothers were playing, so Najwa knew it was something good.

She was right. Spaghetti and his famous three-meat sauce

simmered slowly. Najwa knew he had gone through a lot to prepare the meal and it reminded her of what a true friend he was to her. Najwa leaned back on the couch and for the first time since Keisha was dismissed from school she was actually relaxing. For once she did not care where the pledges were, who was getting expelled from school, or what she would do after graduation.

As the needle moved to the next groove, it began to skip.

"Get that for me." Dakota shouted from the kitchen.

"I thought you said to relax?" Najwa said as she walked over and lightly tapped the head of the needle.

A slow melodic tune with an acoustic guitar strumming sweetly began to play.

"Oh no wonder it's scratched. This must be the song you play for all those women that come over to see you." Najwa picked up the album cover and looked at it.

"Naw, I was saving that one for you baby." Dakota replied.

Najwa laughed hysterically. It was at that moment that she realized in the past weeks she had not laughed at all. She looked in the kitchen at Dakota whose back was turned to her. The long skinny limbs she remembered from their childhood were now replaced with thick, muscle bound arms connected to broad shoulders. His hands large, and fingers long, but gentle. As she watched him maneuver around the kitchen, she began to think he wasn't such a bad cook after all. In fact, he was an excellent cook. She would never dare tell him this.

"See there you go. I knew I would have you laughing before the night was up." Dakota's smile beamed from the kitchen.

With great care, he fixed Najwa's plate. He knew exactly how Najwa liked her plate from the years they cooked in the D.C. back yards. They sat on the couch and ate as they reminisced on the times they had on campus.

Najwa took her last bite and slid the empty plate across the coffee table. Dakota finished, as he always did, well before her. Totally relaxed and full, Najwa looked at Dakota.

"You know you don't have to treat me so good Dakota."

"What was that? Was that a hint that you love my cooking?" Dakota joked.

"Oh shut up Dakota." she laughed again. "I was just real hungry that's all. But thanks. I really needed that. You been more than a brother to me Dakota and I really appreciate it. Even when I act a fool."

"I don't mind. You know I would do anything for you girl."

Najwa immediately recognized a change in Dakota's voice. She knew exactly where Dakota was going and wanted to avoid talking about the day's events all together. She already decided how she would rectify her problem and wanted no assistance.

"So, what are we going to do about this mess with graduate school? As a matter of fact, what are we going to do about everything? We haven't had the chance to talk like we should Najwa," Dakota continued.

His seriousness scared her. Not because of his concern but because of what she may feel compelled to share. No one had ever

315

gotten this close. She kept her feelings locked. The one time she made up her mind to share did not turn out the way she had planned. If she even looked at him, she feared her soul would be revealed. She turned her back to him and leaned against his chest as she always did when they had their "serious" talks.

Dakota gently wrapped his arms around Najwa and pulled her in closer. A chill went through Najwa's body that she had never felt. The feeling she had at the Snowflake Ball returned. And, it felt good.

"Talk to me." Dakota whispered in her ear again.

Najwa closed her eyes for a second. She listened to the Isley Brothers still crooning on the old turntable. She couldn't believe what was happening to her inside. Her body defied her mind as her arms wrapped around Dakota's and caressed his hands. She felt his breath on her neck. Helpless, she surrendered.

"Dakota there is just so much going on with me right now. Sometimes it's just too much. Gamma chapter has me running around like a fool. Not to mention, I would like to graduate this spring. You know I like to have everything under control. Now I don't know if that control is even worth the problems. I started off this year with every intention of making this chapter the best."

"Baby if you haven't noticed, that is what you've done," Dakota assured her.

"Yeah but at what expense Dakota? The strange thing about it all is that I don't think I have done enough."

"But what about you? Did you forget yourself?" Dakota asked. There was silence.

"Najwa you know we are going to get past this. You are smart girl. You can write your own ticket anywhere. So I don't even know why you are concerned about after graduation," he continued.

"Dakota I don't know what I even want anymore. Nothing I ever do is enough." Najwa realized he had opened a door she would have rather left closed. Aside from the music still playing, there was silence between the two of them. Najwa felt Dakota's heart beating against her back.

Finally, he whispered in her ear.

"Don't think about any of that tonight. Everything is going to be fine. Let it go."

Najwa sprung from Dakota's arms.

"Were you even listening to me? I can't just let go, everyone is depending on…."

Dakota pulled Najwa back into his arms as if she never moved, and whispered again, "Tonight, just let it all go. Forget everyone. What about you? What do you want?" He hesitated and then made the decision to tell Najwa how he felt. If he waited another second, the thought of never having another moment as perfect as this one would nag him forever.

"Najwa, I want to give you everything you want. I just want you to be happy."

Najwa was numb. This had to be a dream. If she moved, blinked, or breathed too hard, she feared she would wake herself.

There was silence again as Dakota began to rub the tip of his nose up her neck then down the back of her shoulder. Again, her heart, and not her head, took over. She leaned back inviting him to continue. Dakota leaned back on the couch as he drew her in closer and held her tighter than before.

Finally, for the first time in the twenty years they had known each other, his lips, barely wet, touched her skin. Najwa inhaled a short, quick breath. Dakota gently kissed her neck in an upward path that led to her ear lobe.

Chills shot through Najwa's body, sweet but sharp, as her eyes gently closed and her lips slowly parted. Dakota rubbed his cheek against hers. For a moment, he continued to hold Najwa in his arms gently kissing her neck and shoulders as her hands caressed his face.

Najwa sat up and Dakota turned her body toward him. Still very unfamiliar with this feeling and unable to look him in the eye, Najwa stared at his chest. Slowly he pulled her closer. He lifted her chin and his lips brushed hers. They connected. Deeply, they kissed. Najwa never kissed so deeply. He kissed her gently on her face, cheek, and neck and then moved down.

Najwa was completely at his will. She leaned her body towards him. This was the moment she dreamed of yet she knew not what to do. Her hands had a mind of their own and began caressing the back of his head. She guided him down her chest. He unbuttoned the first few buttons of her blouse and explored her soft chest. As he gently held her, Najwa's heart beat uncontrollably.

"Dakota…wait…I don't know…." Najwa pushed him away and pulled her blouse together.

"What's the matter?" Dakota held her hands.

She gently pulled her hands free, buttoned her blouse and moved away.

"I can't. I'm sorry."

"Is it something I did? Baby you know I wouldn't hurt you."

"Dakota I know. I promise it is nothing you did. Actually, you did everything right. It's me. I just can't. Not right now. I'm so sorry. I just don't know what's wrong with me. I better go." Najwa stood and walked toward her coat.

Dakota jumped to his feet and crossed at her path. Before she could reach for her coat he had already wrapped his arms around her waist and pulled her in once again.

He kissed her lips lightly once again. His forehead lightly touched hers as his nose brushed against hers.

"We don't have to do anything you don't want to. Just stay. Please," he pleaded.

As much as she wanted to leave, she wanted to be surrounded by someone who wanted to give to her for once. She held on to him tightly, not wanting the feeling to end.

*Her body engraved a trail from dirt – to - sand to water. Reaching for life, her hand touched his. The diamond letter "B" sparkled from his monogrammed ring. Grasping at her death, he shoved her from the rocks edge. The water engulfed her body while he moved out of sight.*

# Friday May 17, 1974

"Are you sure you want this article to run Najwa?" The editor of the Tiger Pride asked before Najwa could utter a traditional phone greeting.

"You do realize that this is going to blow the top off of this campus?" He continued.

Najwa juggled the telephone with her notes she was organizing before the call came.

"If they remember anything about this year, it will be Najwa Jackson and you can count on that one," she flatly replied.

"You remember our conversation about accountability Najwa, right?"

"Of course, how could I forget?"

"What about your sources Najwa? I mean, did you do your research on this one?"

"Have you ever had an integrity problem with any of my articles?"

"Not at all."

"Well, I am consistent."

"Najwa, this may be the article to get the Tiger Pride thrown off the campus."

Najwa showed no emotion. "It's your call."

"This is the kind of attention I want. I'm running it," the editor declared.

"It's crucial that this article run the Friday right before finals. The day of the clock nonsense. I want it to run the same day as our rally," she said.

Each year the White students of Casperton University celebrated the traditional ringing of the clock. To all, this event signaled the weekend before finals. When the old clock struck six o'clock on the Friday evening, the White students partied like the end of the world was nearing. On Monday, studying for finals began and the campus became a graveyard. Soon after there was graduation. No one knew exactly when the tradition began, but for years the minutes and seconds were counted before they drenched themselves in an alcohol, and most recently, marijuana frenzy. The clock, another legacy of Bradley Barkston, would sound the loud bell six times. Not a second before the last chime would anyone drink a drop. But, as soon as the last chime sang. The entire Black student body, at the urging of Najwa, took a vow not to attend the event. Instead, they would all meet at the Black House. There they would march to the administration building and protest.

"No problem. It's as good as in!" The editor said.

"Oh, one last thing. Tell our friend Paul to be here with his big time news cameras. This may be the break he's looking for. Tell him this one is courtesy of an old friend," Najwa ended the conversation.

All her pawns were in place. All she had to do was wait and watch.

Najwa felt nothing. It seemed as if the energy from the day before and the rejection letter drained her of everything she had left. It never fazed her that she was hours away from one of the largest events of the chapter, the Founders weekend. There would be sorors coming from all over the country to reunite with the women of the beloved Gamma chapter. She still was not moved. Najwa hoped Berri had accomplished all the tasks they discussed in their last meeting. She decided not to worry if she had not. Nothing could provoke a reaction. Instead, Najwa began to write her welcome speech for the Founders events.

Moments before her editor called, Carla and Lynette phoned to announce they would be stopping by to check on her. Najwa knew they were still worried about her despite their seemingly calm demeanor. Within the hour, her sands arrived. As if nothing happened to abruptly cancel their dinner engagement the previous day, Najwa nonchalantly let them in and continued working on her speech.

"You alright Najwa?" Lynette asked.

"I am fine sands," Najwa replied.

"Are you sure?" Carla asked.

"I am fine. Really." Najwa motioned towards the couch. "Sit down."

"So, are you going to tell us what happened to you yesterday?" Carla asked as she followed Lynette and assumed her position on the couch.

"Do I have a choice?" Najwa grinned as she looked up from her notebook.

Carla and Lynette looked at one another puzzled. They both hesitated.

"Najwa we are just trying to be here for you. Obviously whatever it is, you were really upset," Lynette said.

"Dakota was pretty worried too," Carla added.

Najwa reached over and flung the rejection letter across her coffee table in their direction.

"Here take a look for yourself." Najwa continued writing her speech as Lynette and Carla read the letter and both gasped.

"Najwa, I am so sorry," Lynette said.

"How? That doesn't make sense, you had all the qualifications!" Carla exclaimed.

"Not to mention, you're on the Dean's list. What happened?" Lynette asked.

"Probably the petitions...or maybe even the articles in the Pride paper," Najwa replied.

"You think?" Carla asked.

"They threatened to pull funding of the Pride if I wrote another controversial article," Najwa announced.

"What! Wait a minute. When did all this happen? Why haven't you said anything to us Najwa?" Carla asked.

"Sands it is not important. It's cool I talked to my editor and he assured me that the Pride would be fine. As for the graduate program…well there are other schools I can apply to. I talked to Professor Baker. She was just as angry but not surprised."

"So she is going to help you appeal this right?" Lynette asked.

"It is pretty much out of her hands. Besides, I'm not appealing. Professor Baker has offered to write a recommendation letter for any school I choose to apply to," Najwa replied.

"Wait, I can't believe that you are so calm about this. Najwa, I would think that you would be ready to bomb the administration offices right now," Carla said.

"Naw. I am cool. Really. It is all taken care of," Najwa replied and stared into space.

"What do you mean, 'it's all taken care of' what have you done?" Carla rose from the couch and looked at Najwa.

Carla and Lynette waited for the answer they may not have wanted to hear.

"I am putting it all on the line. I may even be risking graduation. Remember when the year started out Carla? We vowed that no matter what, we would stick out everything together?"

"Yeah we remember but can you give us a little forewarning about what is about to happen," Lynette said.

"No I can't Lynette. I am sorry. But you just need to trust me on this one." Najwa looked at both Lynette and Carla and repeated. "Please, just trust me on this one."

"Okay but Najwa you know this weekend is important. Founders

Weekend is the worst time for surprises!" Carla laughed trying to lighten the mood.

"I know sands. If Berri has done her job then, as with everything else, Founders Weekend should go fine. I was just working on my welcome speech for the social."

"Najwa are you sure you are fine? You just seem so unmoved. You are usually a little more stressed about stuff like this," Lynette said.

"Lynette! Really, I am fine." Najwa changed the subject. "I am more concerned about the pledges. They are going to have their hands full this weekend. Have they learned all their chapter history?"

"We stayed up with them all last night. What all they don't know, that is on them." Lynette threw her hands in the air. "I am sick of those broads."

"I hear you sands. I am not saving anyone this weekend. This is the perfect introduction to their Hell Week." Najwa sat back and started working on her speech again.

Lynette and Carla knew not much more than when they arrived. But as Najwa requested, they never asked another question. After they left Najwa's apartment to set up for the first event of the Founders weekend, there was absolutely no time to worry about the unseen.

The chapter alumnae eagerly arrived to celebrate their sorority's founding. That Friday evening, Gamma chapter hosted a social for the alumnae and Black Greeks on the campus. Saturday was the more formal event for Omega Pi Alpha sorors only. It included a luncheon with one of the prominent alumnae serving as guest speaker. The day was ended with a party in the Barkston Center. On Sunday, the chapter along with the alumnae and pledges attended service at Casperton's local Baptist church.

The weekend proved to be one of the chapter's busiest, yet most successful. So successful, Najwa personally congratulated Berri at their closing event. This Founders weekend marked the largest attendance Gamma chapter had ever hosted. It also marked the beginning of a week they would never forget.

# Thursday May 23, 1974

While all Gamma chapter was still beaming over the record attendance of alumnae who came back to share in the celebration of sisterhood, the pledges were not as happy. Immediately after the alumnae sorors left, Lynette called the pledges into an intensive meeting that moved them into their "Hell Week." Tradition on the campus of Casperton University dictated that all organization's pledges were initiated by finals week.

Being the only sorority on campus still with a line, finally at the end of the intensive week, the pledges were crossing into Omega Pi Alpha. Graduation was less than two weeks away and Najwa's final article with the Tiger Pride was due to come out before finals. Najwa spent the entire week with the pledges and her sorors only breaking away to go to class. There was no way that she would let the smallest detail fall through the cracks.

Tradition dictated that on this day, the pledges would be rushed away from the campus blindfolded at daybreak. Only those who had driven the pathway previous years knew the whereabouts of Gamma chapter's crossing ceremony. For years, every pledge of Gamma chapter in some way or another would finally take this long frightening journey into an unknown location. Nestled in the cornfields twenty miles outside of the town was a farm owned by an alumnae of Gamma chapter. The family had long since moved away only returning during the hunting seasons and usually the summer for a getaway. Here, the chapter had the privacy they sought. Every pledge walked into the large wood frame house on the property in fear and walked out the next morning a member of Omega Pi Alpha.

At midnight, a low flickering candle cut the house darkness.

Najwa read from her sorority ritual.

"My sorors, once again we are assembled to give life and a new breath to the spirit of the struggle and progress. As we begin the process of preparing those to carry on after us, let us be mindful of those who paved the way for us to walk. Bring the initiates into the room."

The crossing ceremony began. The pledges endured a grueling night of proving their loyalty to the organization that had changed their lives for well over six months. Just as they had entered into the process blindfolded six months earlier, by three o'clock that morning, they entered into the full reality of membership into Omega Pi Alpha in the same manner.

Najwa watched as the last initiate fought her way blindly through screaming members of Gamma chapter. Each time she moved closer to finally "crossing over," the sorors pulled and tugged at her legs until she was back at the starting point. Over and over she was subjected to beginning again. Being the last to cross the burning sands, this torn, yet courageous girl would become the anchor of her line.

Najwa too was an anchor and as she watched the pledge, she could not help but see herself on the floor pushing and fighting two years earlier. She knew all too well the feeling. Overwhelmed, Najwa had to step back and gather herself. She watched and thought, if only this girl knew what she was fighting to become a part of. How naive and innocent her thoughts must be. Najwa remembered that she was the same. What picture of sisterhood had she painted for these young women who had such grandeur thoughts of Gamma chapter that they would fight at all costs to become a member?

Najwa leaned against the wall. Her heart could not allow her to participate any more. She stood watching the pledge struggle as her blindfolded line sisters encouraged her from the side. The harder the sorors pulled, the harder the pledge pushed. Najwa knew this pledge was prepared to endure anything.

Two years earlier, Najwa had fought just as hard. It was at this moment, she wondered if what she endured had brought her to this point in her life and why. More importantly, could these women be pushed to the same limits? Would they be willing to lose it all as Najwa felt she had? Would they be willing to endure the pain and disappointment? Would they be willing to continue to blindly push and force their way into the unknown? She could only hope at this point. As much as she loved her sorority, she almost felt guilty about bringing them into a false reality.

Finally, after what seemed to be an eternity, the last pledge was allowed to complete her journey into Omega Pi Alpha. Najwa, still numb, stepped up to the low candle and read the final words.

"You are now trusted to carry on the mission. We entrust you with the spoken promise to Omega Pi Alpha. May God continue to light your pathway." Najwa closed her ritual book and looked around the room at the sorors who were teary-eyed.

The initiates, still blindfolded, were led into the den. Here they were lined up again and finally told to take off their blindfolds. Before them were t-shirts and wooden paddles that bore the Omega Pi Alpha letters and more importantly, their names. As they slowly peeled away the home made blindfolds and squinted at the sight of light, they all stood silent.

"Congratulations Sorors!" The members of Gamma chapter screamed in unison.

The initiates looked at each other again. Still not sure if this was a horrible joke, they did not move. Instead, they looked to their Dean, Lynette, for confirmation that it was finally all over.

"Ladies, it's over. You are members now!" Lynette shouted.

One shriek led to the next until finally all the initiates cried and screamed in excitement. The celebration began.

Najwa celebrated as much as she could before retreating into another room to herself. Genuinely happy for the new sorors, she did not want to spoil their moment. She passed her tears of pain off as those of joy. No one, not even her sands, knew the difference.

"It's finally over! Can you believe it?" Lynette said to Najwa.

"Seems like yesterday doesn't it?" Najwa replied.

"Time for the traditional President's toast!" Carla exclaimed.

The sorors of Gamma chapter passed out paper cups partially filled with cheap champagne. It was the president's job to toast the chapter and it's new members.

"My God we have been through so much," Lynette said to Najwa and Carla.

"Too much," Carla replied.

"There is more to come," Najwa said and looked to the rest of the room who waited for her.

"What do you mean?" Carla asked.

Najwa continued as if she never heard Carla. " Sorors…." She paused and raised her cup.

"Look how far we have come. We have changed. Some of us will never be the same. Sorors, just remember, in the beginning, there was a spirit."

Najwa tipped her cup.

# Friday May 24, 1974
## 12:00p.m.

Friday at noon, in the cafeteria, the last edition of the Tiger Pride came out.

"Oh my God! Are you reading what I am reading Lynette.?" Carla asked.

"Shhh!" Lynette hushed Carla and continued to devour the article.

"Sorors!" Diane and Gloria ran across the cafeteria with the Tiger Pride clutched in their hands.

"Did you read this?" Gloria asked as she stood over Lynette and Carla mystified.

"We are reading it now!" Carla hushed Gloria.

"Has anyone seen Najwa?" Diane asked.

"No not since last night," Lynette answered.

Carla looked up from the article and almost laughed. "So this is what she meant last night."

"Is this true?" Gloria whispered to the two elder members of Gamma Chapter who looked just as puzzled.

"I…don't…oh I don't know what the hell is real any more!" Lynette threw the newspaper on the table. "Carla what is Najwa thinking? What is wrong with her?"

The title of the article screamed, "Blood of Sadie Mae Stained on the Barkston Building!"

"She has lost it. She has really lost it this time!" Lynette tried to contain her voice.

"She is fighting fire with fire!" Carla beamed.

"You have lost your mind too! This is going to get her kicked out two weeks before graduation! We don't know if this story is true or not!"

"Is she accusing the founder of this university of being a rapist?" Gloria interrupted.

Lynette's eyes watered with emotion. "I am not even going to attempt to rationalize this with her."

"We need to get out of here before people start asking about this article. We need to find Najwa!" Diane pleaded.

"She has lost her mind and we are about to be the laughing stock of the campus!" Lynette fumed.

"Look, let's all just calm down. Lynette lets all go back to your place. Let's try to gather the chapter up. We'll all meet back up at Lynette's. Try to make some sense out of this whole thing before the rally at the Black House."

Carla gathered her things. She thought of her sands and how she must have been pushed to her limit. Carla did not believe Najwa would defile the sacredness of their sorority's fallen founder. She knew Najwa would never spread a lie at the expense of the sorority or even to make herself look good. She may even have proof. She wanted to give her sands the benefit of the doubt.

In the back of her mind, she thought the story was brilliant. Carla knew her sands better than anyone. More importantly she understood her better than even Lynette. Nothing Najwa did was by accident or mistake. Najwa was methodic and very calculated even in a state of confusion and panic. The story could not have better timing. The rally was less than three hours away. Carla knew exactly what Najwa was doing.

# 5:30 p.m.

"She is brilliant Lynette," Carla said after reading the article a second time at Lynette's apartment.

"What? She is insane!" Lynette snapped.

"No, Lynette she is brilliant. This is what she was talking about last night. She didn't want to come out and tell us. It would give everyone too much time to react. She needed everyone to be emotional today. Don't you see what she is doing?"

Carla dissected her sands' intentions "She wanted everyone to be just as shocked today. The Black House rally is going to be heated. She is exposing every fiber of this university for what it really is."

Members of the chapter gathered at Lynette's and waited for Najwa's arrival. The new initiates were still in shock from crossing over the night before. They were simply happy to be in the presence of the chapter as members. Their excitement overwhelmed any concern or understanding of what was transpiring.

Robin tried to bring some clarity to the situation. "Lynette, I remember talking to Najwa a while ago and she was telling me about all this information she found on Sadie Mae Wesley at her job. I think this is where her story came from."

"Remember those articles she got in Chicago? Maybe those have something to do with this," Candace added.

"You have to admit Lynette, it's a damn good story. Even people who know nothing about the founding of our sorority are mad. I mean listen to this…." Irby picked up her copy of the article and found a passage.

"She lowered her head to her dying friend's mouth. Sadie squeezed Anna's hand. She used every ounce she had within to draw Anna closer. A promise formed the words spoken to her awaiting friend." Irby put the paper down shaking her head.

"I felt like I was there that night. You don't have to be a member of this sorority to feel the power in this article." She continued. "Najwa didn't make this up."

"We looked everywhere and we can't find Najwa," Diane said as she burst into the apartment with Gloria.

"I just don't understand why she didn't tell us," Berri said.

"She couldn't Berri. There is a lot you don't know. Najwa acted on a lot of things that we never knew about. That's just how she is. She solves everything in her own mind first and then she decides who she is going to let in. But the trick to it is we all play a part in her plan. We just don't know it until we've already reacted.

"Sorors, the only place we are going to find Najwa right now is at the Black House. It is almost five thirty. The rally is scheduled to begin soon. That is where Najwa wants us to be. We need to be there. I bet we will get our explanation," Carla said and walked to the door.

*Sadie could not hold life. She would not wait for assistance. She knew that these minutes were the last.*

## 5:45p.m.

---

The grass of the Black House lawn was covered with Black students already chanting by the time Gamma chapter arrived. Najwa was already positioned on the porch with the rest of the speakers. Emotions were high. They all had read Najwa's article earlier that day. The campus was a time bomb. Only a few yards away across the street stood the campus clock. The White students had to pass the Black House to get to their traditional alcohol fest. The editor of the Tiger Pride positioned himself on the porch in front of the crowd. The two groups heckled each other from opposing sides.

"Light that joint honky and you are outta here!" A Black student cried across the street.

Najwa looked over and noticed the familiar face emerging from a van that pulled up in the distance. She strained to see the figure flanked by another man carrying a camera. As they moved closer, she realized it was her old lover, Paul. She had not seen his face since the summer. She wondered for only a moment if she were over him and whether she had forgiven him for his disappearing act. She had not the time to concentrate on that. She had close to one hundred Black students standing before her ready for anything she commanded.

Najwa looked out into the crowd and saw her sorors. She beckoned for them to move closer to the porch. She had not talked to any of them since the pledges crossed the night before. She knew from the looks on their faces that they were confused and probably surprised. It was too late to wonder about their allegiance. Carla and Lynette were the first to reach the stairs of the Black House porch.

Najwa rushed to explain to her sands. "Sands, this is not about the chapter any more. We made it just like we said we would. This is about me now. This was something that I had to do."

"Was it about you all the time Najwa?" Lynette asked.

"Not in the beginning. I thought I was really doing what was right for everyone. Nobody's name is on that article but mine. If something happens, it is going to happen to me."

"We are in this together. Remember?" Carla assured Najwa.

The editor of the Tiger Pride leaned over Najwa's shoulder. "Najwa we need to get started. We only have a few minutes before that clock chimes. Paul has his camera set up. Let's go."

Najwa nodded. She turned back to her sorors never saying a word. Smiling, she stood, balled her fist and raised it. Lynette and Carla looked at her and returned the gesture.

Najwa positioned herself behind the podium that was set up on the porch. She looked out into the crowd and sucked in their energy and fury. She skimmed the posters they carried that called for fair treatment and cursed the university. Najwa looked out and noticed Paul gazing at her. She thought he must have been in awe. She lived for the day she would make him regret leaving her.

She looked on the opposite side and noticed Dakota. Maybe now he wanted her not because he felt sorry for her but because he saw a strong woman. Her sorors, the newly initiated members, and their alumnae stood to her right, all clapping and supporting their president. Her sands stood unconditionally. The students were ready to move when she said move. This was what she really wanted. This was what she worked the entire year for. Never did she think, while driving into the campus for her senior year, it would end on this note. Maybe it was all about her the entire time. This moment represented everything she worked towards. She took a deep breath, gathering the remainder of the energy exuding from the crowd and began to speak.

"Listen at them over there taunting and chanting 'Turning of the Clock.' They are throwing it in our faces. While we stand over here with our hands tied behind our backs. I said it in my article. The sweat, the tears, and even the blood of my founder and our people are buried beneath the grounds of this campus.

"This land we stand on, much like all the land in this country was stolen. We will not tolerate this any longer! We are going to march over to that administrative office and let it be known we will not be dictated by the hypocrisy of this university! The annual Turning of the Clock on this day will now be known as the annual Burning of the Clock!"

"Burning of the Clock!" Burning of the Clock! Burning of the Clock!" The students chanted louder and louder until Najwa could no longer be heard over the small PA system.

Nothing but the street separated the two groups of students chanting back and forth at one another. The march to the campus administration was not going to happen. There was no way they could now gain control of the shouting students.

"Burn that bastard up!"

"Give me some matches!"

The two campus police cars sitting back on the block were not prepared for the mayhem that would occur on this day. The four officers hesitantly stepped out of their cars and pulled out their nightsticks. Paul's cameras rolled.

The mood of the rally turned to rage. Not a single person was sacrificed in the fury. The White students taunted the Black students by turning beer bottles up to their mouths. They flaunted their inequality.

The police could do nothing. What was usually a traditional event of some kids just having fun was turning into a riot. An officer ran back to his car and called on the radio for backup support from the state police to help maintain control.

In that instant, the shiny empty glass beer bottle that flew across the street claimed the first victim and ignited the spark. The Black woman lay on the ground as a few ran to her rescue. Blood stained the green grass of the Black House. Someone screamed and broke the crowd's moment of silent disbelief. Many of the Black students ran for cover while others ran to the rescue of the fallen woman. Laughter came from the other side. More bottles flew.

"Najwa get down!" Dakota ran from the grass and grabbed her.

"Get him! That White boy over there threw the bottle!" Someone cried.

Black students furiously charged the street. White bodies scattered everywhere. The police were no match for the students. Fists flew from all directions. The fury of every negative experience the Black students encountered in their lives rained down upon the White middle and upper class bodies. The campus ground was the scene of a riot. Crashing bottles and screams masked the sound of the extra sirens in the distant finally arriving to bring order.

The clock rang the first tone.

Dakota wrapped his arms around Najwa and shielded her. He forced her into the Black House.

"Burn that bastard down!" A Black student cried.

Four Black students began climbing the old wooden legs of the clock tower. Before reaching the top, he had already taken a stick to the glass case of the age-old timepiece. Mercilessly, he smashed the face.

The clock would not be defeated. It chimed a second time.

The first spark ignited and it was not long before flames began to peek out from under the base of the clock face. The old wood of the clock began to spark and burn like a match. Fearing the legs would give way, the arsonists jumped at least six feet and began running.

The clock chimed a third time.

Najwa, Dakota, and several other students who managed to run inside the Black House watched from the windows of the top floor.

By now, the State police and the campus police were everywhere trying to regain control.

Paul's cameras never stopped rolling.

The legs of the clock finally cracked and bent as it fell to its knees.

It managed a fourth and one last chime.

*With all her heart and soul, and all that God had given her, she spoke.*
*Sadie squeezed Anna's hand. She used every ounce she had within to draw*
*Anna closer. Her words formed a promise to her awaiting friend.*

## 6:00pm

Time stood still for the first time for the clock planted on the stolen land. The last wooden leg gave way and its face crashed to the ground.

# Wednesday June 19, 1974

The network news ran stories on the Casperton riot. Over ten students were injured and fifteen were arrested before calm was brought to the campus grounds. Paul sold his story and footage to the major networks. It proved the accusations of the Black students were true. The national exposure the story ran was enough for the mayor of Casperton as well as the Governor, to step in and call for a major overhaul of the university officials. To make any Black student "pay" for their part in the incident would have been suicide to the Dean of Students. The Tiger Pride received financial support from alumnae and local dignitaries behind the controversy, which ensured its life on the campus of Casperton University until the doors closed. For the seniors, graduation could not have come sooner.

"So do you really think that article was true?" Lynette asked Carla as she packed the last box into Najwa's car trunk.

"I don't know and I don't care! Not after all we went through. I am just glad that we all graduated. We are lucky that we didn't all get kicked out on our butts," Carla said adjusting the boxes.

346

"Isn't it ironic how, well you know, we got Keisha kicked out and now because of everything that happened, they are letting her back in next semester? Never had to raise a hand. We did everything for her."

What they would not know until two years later was that Irby would eventually tell the chapter of Keisha stealing the money and the incident at the Kappa Land in 1973. Candace and Mark were married a year after Irby broke the news.

"Yeah but we'll be gone. We don't have to worry about her. Let the girls next year be concerned!" Carla waved her hands.

Najwa walked down the stairs with a suitcase in her hand. She threw it in the back seat.

"So Miss Naj, which way you headed? What town you ridin' into next to start mayhem and disorder?" Carla laughed aloud.

"Yeah, so what's next Naj, Omega Pi Alpha National President?" Lynette said as she chuckled and closed the trunk.

"Girl, please! I don't think ya'll are ready for me!" Najwa laughed. "Boy I am going to miss you two! What would I have done without you this year?"

"I think you woulda' been kicked out of here like everyone else," Carla nudged Najwa.

"I just turned over all the president's files to Berri. I'm just so happy it's over. We made it ladies. We actually made it!" Najwa declared.

"My girl is going to medical school in Chicago and my other girl is going to be teaching. I am so proud. I am coming to visit both of you every chance I get." Najwa put her arm around Lynette and hit Carla on the back. "I might even move in. 'Cause Lord knows you owe me Carla."

They walked towards Najwa's apartment.

"So what did you decide Naj? What are you going to do when you get back home?" Lynette asked.

"You know what sands. I don't know what I am going to do. When I started this year off I thought I would do a lot of things. I'm just ready to get on with my life. I feel like I just got my soul back or something. I'm just going to see where the next couple of months take me."

"That's cool. Just take your time. And you know you are welcome any time you want to get away," Lynette said.

"Get away? What would she want to get away for? She's going home and the finest man ever to walk this campus lives right next door!" Carla said.

"Honey, Dakota aint' lettin' her go nowhere! So Najwa, when did you finally wake up and realize that man wanted you? I can't believe you were keeping it from us?" Lynette kidded.

"Yeah did you see the way he rescued his woman at that rally?" Carla laughed.

"Yeah…who was looking like Willie Tyler and Lester that time?" Lynette laughed uncontrollably.

"Aw shut up! I wasn't keeping anything from you two hussies! And who said I was the one who woke up and discovered him? He finally woke up and realized that I was the woman!" Najwa stopped and thought for a moment.

"…And you know what, so did I," she ended.

Najwa realized that she had faced all her fears and still landed on the top. There were still some things she was unsure of but nevertheless she was fine. She had seen and felt the worst yet.

"He did kind of run out of nowhere that day didn't he?" Najwa laughed at herself. "Hey, I am good. What can I say?"

"Aw sookey sookey naw!" Carla hollered.

"So Carla, are you going to be my campaign manager when I run for national president?" Najwa looked at her with a serious face.

They laughed and walked away together just as they did at the beginning of the school year not knowing what obstacles would come their way. But knowing they would overcome no matter what.

# About the Author & the Journey

"There was a Spirit" is a work in the making for over eight years. The inspiration for the story of Najwa Jackson was born in the Chicago apartment of Karen E. Hodge around 1997. From the friendship of Kimberly Noelle and Karen E. Hodge came this haunting yet inspiring novel of promises kept over time, power and self realization.

In late 1999, writing of the book was placed on the back burner when Karen was faced with the discovery that her physical life was being interrupted by pancreatic cancer. In early 2000, during her last visit with Karen, Kimberly made a promise to her sister and friend. She promised Karen that she would finish this powerful story no matter how long the journey. On July 3, 2000, Karen E. Hodge made her transition from her physical body and became a spiritual force in completing this novel. In October 2004 "There Was A Spirit" was finally completed.

The journey of the author after the unexpected transition of Karen E. Hodge is almost parallel to the path of the story. This book is the result of a promise made in a hospital room in Washington D.C. and served as a source of healing for its author Kimberly Noelle. Ironically, the driving forces of the main characters in this story are promises kept over time.

"There Was a Spirit" is Kimberly's first fictional novel. She is also the author of "Break It Down Now!" an inspirational guide to incorporating the art of Fraternity/Sorority stepping into a youth team building activities. In her spare time, she enjoys writing music, traveling, reading, collecting historical memorabilia and working in the community. Kimberly received her Bachelors Degree from Columbia College in Chicago and Master of Science from Northwestern University's Medill School of Journalism. She is a member of Delta Sigma Theta Sorority, Inc. and resides in the Chicago area.

Currently, Kimberly is working on the continuing story of Najwa Jackson and the women of Omega Pi Alpha.

www.knoellepublishing.com